The
Lower Quarter

The Lower Quarter

ELISE BLACKWELL

Unbridled Books

This is a work of fiction. The names, characters, places and incidents are either the product of the author's imagination or are used fictitiously, and any resemblance to actual persons living or dead, business establishments, events, or locales is entirely coincidental.

UNBRIDLED BOOKS

Library of Congress Cataloging-in-Publication Data

Blackwell, Elise, 1964-
The lower quarter / by Elise Blackwell.
    pages ; cm
ISBN 978-1-60953-119-5
    I. Title.
PS3602.L3257L69 2015
    813'.6--dc23
    2015011743

1 3 5 7 9 10 8 6 4 2

Book Design by SH · CV

First Printing

For David,

who once observed

that all novels

are historical novels

Only part of us is sane: only part of us loves pleasure and the longer day of happiness, wants to live to our nineties and die in peace, in a house that we built, that shall shelter those who come after us. The other half of us is nearly mad. It prefers the disagreeable to the agreeable, loves pain and its darker night despair, and wants to die in a catastrophe that will set back life to its beginnings and leave nothing of our house save its blackened foundations. Our bright natures fight in us with this yeasty darkness, and neither part is commonly quite victorious, for we are divided against ourselves and will not let either part be destroyed.

REBECCA WEST, *Black Lamb and Grey Falcon*

The human body was entering a machinery of power that explores it, breaks it down, and rearranges it.

MICHEL FOUCAULT, *Discipline and Punish*

PART ONE

Inherent Vice

Johanna

TAPED into stiff brown paper, the small painting sat atop
her feet, tilted against her shins—a slight felt weight.
Johanna worked the padlock's combination with the pre-
cise strength of someone who gardens or sews, though she
practiced neither skill, and uncoiled the length of chain she
had used five weeks earlier to secure her workshop door's
handles. Lifting the painting to her hip with one arm, she
pulled open the door with the other. The room released the
dank smell of earth turned inside out, of something brought
up that should have been left buried.

Water stains bloomed on the walls like flat moss, and
moisture coated the floorboards, staining the wood darker. She inspected for pooled water and loose wires before
touching the fuse box. The damage appeared to be two-di-
mensional—not lethal, not here. She carried the painting
upstairs to the spare living space squatting between her
first-floor workshop and the building's roof, laying the can-

vas flat on her table with the regard she gave to every painting under her care, this one no less.

Her first move was an act of optimism: Turn on the air conditioner. Next she hauled up from her van the suitcase of clothing and books, the boxes of food she had purchased ahead of her return, and one of the two HEPA filters that would clean the invisible dangers suspended in the air. She closed the door on her apartment at the top of the open staircase and brought the other filter into her street-level workshop. With a surgeon's mask covering her nose and mouth, she set to returning her favorite room in the world to what it had been before the storm. The work she performed for others would be needed now more than ever, and she would be ready.

Though restoring surfaces injured by water was her expertise—her vocation, she might even have said—a room is not canvas and paint. The wood floors she would have to leave to chance. The companies that owned the specialized equipment capable of extracting water collected under floorboards would be booked for months, a year, longer, and at prices high enough to ensure that the very rich would be the first to recover.

Clay, she thought, but she would not ask him for help.

Eventually she would call him; perhaps she could wait until he tired of telling the story of how he'd stayed in the city through the winds, through the flooding, as though the storm had come just for him. Even then, she would not ask for his help.

Johanna could not extract the water under her shop's floorboards, but she at least knew better than to sand the floor as soon as its top dried—a common mistake. She had no choice but to wait and see if her floor buckled. Either it would or it wouldn't, and she was a person who understood better than most what can and cannot be controlled in life, what is in a person's power to alter and what must be endured. A buckled floor is not such a bad thing. It wasn't as though she worked in the hermetic rooms she had trained in or a state-of-the-art restoration center. She imagined her bare feet comfortable on the warped wood, a smooth and eventually harmless surface.

Concentrating on the room above the floor, she worked across the warm morning to transform the space into a safe house for the paintings she would salvage. One of her early mentors had tried to lure her into preventive conservation, wanting to train her to help some off-top museum *do no harm* to the treasures it found under its watch. In the years during which she studied—and still, really, among some circles—stabilization was the shrine worshiped. Her teachers and most of her peers thought always of the Rembrandt that no one would dream of touching with a brush dipped in fresh paint. *Preserve. Do no harm. Clean only when there is no risk. Leave the cracks be. An imperfect masterpiece is a masterpiece.*

But Johanna had planned all along to work for herself, or, more accurately, never again to work for someone else. This meant moving in the world of lesser works, among people who treasured paintings unwanted by institutions—good paintings and bad paintings but always paintings whose damage they wanted undone. At the least, they wanted harm hidden.

Circulation: first air, then light. Johanna removed her mask. Using the claw of a carpenter's hammer, she removed the plywood she had secured over the windows facing Decatur Street and assessed the shattered rectangles. A loss easy to accept: two panes of twelve. The broken rectangles were small enough that she could leave the frame intact in the wall as she knocked loose glass, chiseled out the old putty and glazer points—difficult work in cold weather but fairly easy in the still-warm early fall. She painted the wood with thick stripes of linseed oil, not minding the smell that many dislike: a spine-straightening sharpness wrapping the sweetness of decaying fruit.

The humidity outside was heavy enough to be visible; even the empty panes gave the effect of filmy glass. Looking across the vacant street was like looking through water, as though the Lower Quarter had indeed flooded and was aquarium still.

Or not a real place at all.

Lights blinked on, and the doors opened to the small restaurant and bar where Johanna had eaten her lunch nearly every day for three years. This could mean that her life would return to normal, to the normal it had become before chance had again dislocated her. *Bad luck, but not so bad this time.* She would walk over while the oil soaked in.

In the middle of the street she paused to look left, down Decatur toward the Marigny, and right, up Decatur toward the still-closed French Market on the river side of the street and Jackson Square on the other. With the exception of the evening she had driven out of the city, she had never seen the Lower Quarter so abandoned. The effect was the same as looking at an old black-and-white photograph, as though the colors she saw were superimposed, painted on years after the fact by a moderately skilled artist.

She wasn't the first customer back. Two others already sat at the counter. One she remembered: the lovely, buxom singer with a vodka-tonic habit and a litany of grievances that ranged from minute quotidian irritations to fifteen hundred dollars in unpaid parking tickets. Johanna could fit the woman into the history of the Quarter that she had learned and arranged in her mind. The other patron was a young man she'd never seen before. He wore work boots and rested his wrist on a drab-green hard hat. Part of the new history, she supposed, jarred by the idea of change from without.

The bartender she knew as well as almost anyone in town, which made him an acquaintance: Peter.

"You're one of the first to swim home," he said.

Johanna nodded.

"You think they'd at least clear my tickets, give those of us coming back a clean start," the singer was saying to the worker, whose face was turned away from Johanna as though this were a dream her mind had failed to populate fully. A world conjured by a tired god, or perhaps merely a lazy one.

"The usual?" Peter asked Johanna as though they'd both been there the day before, as though every board game and newspaper in the place were not stacked soggy in the corner. As though the place always smelled like sulfur and wet dirt and mushrooms, and that's what people wanted.

Her nod had its effect. The pencil came from behind his ear, scrawled the name of a sandwich on the ticket. Peter's hand ferried the ticket from the counter to the bald cook, who smiled at the order but didn't look up.

"He's happy to be back to normal," Johanna offered.

"Normal?"

"For this town." This was something she'd heard people say. The people who said this had certain kinds of bumper stickers on their cars, but she couldn't remember which ones. She was still figuring out the zoo, its more straightforward taxonomy, and had not yet quite ordered her history of the city—based on types, ethnicities, currents of arrival—to the present. She wasn't sure she would ever graduate to living human beings, though some categories were simple enough: rich or poor, free or not free, good or evil. She was not simple enough to deny ambiguity, to deny that there are shades of gray, but neither was she so naive as to believe that black and white don't exist in this world. She'd seen good and she'd seen evil, enough to know that both were as real as their more complicated mixes.

Peter laughed. "But maybe abnormal enough for you to

drink a whole beer? Nothing on draft yet, so our arrangement is off for a while."

She shook her head. "Charge me for a whole bottle, then, but pour the usual amount."

He pressed his hands into the bar in front of her, leaned weight into them. "I never asked before, but now is different."

She scanned the place. The window-doors were bright with the day, making the rest of the room darker, dim enough to obscure change. The single pool table still occupied the open area just inside the doors. The floor's concrete remained a dingy color, not something to notice. "Different, yes, but different how?"

"Because now I know if you don't ask people what you want to know, you may never get the chance. Sometimes you see them tomorrow, sometimes not. Don't people where you're from drink beer for breakfast?"

"Beer?" Johanna removed her hands from bar top to lap. "I think beer for breakfast is more here, more New Orleans. For me, it's just that I like the taste but not the rest of it."

"AA, twelve steps? That'd be against their rules, no? Having a taste?"

"Nothing like that. That's not a problem I have. Even if I did, I don't like groups. I just don't like how it makes me feel, fuzzy, not in control." She drank the beer he'd poured in two small sips and tasted hops on her breath. "So what was something you wanted to ask somebody and can't now because they're gone?"

"Besides you and the beer?"

"Besides me, yes. You got your chance to ask me your question, it turns out."

Peter was cleaning the bar with a white towel, in small circles. He looked down at his hands as though just now realizing that they belonged to him and did his mind's bidding. He stilled them and looked up. Again, even though she knew to expect it, the green of his eyes surprised her against his black hair. "Black Irish except we're French," he'd said to her once in the flat accent that he said everyone spoke with where he grew up—a small town somewhere west of New Orleans, a place she was unlikely ever to visit.

"Okay," he said. "There was a girl who used to come in here once or twice a week, usually pretty late, say three in the morning, and she'd nurse one drink and smoke a whole pack of cigarettes like she was really mad at someone. I always wanted to ask her who she was mad at and what for."

"Everyone's mad at someone, right?"

"I was just curious, specifically. It was a thing I wanted to know. Don't you ever look at people and wonder about them? Wonder what makes them tick, or what's going on inside their brains?"

Johanna shrugged and pulled her wallet from her back pocket to pay. "I guess I tend to take people at their face value."

"What you see is what you get?"

She handed him a twenty-dollar bill and watched him from behind as he counted change from the till. Before he turned around she said, "Not what you see, maybe, but what they do is what you get. Thoughts are between a person and himself. What someone does, that's what matters to other people, what changes the world."

"I'm not sure I agree."

"See, whether or not you agree is between you and you. Only if you argue with me does it have anything to do with me."

Peter stared at her, head barely tilted but tilted.

Johanna offered the closest thing she had to a smile. "And now you are thinking that it was better when you didn't ask your customers questions."

He shook his head, grinned. "That's between me and me, but what I was thinking is that today is the most you've ever talked by a long shot. Anyway, as soon as I get some of this stuff cleaned up, we'll do what we can about getting some beer on tap again. Even the check pads are soaked." He gestured to the tall stack of wet newsprint, game boxes, and receipt pads in the corner behind the bar. "This is the only dry paper in the place." He pushed a folded paper on the counter toward Johanna.

She flipped it open: the back of the front section. The headline read, "Tourist found in Hotel Richelieu victim of murder, not storm." Under the headline stared out a face she had not seen in ten years or on this side of the ocean. The same wide cheekbones, but the washed-out eyes were locked rigid, the pupils smaller than life.

Peter cocked his head. "Good time to kill someone, I

guess, right when a hurricane hits. Not like it's going to be a top investigative priority."

Ladislav had been less than two blocks from where she lived and worked. He had died there, that close to her. He had seen her, maybe, without her knowing it. The room went from warm to cold, and Johanna shivered with the recognition that there is no such thing in the world as a coincidence that large.

She looked directly at Peter, willing her face to form a flat surface with nothing behind it—words on a page that signify nothing in the real world. "I guess that would be a good strategy." She repocketed her wallet and walked back to her studio, leaving the newspaper where it lay, as though it held nothing of interest to her.

Eli

ELIZAM smiled at the congratulatory email on his screen. It had been his first real job for the Lost Art Register, the first investigative work that had gone beyond a basic due-diligence search to ensure that some painting about to go on auction had not been reported stolen. This had been his first recovery job, and it had been successful. It had been Eli who had recognized the hand of amateurs, who had flown to Kansas City and suspected at first glance two security guards taking a cigarette break outside the art-storage facility from which the small Henry Moores had gone missing. It had been Eli who had followed them for three days, who had got the cops—that old enemy—to the right place at the right time: the moment the thieves met up with their loser local fence, statues stupidly in hand.

Prior to his first real investigative assignment, much of Eli's work had amounted to little more than telemarketing: phoning people reported to have had—or even just likely to have had—art stolen to convince them to list their works with the Register for a fee. Or occasionally there was the slightly more delicate job of phoning someone whose stolen property the Register had a lead on to see if they were willing to pony up a finder's fee in an amount to justify the staff hours that might be involved in its recovery. This work managed to be boring and tickle his conscience at the same time, but Eli's release from prison had not brought with it full autonomy. He needed his job. What helped ease the pangs was this: Everyone he called was either rich or institutional. Millionaires and billionaires, well-endowed museums, insurance companies. What he was doing was just a matter of moving some money around among those who could afford the give-and-take. Back and forth, forth and back. There were lines he wouldn't cross, and he felt secure in his knowledge of just where those lines lay.

Eli's desk backed diagonally into the corner of his office farthest from the door, which allowed him to face the door while keeping the office walls as distant as possible.

"You've got a knack for this work," said his boss, stepping through the open door. "Takes one to know one, right?" Ted closed the door behind him and sat on one of the twin chairs facing the desk, his large hands capping his knees. The desk now separated them, as had the visiting-room table the day they had first met face to face.

"You have me all wrong," said Eli, spreading his hands to give the appearance of humor, though he meant his words. *You have me all wrong.* He was nothing like those Missouri amateurs, who'd stolen what wasn't theirs from the place that paid their bills, who'd been too dumb to know the value of what they had, too dumb to find a buyer to make the statues disappear without an incriminating trace. When he'd been on that side of things, he'd been good at what he'd done, and there was earned pride in the difference between *criminal* and *art thief.*

But Ted knew that. Eli's skill was why he'd been offered this job and the early release it had helped secure. The distinction Eli wanted Ted to understand was this: He'd never taken anything from the person it really belonged to, never taken a beautiful thing from someone who deserved to possess it. His mission had never been to steal from but to give back, to turn tables needing turning. *Repatriation.* One rung up from Robin Hood. The joke of it all was that when he'd finally been caught, it had been for stealing something with his name on it: a painting by his own hand.

But Ted knew all that, too. That first visit, when he'd flown east to recruit Eli, Ted had led with a smart if easy line. "So," he'd said, "I hear you like to return things to their rightful owners."

So now Eli kept his mouth shut and the good mood on. "There's another case I'm sniffing," he told his boss. "The Mercury paintings. I'm pretty sure the lawyer's got them. Slimeball after the finder's fee. Should be easy to smoke him out, use a few dollars as bait."

Ted had extraordinarily thick hair, going from dark to silver in a way that made it look like he'd been born old and was passing through middle age on his way to young. It lifted from his head like water leaving a fountain and moved in unison when he nodded. "You have good instincts, and I'll put someone on that. But I've got something bigger for you."

Eli straightened. Something that he couldn't identify had entered Ted's voice, some groove in his throat that gave it a more complex texture. Eli had no experience to draw from with men like Ted. Men born into easy citizenship, who belonged to clubs with golf courses, who had wives who were beautiful but so thin they looked frail, looked like someone you could sit across from but not lie on top of.

Ted had done him a good turn, and Eli even liked the man, but he couldn't trust someone he didn't know how to measure. Maybe Ted could be trusted and maybe he couldn't, and Eli saw no reason to put himself in a position where it would matter which way it was. A caution with others that he'd learned the hard way, the cost being more than a decade of life as he would have lived it and the only woman he'd ever met whom he thought he could live with.

The image of dark hair against a smooth shoulder came to him when he blinked, real as taste, and he swallowed it.

"Bigger sounds good," he said, "but remember I'm a rookie."

"Well, the painting isn't very big at all." Ted tipped his chin toward Eli's closed briefcase, which sat on the floor next to his desk. "Fit in that, maybe, if you needed it to."

"So the price tag, that's where the size comes in?"

Ted nodded. "Pretty big, but it's more about the need for

quiet, which may or may not be easy. There's a body, too—
that's a problem. It seems that no one may care because this
body got caught up in a sea of bodies. With a body, though,
you never know whether there's someone who cares but just
doesn't know yet. Or someone who cares and already knows
but is playing it close for some reason or another."

Eli sustained eye contact with effort and said, "Usually
your lines are easy enough to read between, but I don't know
what the hell you're talking about."

"The Crescent City, Eli. You're going to New Orleans.
Right before the hurricane, guy turns up dead in a hotel
room in possession of two paintings that have been missing
from Europe for a dozen years."

Eli did the simple math. "You don't think?"

Ted smiled, shook his head. "It may have happened just
before you went in, but definitely not your work—or really
your part of the world."

Eli swallowed again. "You said the paintings have already
been found, so where do we come in?"

"I said two paintings were found, but, back when, three
were stolen together. Your job is to find the third. The police
are probably thinking that if they find the painting, they'll
find the killer, but for us it's the reverse. Vice versa. I'm not
saying you should catch a murderer, but if we can find out
who might have wanted this guy dead, the third painting
just might turn up."

After Ted left his office, Eli read the file, which included a *Times-Picayune* story with an artist's rendering of the

unidentified man found dead on a bed in the Hotel Richelieu in a city waiting to hear whether it would take a direct
hit from a powerful hurricane. The choice to use a drawing
when someone could have photographed the corpse seemed
strangely inefficient. Indeed, the artist with the charcoal
and pencil had probably worked from such a photograph.
A prohibition, probably—some taboo against publishing
direct representations of mortality. Protect readers' delicate
sensibilities by rendering the dead in soft graphite, as something that might be fiction.

The suspicious circumstances mentioned in the article
might have warranted a focused homicide investigation
if that storm had never hit—a tourist dead inside an al-
most-tourist-district hotel is a problem no matter what
crime rate you're accustomed to—but a lot of bodies had
journeyed through the morgue in the weeks that had followed the murder. Eli wondered if the perpetrator was
smart that way or just lucky. Not smart, he decided, given
that he seemed to have left behind two paintings that were
as valuable as the one he'd taken. Or maybe smart but un-
lucky—interrupted.

Or maybe it was more complicated. Perhaps the missing
painting had been sold earlier, and the murder and paintings were unconnected. If that was the case, the identity of
the dead man would still be the only trail to the painting,
but it might be a very long trail. Eli's thoughts circled back
to the paintings: There would be a reason the dead man had
brought them to New Orleans. Or had found them there or

bought them there or stolen them there from whoever had stolen them in the first place.

Horizontal windows opened a narrow, broken line across the wall to his left—a series of dashes—giving the effect that he was looking at the world through squinted eyes. Not the world: a single stratum of the Hollywood Hills. "You're lucky," his prison friends had said when they'd heard where he would land. Lucky to be out, yes, but he found the monotonous sunshine melancholy. He had always thought of Los Angeles as a place where people's dreams are disappointed, a disappointment made sharper by the presence of those few whose dreams have come spectacularly true. As for the beautiful women, he remembered having once been good at talking to them, convincing them into bed. But he could not remember how he'd gone about it—not the sex itself but the getting to it.

Most often now when he saw a woman he found attractive, the effect was the same as looking through the windows of the Beverly Hills stores he walked by on his way to work. The paintings at the L.A. County Art Museum, the fossils in the tar pits behind it—these he felt closer to having. Sex had become a solo operation.

One evening about a week after he'd first arrived, he and Ted had met a client at a bar of the client's choosing, and Eli had noticed that the women were younger than the men in suits, better-looking, more available than they should have been. While the client was in the bathroom, Ted told Eli what should have been obvious to him but that, in his new naïveté, he'd missed entirely: "They're hookers, albeit of varying levels of formality."

A few nights later Eli had dressed in one of his two new suits, knotted his tie the best way, and gone back to that bar alone. The place was empty of women and almost of men. Eli ordered a beer, realizing that he was more relieved than disappointed. What would he have done, he wondered, if a woman had been there, available for the asking, for the paying? The mechanics of it all were beyond him: broaching the subject of money, settling on a number, choosing a place, protecting himself against disease and against theft. Even once the transaction was settled he would have been lost, unsure whether he would be expected to kiss the woman or cut to the chase, whether she would fawn over him or dispense with the pretense of liking him at all, whether he got to choose the position or was expected to take what he got. It was the same in taxis, even: He never knew whether he'd bought the ride or rented the space, whether it was within his rights to ask that the radio station be changed, the volume lowered, the window rolled down, the cigarette extinguished.

And he thought of how awful the sex itself might be: the uncovering of bruises with worrisome origins, the revelation of objectionable tattoos or piercings, the enacting of theatrical orgasms. After the one beer, he went home and hung the suit on its hanger, amused and embarrassed by his folly. Even comedy and shame, it seemed, were now solo operations.

But California was as good as anywhere; he felt at home nowhere. He'd spent the three weeks between release and the start of his new job visiting the places of his past, standing outside apartment buildings in Chicago, in Harlem, in the Bronx. He flew from LaGuardia to San Juan on a large plane full of tourists and Ricans visiting family. He circled the island clockwise in a rental car, finding that oldest home an amalgamation of the worst the United States and Latin America had to offer with the virtues of neither. In Fajardo, his visit with his parents and much younger sister was pleasant but formal. His father stared at him when he thought Eli wasn't looking but talked mostly about weather and sports, eager to agree with Eli's views on both topics. His mother was warm at first but retreated into harmless gossip about distant relatives. His sister, busy planning a large wedding, stayed only a couple of hours.

Friends in Ponce from the hard-core old days threw him a party—perhaps toasting his incarceration more than its ending—but even they were more interested in talking about remodeling their kitchens than about Independence. The wife of one, an advocate of statehood and visibly drunk, asked Eli how it felt to have given up twelve years of his life for a cause that was now obsolete.

"Okay," he whispered. "It feels okay."

The next morning he rose earlier than his hangover to complete the circle. In Rincón he sat on a small cliff, the wind in his face, and watched novice surfers smeared over and over by waves. He did not drive by the house where the only woman he'd ever met that he thought he could live with either lived or had once lived—he didn't know which. When he stopped at a gas station even though he had half a tank left, he recognized the small hope that he would run into her, chided himself, and continued his drive without topping off.

Only back in San Juan did he feel something that approximated closure enough to call it that. Two of his paintings hung in the Museo de Arte. One was the canvas he'd been arrested for stealing from a small Brooklyn museum—a work subsequently repatriated to Puerto Rico, which had been his mission in the first place. He'd been a different kind of naive back then and had never considered that there might have been other solutions to the problem than breaking and entering. He let his eyes pass over it only briefly, not because of that memory but because of part of its subject matter, because of the dark-haired woman lounging in the foreground.

The other painting was a self-portrait he admired but barely recognized and couldn't remember painting.

The plaque between the two works held his name, noted his place and date of birth, and identified him as "celebrated visual artist and Puerto Rican nationalist." He was grateful that the summation left out the nuances, the truth of what those things had meant for his life, the fact that he was no longer either.

Afterward he had a beer and *sorullitos* near the Mercado Santurce, eavesdropping on the conversations around him, happy to hear that they were in Spanish. *Familiar but not home.*

So maybe Los Angeles was better: unfamiliar and not home. No chance for mistaking his situation.

The manila folder Ted had left with him included descriptions and photographs of three paintings by Eugeen van Mieghem. All were on the small side, according to the dimensions recorded, and all were portraits of emigrants waiting to leave Antwerp by ship. The two that had been found were of a man and of a family. Despite the often wistful brushstrokes and liberal use of red, the overwhelming mood of the paintings was bleak. The sad helplessness of hope: people waiting to find out whether their lives would change for the better, the answer only marginally in their control. The painting that had not been recovered was of a young woman, maybe a teenage girl, gazing at the ocean she waited to cross, hoped to cross. The Belgian artist had painted it in 1926.

An online search revealed recent renewed interest in Van Mieghem, including the opening of a small dedicated museum in the artist's hometown. Still, given the size and simplicity of the paintings that had been recovered, and of the one still missing, they would fetch only a few thousand dollars apiece at auction. Real money, to be sure, but not what a man like Ted would ordinarily call big.

Unlike the case files Ted usually assembled, this one said nothing about ownership or the details of the theft beyond the date and the city: Brussels, 1993. It was unclear who the client was—whom the paintings had been stolen from, who wanted the missing painting found, to whom it might be returned, who was paying the bills on this job. Ted hadn't mentioned what had happened to the two paintings that had been recovered.

Dirty provenance, Eli guessed, which—given the location and when the painting had been done—probably meant it had run through Nazi fingers, fascist banks. The artist had died in 1930; it was unlikely that the painting would have left Western Europe before the war unless the owner had left and then returned.

Eli hoped he was being hired on behalf of the rightful owner because that was the person he planned to give the painting to if he found it. As always, he would depend on his own definition of rightful.

Alone in the room he nodded, physically reminding himself that he did indeed know where the lines he wouldn't cross lay.

Marion

THE brakes rubbed tight against the front tire, so Marion had to pedal hard as she biked down Frenchmen Street, as though she were going up a steep hill and not steering across the flattest city there is. She gripped the handles tightly with hands oversized enough that she'd known from a young age she was meant to work with them.

As she passed, she noted which bars were closed just because it was morning and which were still locked up altogether. If a place could start over, then so could she. That's what she was waiting for: the return of hotel spa business, the return of legitimate clients, the return of the career that used to pay the bills. Volunteering do-gooders, on-the-make construction workers, and locals returning to huge repair bills were not interested in what she was trained to do. They were not interested in her, and she had no use for them. Right now her needs and plans were simple: Do the work she could while waiting for the blue bloods and tourists to return and spend money. *When* was what most people said, not *if,* so maybe optimism did have its place. Meanwhile she was leaving a résumé at every hotel and day spa that was reopening or looked poised to, trying not to think about the fact that most of the people preaching optimism were those who'd stayed through the storm or come home quickly after—in other words, not actually most people.

Maybe if she could get back her real job it would lead to the return of the other career as well. *The vocation.* But she wasn't ready to think about that. The owner of the rubbled Ocean Springs gallery that was to have hosted her first show had told her the story of a famous writer—Hemingway, maybe, or someone like that, definitely a man—who lost an entire novel to fire or theft or because he left it on a train. He then sat down and rewrote from scratch what became a classic. That was supposed to make her feel better, but it infuriated her.

Weeks later, though, the thought of starting over no longer made her angry, just tired. One weekend after a double shift, she'd slept sixteen hours straight, waking up dehydrated and uncertain where she was. Her bedroom had materialized slowly, like an old-style photograph being developed. She no longer even saw the damaged canvases stacked against her bedroom wall except when she swept the floor, which wasn't often.

On Decatur, two blocks before she reached Molly's, she noticed two doors newly unpadlocked, two new lights on. There was a woman inside the first, turned sideways to the storefront, scrubbing or sanding a table against the wall.

Blond, tall, older than Marion but not old. There was no sign on the door, no clue hinting at what the business might be. Marion hopped off her bike and walked it down the middle of the street. The second new sign of life was on the next block, just past and across from the Mojo Lounge. No person visible, just a light and a sign. A tattoo parlor. A new establishment, as far as Marion could tell.

She locked her bike to a column in front of the bar and breathed in the smell of the Lower Quarter, an experience like standing outside a dryer vent except dirty instead of clean. Not quite sewage but stagnant water. She steeled herself to face the men inside, telling herself to be nice, that their dollars were worth smiling for. She told herself this every time, but usually she just slammed their beers down in front of them. It wasn't like they had many other women to look at outside those Bourbon Street strip joints that had stayed open or reopened fast, their girls looking more bedraggled than before. And of course some guys are attracted by disdain, determined to win you over, overtipping for rotten service. Anyway, they were glad to be served from behind a bar. In the first days following the storm, the bar had made do with beer bottles stuck into a pile of ice on the floor, compliments of a firefighter who had been a loyal customer. The owner took pride in not closing at all, said the city's thirst was stronger than any natural disaster.

"Tag. You're it." Suzette threw a towel at her before she even rounded the end of the bar.

Marion let it fall to the floor and walked through the

ceilingless corridor to the bathroom, stepping around puddles from an earlier rain, to use one of the stalls carrying the warning sign that tourists snapped pictures of: *One customer per bathroom or you will be asked to leave.*

She retrieved the towel from the floor when she returned, more or less ready to face the customers. High on the wall behind her, above the mirror that reflected a thousand bottles back to those who would drink them, hung license plates from every state—most of them quite old, but a few (Hawaii, South Dakota, and for some reason the relatively proximate Alabama) were newer. When she'd first started working at the bar, Marion had assumed the plates were some sort of tribute to tourists from every state who had set foot in the bar. Now she thought of them as representing not so much those who passed through but those who came and stayed. Despite claiming tourism as its main trade, the Lower Quarter was a place where you could become a local faster than in most places. Or maybe it was because of the tourist trade, not despite it, but Marion knew that other parts of the city were not the same. Uptown you were considered to be of the place only if your grandparents had been born in New Orleans, and there were families who thought even that definition was too generous, that true belonging required the commitment of additional generations.

Coco Robicheaux sat at the end of the bar, where he often sat, wearing an orange fedora with a bright blue band. A clear act of calculated outrageousness. A few stools in from the windows that opened onto the street, two long-haired guys were talking about snakes. Suzette—Marion was pretty sure that was her name, but business was down enough that none of the bartenders ever worked together—had taken care of all of them: tequila shaken with ice in front of Coco and two Pabst longnecks in front of the amateur herpetologists. Sitting farther in, near the taps, was a new arrival. He had a shaved head and brown skin and wore a white sleeveless undershirt showing off a thick torso and arms covered with tattoos.

"Hey there, fully illustrated one," Marion said. "What are you drinking?"

She could generally tell if someone was a tourist by the answer to this question. Bud light meant yes. Bayou Teche, no. Hurricane, yes, and get the fuck out of here and stumble your way to a tourist bar farther up in the Quarter. Bourbon on ice meant local and okay to stick around all afternoon. But this guy wasn't a giveaway: vodka with a twist. His accent was slight but present, probably Latino but what kind she had no idea. She made the cocktail, choosing lemon over lime without asking, and leaned back against the bar · to watch him drink it. He took two long sips. *Not a tourist but not local.*

"I'm guessing you and the new tattoo parlor on the next block are related," she said.

He smiled, maybe pleasantly surprised by her calculation or maybe only polite. Not flirting, she was pretty sure. "You're the only girl I seen working here with no tats at all."

His tattoos were botanical, making rain forests of the

large muscles of his arms and shoulders. They had less black and more color than she'd seen in tattoos before, multiple shades of green—dozens—and several of blue and red. She searched his neck, but he'd left that alone, passing at least one IQ test. There was a mole just above his left collarbone that made a diagonal with an identical beauty mark on the outside corner of his right eye. The imaginary line made her think of a Da Vinci drawing of a bisected man that she'd seen in an art history book.

"You should hire me," she said. "Teach me what you know."

"You wouldn't be much of an advertisement, blank slate like you." His voice was low in register, gentle in volume and tone. Now his accent just sounded big-city, not Southern—maybe Brooklyn or Detroit. "Afraid of the pain?"

She smirked. "It's not that."

"Nothing to be embarrassed about. It's smart to be afraid of pain, right? Evolutionary. But it's not so bad, the pain. And it's all for gain."

The rhyme should have put her off, but he said it like he knew it was stupid.

"Really, it's not that." She paused so he would hear the truth in what she said. "Not even a little. More like I'm afraid of commitment."

"We could start you off slow, something that could change over time, make you a living work of art, a thing in flux. Not like I'd stamp you with a tacky rose or heart or some guy's initials and send you home to live with it for the rest of your life."

"But what if I want to be an employee and not a customer?"

"Ink's not something you just start doing. There's talent and training and shit."

"An art form, I get it. But you just started doing it, back when, at the beginning. That's how anyone starts anything, right, how people start over?"

The snake guys caught her eye, and she delivered two more longnecks and added the price to their tabs. If the new guy's tattoos were art, theirs were cheap comics—a bad collection of individual figures, a graphic record of sloppy choices made one at a time. Some people don't learn from their mistakes—this was something she'd seen. Empirical knowledge she trusted.

While her back was still to the new guy, he said, "What makes you think you'd be any good at what I do?"

She turned around, spoke with a speed that surprised her. "Because I know both things—I know how to draw, and I know the body. I know line and color." She stopped short of calling herself an artist. If the show had happened, then she might have felt some claim to the word, but it hadn't and she didn't. "And I trained as a massage therapist—the real kind—have the certificate and everything, and I'm good. So I know skin, the shapes of muscles and how the shapes change when they flex and relax." She was struck by her own idea: art in motion on skin.

She watched his biceps shape-shift as he helped himself

to a napkin from the plastic barkeep and pushed it toward her. "Design something."

She rummaged around the cash register and found blue and black pens and a pencil. No green, which she wanted, but maybe that was for the better since green seemed to be his color. "Just remember: I'm using a ballpoint pen and a crappy napkin."

"No problem, I get that limitation, but the trick is you have to design something you would wear."

Shape moving on skin. Undulating. The ocean. She wanted to draw a jellyfish, translucent, shimmering, moved by waves, with waves. Painful when touched, yet beautiful. So beautiful that you touch it anyway, knowing the pain is part of its beauty, part of all real beauty.

But with pen on a cocktail napkin, the form would be amoebic, nothing but a blob. She would be laughed at. So she drew instead a stylization of a squidlike creature she had seen in a book of photographs of animals that live in the deepest parts of the ocean.

When she looked up after—how long? minutes? more?—Robicheaux was standing at the end of the bar waving, wanting to settle. After she'd taken care of him, she avoided eye contact with the illustrated cholo, wiped down the bar with the dirty rag. Out of the corner of her eye she saw his wallet come out of his pocket, money come out of the wallet. She had no choice but to go over, see if he needed change. She made his change and set it in front of him so she wouldn't touch his hand.

"You're a weird girl. I like that." He took his money, leaving a dollar on the bar—reasonable but not an overtip. "Stop by the shop sometime and I'll show you a thing or two."

Marion knew the value of clear statement. Once in high school a boy had asked her if she had a date to a dance and she'd mistaken his curiosity for an invitation, purchasing a dress that she never wore. When her parents bequeathed their furniture store to her brother, she learned that *Take care of your sister* meant *Shoot the business straight into your veins and leave her with nothing.*

"Are you saying you'll hire me?" she asked.

He laughed. "Why would I hire a girl with no experience who hasn't even bothered to ask my name? What I'm saying is that I'll think about it. Mostly what I'm saying is what I said—stop by sometime and I'll show you a thing or two. Decisions aren't always something you make in one moment, right?"

"I'd think in your line of work, you'd hope that wasn't true." Marion thought to smile at him, but by then his back was to her, and she didn't realize that his comment about her not asking his name meant that she was supposed to introduce herself.

That night, after she pedaled back to the Bywater, where she rented the left side of a double shotgun that had been rehalved into a duplex, Marion searched tattooing online. She combed through designs. Knowing better, she clicked on "most disgusting tattoo ever" and saw the photograph of a man's abdomen turned into a cat, his enormous misshapen navel the cat's vulva and anus. At least it was a design meant to be put in motion. She started to read what she could find on training, instruments, sanitary procedures, rules and codes. Like everything that has to be learned to acquire the kind of credentials that can get you paid for something, it was boring.

Without planning to, without even knowing she was about to do it, she typed in the website address she was too embarrassed to keep bookmarked even though she lived alone. She read through the posted ads, telling herself it was just because she needed the money, telling herself it was just something to do until she could get back to her real work.

She looked at ads on both sides—the ads she knew were too dangerous to answer and the ones on the side she could answer prosperously while managing her personal risk. As she read through the second batch, she stopped on the phrases *resolved through abnegation* and *cleansed by pain*. Certain she had just read the same words elsewhere, she went back to the ads for submissives, and there they were: *resolved through abnegation* and *cleansed by pain*. She wondered if it was a coincidence, a copycat, the work of a switch, or something else. When she woke in the middle of the night, those were the phrases she repeated to herself while she waited to fall back asleep.

Clay

CLAY pulled the second drawer of his filing cabinet out as far as it would go and removed from the second-to-last folder in the second-to-last hanging file the neat sheet of paper with his identities and passwords typed in columns and rows. He slid the drawer halfway in and pulled from the second folder in the second hanging file his ledger dates, times, and website addresses. This was a messier affair than the typed words and codes on the other sheet. The soft graphite numbers and letters had smeared from the weight and oil of his left hand as it followed, heavily, the pencil it pushed across the paper—a technique no teacher had been able to break him of.

Outside he heard the occasional vehicle: rarely the sound of a normal car, most often the mechanical buzz of the top-less Hummers driven by the private security forces still patrolling Audubon Place. Israeli tactical forces had been hired, some said, and others said no, but rather the American contractors who had misbehaved to notoriety in Iraq.

He'd seen an action star riding in one—a guy he'd seen in a movie some years back but couldn't name—bandoliers criss-crossed for show or fun or real sport. Clay knew he didn't have to worry; his skin color made him invisible, and the address and last name on his driver's license marked him as one of the protected.

He worked methodically, careful to use the correct computer for the correct identity on the correct blogs and accounts, a different one for the work he would do under his identity as Wikipedia editor, and the third for the reader reviews he posted to online bookstores.

Three of his targets had been there from the beginning—old friends, really, names that comforted with their familiarity. Others rotated in and out as people caught his ire and then bored him or when he determined that the damage inflicted was proportional to the injury deserved. The punishment should fit the crime, ideally in kind and certainly in degree. This was part of the unwritten but strict code he'd developed since he'd graduated from his youthful commitment to general mayhem and havoc by superglue to the more purposeful enforcement and revenge he now thought of as a practice.

He'd started small, canceling the newspaper and cable television service of an out-of-town neighbor who had smacked her gentle dog's nose with a rolled-up weekday edition or gluing together the pages of a library book by a local historian who was piggish in interviews. Rarely, but sometimes, the target was personal: a former schoolmate who'd popularized the entertainment of mocking Clay's gait. That gait was compensation for the small, crucial fact that his left leg was three centimeters shorter than the right, stunted as it had been by a large fibroid tumor in his mother's uterus.

His father's voice: *See, she gave you more than your money.*

He couldn't do much about his parents—his mother dead and his father seemingly with impunity in all situations—but a series of minor misfortunes had befallen his high school tormentor until the fellow had finally transferred to a parochial school with significantly less impressive college-placement results.

Kiddy stuff, he thought of all that now, but you have to start somewhere, and in those early pranks he saw the genesis of the artist he'd matured into. Though he'd never say it out loud to Johanna, what he did was a kind of art. His medium was the lives of others. Most often these days it was their virtual lives, though Clay understood that the relationship between who we are and whom we present ourselves to be is a strong if complicated one.

Once in a while he actually finished someone off—like the British graphic novelist he had tortured into obliterating his own web presence in the wake of a nervous breakdown, committing a digital suicide nearly as satisfying to Clay as if the man had actually hung himself from the rafters in his attic and not been found until the odor raised the neighbors' suspicions. But most often the feebleness of the bad actors he targeted educed his leniency. Narcissists are easy to punish. Even as they are quick to generate ego-protecting narratives, they are prone to shame and injure readily. It was hard not to feel sorry for them, really.

Only after Clay had moved item by item through his list, visited each social media account, commented on the blogs and sites he'd scheduled for that day, and read up on a critic he was weighing as potential victim—though lately he preferred to avoid the word victim, thinking instead in the terms of justice—did he search the Czech's name. How anyone could keep his name off the Internet in this era, even a sewer dweller like Ladislav, he couldn't fathom. But the only bearers of his name Clay could find with any search engine were human homonyms: an elderly resident of Prague and a middle school swim champion in East Chicago. Only by searching "Hotel Richelieu" and "death" did he produce a representation of Ladislav's face on screen.

John Doe was what they were calling him. *John Doe* was what they were calling the man responsible for the only time Clay had hurt someone who didn't deserve it. *John fucking Doe.*

Still, when he closed his eyes—not every time he blinked but often enough if his lids fell for more than a split second—he saw the small rectangular room, the cheap but sturdy headboard, her hair stuck to her wet neck. Still he smelled her sweat, more sweet than sharp, the specific smell of fear. Still he heard her whisper—beg—for him to get her out as his stomach hardened with the comprehension that her plea was not part of the game. *An innocent.* It embarrassed his pride that he hadn't noticed on his own, that it had been his third visit. It had taken a week, a little over a week—nine whole days and a few hours of the tenth—but he had got her out. *Out of the room, out of the building, out of the country.*

He'd sacrificed for it, too, by consenting to additional years under his father's rule in exchange for his help. But that never felt like enough because Clay could not undo what he had done three times over. When much later she thanked him for helping her, for getting her not only out but on her feet, more or less saying that he'd evened the score, he had screamed at her, "I don't want to be forgiven."

Instead of sitting down at his drafting table to work on the wolf drawings for his new book, Clay lay back on his unmade bed, typing now on the laptop with one hand. "Adult services: niche."

"The punishment should fit the crime, ideally in kind and certainly in degree." This he said out loud, to an empty room in an empty house on an almost-empty street in an almost-empty city.

Johanna

THE Lower Quarter repopulated slowly as people returned and new ones arrived, one at a time and then in
clots. One day there was an extra lunch customer across the
street. A week later Peter served a handful on the same day.
Before Johanna could worry about money, or just as she was
beginning to worry, customers appeared with damaged oil
paintings and watercolors.

A middle-aged woman with a painting of a covered
bridge: "I know it's dreadful, but my mother painted it before she died."

A gallery owner who'd purchased a large abstract canvas
covered in red and blue by an artist whom he'd given a show
right before the evacuation: "I bought it to be nice, because
he didn't sell anything else that night, but I also kind of like
it. And it wasn't cheap."

A young married couple who didn't realize that the
framed picture they'd bought from the hallway of the fancy
San Diego hotel where they'd honeymooned was a print—a

poster, really—and what they had purchased was not a great steal but rather an expensive frame: "But can you fix it?" the woman asked, her voice rising. Johanna tried to explain that there was no paint on the paper, that a replacement could be ordered easily.

Another couple phoned from Italy. They were university-based artists who had been on sabbatical when the storm hit. A house full of paintings and drawings, they said—luckily many on the second floor. They wanted to send Johanna a key, have her survey the damage. They would give her a list of where to start, which works were most important to them professionally, personally, one for no good reason at all. "Also, our cat," they said, speaking at the same time into two receivers.

Johanna told them she'd think about it, planning to call them back in a day or two with the name of someone else they could call, either explaining or making an excuse. She did not like to go into other people's houses without knowing exactly what she would find there.

It didn't take long for people—the lunch crowd across the street and the customers who carried framed canvases into her workshop—to speak in terms of before and after. Nor long for the lovely word *Katrina* to morph into something more generic and less dreadful. *Before the storm. After the storm.*

Johanna could understand this language. She had long described her life to herself by a similar equation: before and after. Sometimes she thought about what fell between the two, which her mind avoided in its details, as *the bad time*. Her version of the generic. But mostly it was this: *Before Belgium. After Belgium.*

Both before the storm and after the storm, she dwelled mainly in *after Belgium*: her daily routines, the people and shops of lower Decatur, her weekly trip by foot and then streetcar to Audubon Zoo, where sometimes she met Clay but most often did not, followed by a rest in front of Bird Island, which Clay, whose family had lived in New Orleans since forever ago, called Ochsner Island. And her work—her work had come after and now occupied most of her life.

There were times, though, when she skipped right over Belgium and allowed herself to think, for short spans, of *before*. Her memories of her father were from before. Most were fragments—wispy images with the quality of a morning dream just before waking. Even those few memories that were crisp were isolated. Single images: the side of her father's face, his hand turning the page of a book, the smell of leaves on his shirt. Only one was more extended, possessing the quality of narrative.

A beach near a city, a vacation. The only time in her life when she will be a tourist and not some other category of migrant. The ocean is flat: a thick stripe of turquoise water close to shore and then the wide block of dark blue, the line dividing them clean and straight. A child's painting of the sea. Unlike the pebble beaches closer to where they live, this one is sand, and her father shows her how wet the sand needs to be to make a fort. The one they build is large, protected by multiple sea walls. As they finish the tide breaks over the wall farthest out, filling the moat between it and the next. She sees, then, what will happen.

"The people will have to move." Her voice is somber. She looks to her father.

"Maybe that will be a good thing," he says. "They thought they wanted to live in a fort, but the rooms are very cold and the floors are very hard, and when they move they will find that they like their new home much better."

Later in the day they are in the city near the beach, walking hand in hand in a museum. Her father is telling her about the statues in the Greek wing, how once upon a time their irises were green and brown, how they were brightly painted from head to foot, how now they are just silhouettes, bland copies of their former selves. Not what the artists meant for them to be at all.

"Now they live in a fort," she says in her child's voice, "where the walls are cold and the floors are very hard."

Her father kneels, looks at her as though seeing something previously unnoticed, kisses the top of her head.

Yet, memory being untrustworthy, she doubted this recollection. There had been a photograph of that morning on the Dalmatian coast, which she had seen several times after the excursion itself, seen while her father was sick and again after the cancer spread from his bladder and killed him. As much as she wanted the memory of her father emerging from the turquoise water to be direct, she admitted to herself that it may have been the photograph she remembered.

A memory of a representation—not direct and so not real.

The conversation about the color of the statues' eyes, though, that she remembered herself and not from a photo. But it was entirely possible that the conversation had not happened the same day or the same week or even the same year of the trip to the beach. It was possible that it hadn't even happened in a museum but over a book opened on their little table at home. Before he got sick. Before the bad time. *Before Belgium.*

She picked up the phone and dialed Clay's number, wishing that the sequence of digits wasn't rote after all this time. Yet there were few numbers—none—to displace the knowledge. Clients' numbers she called only once or twice so did not memorize, and there was no one else she called.

When Clay did not answer, she hung up without leaving a message. The information she had to give him, if he didn't already know it, and the questions she knew she was supposed to ask him should not be entrusted to a machine. She would eventually have to see him.

She called the couple in Italy, not accounting for the time difference. They were grateful to be wakened when she told them yes, she would go see about their work. And yes, their cat.

She trembled when she hung up, bracing her fingertips on the counter of the narrow galley kitchen. She had not meant to make the call, had not known in advance that she was going to accept their offer. Indeed, she had decided as soon as she had first talked to them that she would not take the job. She delayed only out of respect for what they did—to make them think that she had at least deliberated, perhaps to give them another name or to offer to look at their work if they could hire someone else to retrieve it and bring it to her. She did not care to go into other people's houses, she had planned to explain, and she was no good with cats.

Though her back was to the small painting in her sitting area, she could feel it there—like being in the room with another living thing, an animal unseen but whose sentience you feel. She carried it now to her too-soft sofa, loosened the twine, opened the squares of smooth brown paper, revealed paint and line and figure.

The first time she had seen the painting, grime had obscured its colors. She'd had to strain, her head twisted unnaturally to the left, to see the human figure—a young woman—waiting to trade one life for another. It was then, in that horrible and undeniable moment, that she had first experienced the curiosity that would become her vocation. Lying on the floor, level with the painting slanted against the wall, her head bent away from what was happening to her, she had wondered how a painting might be cleaned, its colors restored and released.

Eli

W HEN he was a younger man, Eli loved not only to travel but the travel itself, the flying from place to place, inhabiting a space between lives and friends and countries. He was a nationalist, yes, in that he believed in independence for his people, his home. Personally, though, he identified as something else. Cosmopolitan was a word pretentious to him even back then, when, feeling as untouchable and certain as all bright and handsome young men, he'd been at his most pretentious.

Yet there was also a simpler appeal to travel: the coincidental crossing of lives—whom you might meet. In his fantasies it was often a beautiful woman who shared his tastes in paintings and books and politics. But sometimes he imagined sitting in a window seat and looking up to find an artist he admired storing his satchel in the overhead compartment, taking the seat next to him. Eli would imagine how he would hold his body next to the famous one, respecting his privacy too much to speak but following the illustrious gaze with his own, seeing what it landed on and for how long, as though perspective were a skill that can be learned through observation of another rather than through study.

While Eli had never had the good fortune to sit next to either a woman or a painter worthy of a pedestal, knowing that it could happen was still a pleasure. And often enough he sat next to someone who was at least interesting, or who could recommend a good park or bar in the city he was heading to, or who told him some strange fact he found himself pulling out at a party a week later. If nothing else, he'd learned that most people hold jobs you've never heard of or at least never thought about doing yourself. On various flights he'd been seated next to an actuary, a man who investigated train wrecks, a woman who managed a factory in which single-use coat hangers were manufactured for (as she called them) high-volume department stores, a couple who had started a company that arranged food for photo shoots, a pro bowler, and a guy who called himself a user-experience designer. "I make it more pleasant for people to interact with things," he'd said. "My favorite work is with board games, but I'm working on cash machines right now. You take the work you can get."

Airline travel had changed while Eli had been away. He'd done enough of it in his first year out to get used to it, but now he didn't like flying as he once had. The surveillance, the assumption of guilt, the routine inspection, the line of adults rendered shoeless and harmless as children, it was all too much like where he'd just been. The security line this time wasn't too bad. The first-class ticket arranged by Ted's assistant landed him in the shortest line. "It'll help make up for where you're staying," Ted had said. Plus he'd worn loafers—not on purpose but by good fortune. He'd boarded early and been handed a free mimosa, a newspaper, a pillow pristine in its plastic case.

The suited man across the aisle from him lifted his glass and said, "Everyone's always in a good mood on their way to New Orleans. Different story coming back. At least that's how it used to be." He drained his glass, then shook his head. "Damn shame, damn shame. But at least there are direct flights again."

Eli had never given any real thought to New Orleans, which perhaps was why the recent television images of the city felt as remote as news from the other side of the world. He'd wondered before, now and again, what makes some lives more mournable than others. So often it was proximity—not merely geographic but social, economic, cultural, ethnic. The more like us someone is, the more we empathize. For those more distant, it's too bad and we're sorry, but we rest certain that their misfortunes won't strike us. *It couldn't happen to me.*

Trite observation, he knew, but one whose truth felt close because he knew that's what people think about those who go to prison. Even the exonerated are presumed to have done *something* wrong, even if not the thing. Eli had been guilty as charged, making his story an even harder sell to the sympathies of the never-incarcerated. What had happened to him could not have happened to just anyone. His fate was specific to him, and he knew better than to expect anyone to feel bad for him. He was lucky to be out. The fact that his luck could be reversed with very little paperwork by others was enough to prevent him from taking his freedom for granted. He enjoyed the hell out of his free mimosa and then gave into the resulting drowsiness.

Eli woke when the captain announced the descent into New Orleans. With his forehead pressed against the peculiar plastic of the window, he watched the city grow closer and larger. He'd never seen such a flat place, or one where the borders between what is land and what is water were so vague.

He'd expected the airport to smell like humanity—like the hundreds of people who'd camped there hoping to fly out ahead of the hurricane—but the only signs of the storm were ladders and plastic and tape, presumably from repairs being made by workers currently on break. A jazz band played in the terminal, just outside security. Old style with clarinets, a trumpet, a trombone, and an upright bass. Music Eli had heard before, probably in a movie: music intended to indicate both a mood and a place. Giving tourists what they wanted. *More symbol than song.*

He'd known two women once, from the old life, who'd ventured no deeper than the airport when they'd flown to New Orleans one year for Mardi Gras. "You could feel the place was evil," they told him, explaining why they'd imme-

diately changed their return flight and left only hours after
arrival. He'd dismissed the story as nutty when he'd heard it.
Now he wondered if their irrational and expensive response
didn't have something to do with the smell of the place—
not a bad smell, exactly, but like something turned inside
out so what should have been obscured was instead bared.
An animal without its hide.

Outside he was third in the cab line and rode into the
French Quarter with a driver he identified as Haitian by
his accent. "You people are starting to come back," the man
said, "and this is a good thing."

Eli named the hotel where the murder had occurred,
where two of the missing Van Mieghem paintings had
turned up. "You know it?"

"Sure, sure," said the driver as he fed into thin traffic.
"That's in the lower part of the Quarter."

Eli felt unmoored and put it down to the drastic increase
in humidity as well as the flatness of the land, which offered
no vantage point, no contours by which he could get his
bearings. He put his trust in the cabdriver and watched the
short view along the highway, which—aside from hit-and-
miss damage and the sense that the foliage might overtake
the man-made—was not so different from any other drive
between a city's airport and itself. Already he was getting
used to the smell.

Though Eli could not name the streets unless the cab
slowed enough for him to read the green-and-white signs,
he knew enough to tell that they had passed the Super-

dome, made their way across wide Canal Street—split by streetcar tracks not in use—and penetrated the Vieux Carré.

"I'll drive you down Bourbon," the driver said, "just because I can. Before, it was not possible—always blocked to traffic—and I believe you take what is good from what is bad. It won't be open for long, not if you folks keep returning and the young ones keep moving in."

"A good philosophy," Eli said, though it was the type of sentiment that had angered him in those early locked-up years. *Make the most of it. Like hell,* he'd thought, but then he continued living his life because that's what a person does. All the clichés from the movies, because for the most part that was what was on offer: the prison library, the weight room, meditation classes, even a little drawing, though he'd never asked anyone to send him paint and was still determined never to paint again.

And now Eli made the most of the drive down Bourbon Street, its mix of open and still-shut. Stores mostly shut, bars mixed, strip joints open, the girls even standing in the doorways, trying to wave in the scant pedestrian traffic.

"Before the storm," said the driver, "there were better girls. Not too round but not drug-skinny. More clean. The best ones left not to come back. These are the ones with nowhere better to go, plus some who came after. What's the word?"

Eli made eye contact in the rearview mirror and shrugged. *"Professionals?"*

"Opportunists," said the driver. "That is the word."

"Making the best of what's bad?"

The driver laughed, his eyes squinting in the horizontal rectangle of glass. "I suppose so, making the best for themselves of what's bad for other people."

A few blocks more and the car slowed at a curb in the middle of a block that looked deserted. "This is you," the driver said, his hand indicating a three-story brick building with a few sad flags hanging over its short front steps. "I know what you are thinking, that Richelieu is such a grand name."

"It's all right," Eli said, smiling. "This is what I expected. This is what I always expect."

Marion

As a child, Marion had wished her parents dead, at least in make-believe. She'd grown up on stories of orphans who lived in boxcars and intrepid motherless girls with special powers. Across the happy years of late elementary school, she and her best friend had played a game called "Runaways." They chose names—Tatum and Tara—and invented a stern older brother (Terrence) who protected them and an annoying younger one (Tommy) whom they often had to rescue from self-inflicted danger. Orphans, all of them, they'd fled a cruel aunt and fended for themselves on scavenged food and the close sibling bonds of brothers and sisters named with the same letter of the alphabet.

But life was nothing like the comforting game when her parents died in quick turns—too late to turn her into a storybook heroine but before they could help her get a start in life. Her brother, her only sibling, was no Terrence, and their names shared few letters. He was just a fuckup who hadn't really meant to screw her over but had done so just as surely as if he'd tried. It had taken him less than two years to shoot up not only the furniture store her parents had made their modest living operating but also the second loan on the Ocean Springs house she had grown up in—a house recently obliterated, not that it mattered anymore.

Marion had dropped out of Mississippi State, where she'd done well in her art classes and well enough in the others, and racked up more loans to earn a massage-school diploma. Before the storm she'd worked at Beau Rivage Casino and Hotel in Biloxi and then after the storm trekked up the Delta to the spa at the Alluvian Hotel, where there weren't enough clients to cover her expenses, not even in the Viking Range–subsidized town of Greenwood.

Beau Rivage was rebuilding quickly and would have had her back, but she didn't want to return to the coast or to a casino—a place where people wagered their lives away one small stake at a time. If she was going to start over, then she wanted to start over. She had no people left on the coast, anyway, besides a few old friends who weren't much good for her and the brother she no longer talked to. He'd evacuated to Houston, someone had told her, but she didn't know for sure or much care.

Marion had never minded the massage work. She'd discovered that you learn a lot about people from their bare backs. She could name her clients' ages to within a few years—the older they were, the more accurate her estimate, a fact that seemed backward to her, as counterintuitive as the rest of her life. If they were fat as well as old, she could glean how fast they had got that way, whether suddenly from a recent addiction to packaged food or slowly, perhaps from alcohol's secondary depositing of internal fat or a happy lifetime of rich food. She could read less of the younger ones' lives, their bodies still mostly unmarked, undetermined. Blank like their fates. As bad as she had always been at understanding the past, she'd never been able to see the future in any way that came true.

Often but not always she could tell if someone's visit was the regular maintenance of the wealthy or a rare luxury, perhaps a birthday gift from another or to self. When she could tell this, which wasn't always, it was by how much pleasure they pulled from her touch and, sometimes, by how easily they submitted. Though she loathed the wealthy, she never varied the quality of her work. When she worked, she did what she was paid to do as well as she could every time—mostly but not only for a good tip. She'd been able to discern no relationship, positive or negative, between wealth and tipping behavior. Sometimes the rich were generous, sometimes stingy. Sometimes the poor were frugal, and sometimes it was easy to see why they didn't have two dimes to rub together most of the time. She took note of all of them, finally determining that the middle wasn't a bad place to be and would be her goal if she ever in her life had any money to squander, which usually seemed like never.

It is no small thing to make people feel good, to give them an hour of respite, press away knots in their muscles, make them forget their lives. Yet she'd never confused her work with a noble calling like some of her New Age co-workers. It was her day job, though not the worst she had held, and she was always glad to have finished the shoulder blades of her final customer, to pull up the sheet and turn off the light and say, "Stay as long as you want, and check out up front."

How easily her expertise transferred from giving plea-sure to giving pain—or pleasure through pain—surprised her when she thought about it, which she mostly did not. If a person could live an unreflective life by choice, then that was what she did. Besides, she was just doing it for the mon-ey until the tourists came back. That she should have gone farther than New Orleans was an idea that came to her reg-ularly and one she pushed away each time. She'd gone as far as she could afford to go, and later, when the tourists came back, it would look like it had been a good idea all along.

She chose not to meditate on her life generally, but it was harder than she would have thought and had to be enforced in small ways nearly daily. As she biked up St. Charles, she felt a thought at the border of her mind, felt it like water seeping under a door. She sealed the crack and pedaled on, navigating occasional piles of rubble, small mountains of stone, a toilet inexplicably sitting on the streetcar tracks. As she rode, she looked left and right at the fine old houses, many of which looked not merely evacuated but long empty, like a restored ghost town or the set of a movie.

At least one blue blood was back, though, if the address in her pocket could be trusted as an accurate indicator. Almost to Tulane, she thought the number was, and pedaled harder. He would not appreciate her being late. He would be the kind of man who was accustomed to others waiting for him—probably why he was hiring her to put him in his place. Not a true masochist but a man who enjoyed handing over power because he had so much of it. A short respite from responsibility, that was what most of them wanted. Yet she was still fairly certain that he had written both ads, the one she'd answered and the one she'd wanted to answer, which made him something other than most of them. That this was why she had come was another idea she sealed out when she sensed its approach.

She'd heard the stories about Audubon Place, how the rich people who lived there had hired Israeli military to guard their houses when their own federal government wouldn't even drop bottles of water over the city. Macho movie actors with too-long, thinning hair cruising around in Hummers with bandoliers strapped to their chests, guests of mercenary security outfits. People at Molly's said it was all true, and that wasn't the half of it. Shots taken at black men for sport, on a bet, and worse still. She gave her name at the gondola next to the gate and was waved through by a tall, square-jawed man whose looks made her believe that any of the stories could be true, though she couldn't spy a gun in plain sight.

The house was grander even than she had imagined but ugly—not a whimsically painted Victorian, like many of the large houses on St. Charles, but a vulgar stone thing. A fortress with small and opaque windows. An obscenity, really, surrounded by ridiculous statues of perfected nymphs, thorny rosebushes everywhere. Unlike most of the other houses nearby, it had no front porch. Its architecture was designed to keep out rather than to welcome. If she disappeared into a basement dungeon, no one would ever know except perhaps the guard in the gondola, who would be the one to help cover up the crime. She should have run this through one of the agencies. Instead she risked a lifetime of torture so she could pocket the full fee, or perhaps for the reason she kept at bay.

She had left at home a letter detailing where she was going and why. It wouldn't save her, but it might stop him from getting away with it. If some asshole was going to kill her, she wanted him to get caught and sit in his jail knowing it was because she'd planned ahead, knowing that he'd underestimated her. She pictured him vague-faced and tormented, the bars of his small cell casting shadows diagonally across his face, the sound of heavy breath—a menacing presence one cage over. The future girls whose lives she'd saved would never even know they had been in any danger, making her act all the more noble.

A moving shadow revealed him now, in the recess of a side door: average height and looks, thin, indoor-pale, straight sandy hair snipped short in back but with long bangs almost concealing light eyes, probably blue, maybe green. Weirdly, he was young. Usually they were at least old enough to have made a lot of money and sometimes really old, but this guy was *maybe* thirty. Inherited wealth, this meant, which was rare. Her clients were mostly self-made men, and if she thought about it there was some pride in this for her.

"I didn't expect you to be on a bike." His voice was soft but carried, like an actor whispering from a stage so that an entire audience can hear without mistaking the whisper for something louder. "I thought you'd have some sort of costume."

"Backpack," she said. "I need to change. And somewhere to lock up my bike—couldn't very well ride the streetcar."

"Bring it in." He went inside, letting the screen door slap closed behind him, forcing her to open it for herself while balancing the bike with her other hand. She negotiated her way in, fitting awkwardly through the narrow side entry with pack and bike. She stood in a library—no furniture but a table and two heavy chairs covered in thick plastic sheeting. Walls of hardcover books climbed to the high ceilings. She tapped down her kickstand, wondering if it would damage the Turkish rug and if he'd hold her responsible if it did. She could see into a larger room, perhaps a living room, with formal furniture, a shiny grand piano, and paintings covering most of the walls.

"I only use part of the house, upstairs." He gestured toward the second floor with a stab of his head.

Perhaps he was just a house sitter, in which case it would be even more important than usual to make sure up front he had cash on him.

The stairs were broad and spiraled slowly up. Only a huge house could afford to yield so much room to a staircase and have it make sense. He motioned her to go first. Now a gentleman, she thought, but corrected her interpretation as she felt him watching her climb. She wondered what his gaze focused on: legs, ass, waist. She'd been clear, as always, when she'd answered his ad: "No intercourse, and my clothes stay on."

Upstairs they walked by a bedroom's open door. On first glance it looked like command central for some sort of low-level spy or police operation in a movie—computers everywhere, some of their lights blinking and others constant. But beyond the distracting barricade of technology were an unmade bed and an almost equally large drafting table covered with neat stacks of paper and pens lined like logs for transport.

"Do you sketch?" Marion asked, remembering the advice that a victim always try to humanize herself to a perpetrator—advice she applied to clients who could become perpetrators, which was potentially any one of them.

"Farther down," he said, "last door on the left."

The door opened onto a much larger, grander bedroom with tapestrylike curtains and an enormous canopied bed.

"You can change in the suite bath."

She turned, almost expecting him to be holding a gun or a knife. With his frail body and slightly entertained expression, he looked harmless, at once belonging to and seeming out of place in the stuffy, old-money room decorated by someone else.

"Great," Marion said. "First, we'll go over what you want, special requests, your no-list, limits."

"Doesn't that undermine the whole experience, if it's choreographed, if I know you won't go too far?"

"It just gives it a container. Once I come out of that bathroom, we'll be in scene. Taking care of this now will make the whole thing better."

"For you." His voice was accusatory, but the accusation was amused, and Marion couldn't tell if it was playful or real.

"And for you," she said flatly.

"You can do anything to me, but make it hurt. The less I like it the better. But no baby talk either way. I'm not looking for a mother. Just pain. I know some of the men who hire you are just playing. A little rough talk, a little humiliation—kiss my boot and all that—but you can't leave a mark on them without them crying for real. Am I right?"

She assumed his question was rhetorical, but he waited for a response, and finally she nodded so he would resume.

"I'm different. I want you to hurt me. I don't care about the rest of it." His blink was deliberate.

Marion did the sorting: more masochist, less submissive. "Do you want any kind of frame?" she asked. "You know, roles? Cop and speeder, teacher and student."

He shook his head but then said, "Sadist and captive, if anything. Or better, let's just be who we are." Again the blink. "Or best, tell me what you would pick if we switched places."

She didn't know why, because she generally followed her

instincts and this violated them, but she answered with the truth. "I would start with who we are. You're rich, and I'm not, so there's power already there. Maybe you had me taken here because I insulted you, and I know I can't get away because you could find me again."

"Psychological power is better than locks and chains?"

"Always. So maybe I'm an intruder—a looter or trespasser or something—and you discover me. I do what you say, submit to your form of punishment, or you call the cops."

"The cops are too busy to answer the phone these days." He tossed his head once, flopping the bangs out of his eyes. Blue, not green, and unattractively pale as though whoever colored them hadn't finished the work.

"They're never too busy to answer calls from this address," Marion told him. "I bet you have all the direct lines, red buttons or whatever, but we can say you'll call the asshole security guards who patrol this place now, like that goon I had to pass through to get here. So I'd be better off taking my chances with you, or so I would wager."

For just a moment, his mouth collected itself, became smaller, as though stopping itself from saying something he had thought better of saying. Instead he said, "We'll just assume that you have this house's power and that I have no means of escaping lightly. As I said, I don't care much about the frame. You can change in there."

The bathroom was as large as she would have expected, with a separate walk-in shower and huge soaking tub rising into a wall-sized mosaic of tiny multicolored tiles, ridiculous bidet next to the toilet, triple sinks, and what even she could tell were expensive fixtures. There were three small paintings of blue horses on one wall, paintings she recognized well enough to wonder if they were real. It took her a moment, but she came up with the artist's name: Franz Marc. She'd liked him when she was young—in high school—and then convinced herself that she wasn't naive enough to like Marc until a teacher she admired gave her permission to like him again. "There's a lot more irony there than you might think," he'd said, but mainly what had won her back were his brushstrokes and the deceptive saturation of his colors, especially the blues. She looked more closely now: definitely paintings and not prints but perhaps copies all the same. There were people who collected such things, she knew, because she'd looked into every potential career choice before she'd settled for what she'd settled for. She'd have broken into real forgery if she'd known how to and had that particular artistic gift. But, no, these paintings were probably originals, and she wondered how much something like that cost.

Her hands trembled as she rolled up the stockings and hooked the absurd bustier. Even with dark red lipstick, she looked like a freakishly dressed-up child. The man wasn't tall, but he would still be taller than she was in the spiked heels. He was right about it being all play. She had never really hurt anybody before. It interested her, but only indirectly, as a student of herself. In the end she was nothing like her clients, not in life situation and not in the way she was wired—not that psychology interested her as anything other than instinct.

He called through the door, "What about me? How much do I wear?"

"Up to you," she said. Realizing her voice wasn't loud enough to carry through the thick wood, she repeated it with forced volume: "Up to you. I can hurt you through your clothes. Most guys wear boxers. A few need to be naked."

"What's your preference?" Even at its raised pitch, his voice was patrician. Something in the accent or intonation—she couldn't identify it, but she recognized it all the same. Yes, the paintings were the real thing.

"Doesn't matter to me either way, but my clothes stay on."

When she came out, face set to make it look older and more serious, he was wearing jeans and nothing else.

She thought she might start with him over the bed, testing whether what he said about pain was real before striping his back or his feet with the single tail, which she had used before but only lightly or to make noise—all pretend. But that felt wrong. She chose a leather strap, drawn by its simplicity, its ability to leave marks but not draw blood. "Grab the doorway," she said, "up high."

He smirked but did as she said, his feet on each side of the door as he faced the hall, his hands holding the frame near the top on each side. There was something off about the shape he made—a star tilted because his hips weren't even, the left one lower than the right, leaving him slightly cocked to the side. The imperfection appealed to her. She bit her lip just hard enough to make it hurt, for her to imagine the blood near the surface seeping through the skin.

She hit him hard across the back of his jeans, but not as hard as she could. The next time a little harder and then again, settling on what she calculated to be severe but short of what she was physically capable of and counting to twenty. She'd show him his pain threshold wasn't as high as he thought it was, that he didn't really want what he said he did.

His body stiffened with each strike, resisting rather than giving in, more brittle than relaxed. When she told him to look over his shoulder at her, his expression was hard and unreadable. He was not pliant, and he had not been transported to that other place, the place of permanent now with no responsibilities. She wielded the belt as hard as she could, and he glared at her. His eyes showed no pleasure, no connection, no release or escape, no fear or desire. Nothing.

She stated the simple fact: "You're not a masochist."

He shook his head, still glaring at her. She couldn't tell if it was due to the light through the plantation blinds or if his eyes were really wet. If what she was seeing was the beginning of tears, they were tears of physical pain, or perhaps of anger, but not of humiliation.

"And not a submissive," she said, letting the belt fall against her own thigh. "So what the hell is this? Did you lose a bet or something?"

He dropped his arms and turned toward her, taking a step closer. This made her want to back away, but she held her stance and looked directly into his eyes, nearly see-through in color but opaque in expression.

"I wanted to feel what it's like to have something done to you that you don't want done," he said.

"You want to be punished for something." She knew that she should be afraid of what the something was, yet she no longer perceived him as a potential threat. It might have been because of his off-kilter stance, though that would be dumb; a physical flaw can make someone more dangerous just as easily as not.

His lips parted as though he was about to answer her, but they closed before they opened again with what she was sure were different words: "You could say that, yes." The blink again, slow, as if for effect. "How could you tell I didn't like it? I'm guessing it takes one to know one?"

His voice was louder now, direct, accusatory, and she felt the place inside her unlatch. Her knees bent just slightly. A patch under her sternum quivered. "It's from this side"—she handed him the strap she'd been using—"that you learn compassion and forgiveness."

His laugh was almost a snort when he shoved her over the bed. "You think I should be rehabilitated instead of punished? Or that someone can learn to use power with restraint?"

When he struck her across the back of her thighs, the

sting was sharper than any she'd ever felt. She heard her breath catch, and then she relaxed into pain, never knowing quite when or where it would come.

An hour later, she had broken both of her rules. Surprised by the strength of the weak-looking man, she was nude and had been fucked bound on the floor, bent over the bathtub, pressed against the wall. She'd been whipped and pinched and forced to her knees, her hair pulled hard. He'd taken her across her pain threshold, and she'd let him, afraid that if she broke the scene it would end instead of soften.

When he was done with her, finally, he lay on his back on the bed. She lay on her side, looking away from him and at the wall, smelling his smell coming from both of them, slightly metallic but also like sanded wood.

"Do you want to know what it feels like from this side?"

Her question was quiet, but he heard her and responded: "I'm not interested in your psychology, and I don't want to hear any stories about how your self-esteem was injured as a child by the teacher who threw away your dandelions or the daddy who didn't like the poems you wrote."

"But you are interested in it, because it's my reaction that gives you pleasure, and you're wrong about it. I've never written poems, and I don't have self-esteem problems or daddy issues."

"Well, then?"

She changed sides, facing him but maintaining the distance between them on the high bed. "Clarity. There's no indecisiveness, because there are no decisions. There's not any regret, because there's no past. There's no anxiety, because there's no future."

"Indecisiveness is not my problem. I like making decisions."

"Obviously you like control. I won't ask why."

He remained looking straight up at the gauzy canopy that made the bed into its own room. "If you ever want to do this again, you need to stop with the psychology right now. It bores me, and its little equations are almost always wrong."

When she left she felt something close to exhilarated, barely noticing the long bike ride home. Maybe she had found him: the man who could show her who she was outside time and place. If he happened to be an asshole with a limp, that was probably part of the territory. His talent was rare.

Most guys would play at the role if asked—most guys will do anything to get and keep getting sex—but only for very few was it not play. She didn't know what it meant that it came naturally to this man, or what it meant that her role came naturally to her, but the man was right in his condemnation of easy psychology. She knew that as well as anyone and again resolved to return to her intentionally unreflective life. She liked what she liked and had finally found a place to get it.

Only when she arrived home did she realize that she had not returned his money to him. For a moment she thought she would keep it—after all, she'd ridden all the way uptown and started to do what she was being paid for—but then she recognized that she could not because of the words she would be if she did. She was none of those words. She was her own person.

Eli

THE hotel used real keys with cumbersome rings, making practically appealing its rule that all room keys be left at the desk. Behind the down-on-its-luck reception desk and the surprisingly crisp woman staffing it, a partial wall of small numbered cubbyholes held the keys of guests out walking the Quarter. Eli counted: his key would make that number three.

"Were you working here before the hurricane?" he asked the woman, guessing that she looked younger under her makeup, was playing at being professional.

"No, sir." She smiled wide, her small teeth not quite enough to fill her mouth properly or she would have been a beauty. "I'm new."

He wanted to ask her if the key system had been in place long, but it was obvious that it had been, that the hotel was one of the very few that had simply never updated to the key cards that were now ubiquitous but were new enough to be rare the last time he'd stayed in a hotel before going to prison.

He wanted to ask her if she knew which room the dead man had been discovered in, but even as little as he knew about people, he knew that was a creepy question, one that would make her more cautious with information rather than more forthcoming. Embarrassed to be standing there mute, he asked directions to the nearest place for coffee, and she directed him a block toward the river.

"Welcome," he said.

"That's what I'm supposed to say to you, at least what I should have said when you checked in."

He felt his face warm and hoped that the flush was not visible, that she would not think he was trying to hit on her, given their clear age difference. "I meant welcome to your new job."

Her confused look told him he was a terrible detective, though perhaps a talent for confusing people could prove a useful skill. To confuse the right person at the right time might loosen a tongue. He'd seen this in prison—someone disarmed by a friendly response when they were expecting defense or a direct comeback when they were expecting fearful evasion.

As he opened the door, warm air reached into the air-conditioned lobby. As he walked down the steps, it swarmed him, then penetrated. Soon an equilibrium was reached, and he and the heat no longer felt like separate things. He followed the clerk's directions, walking toward the river. In a narrow ice-cream shop, he drank a double espresso standing at the counter. Like the hotel clerk, the worker was young and seemed new to the city. His frequent eye movements made him seem not wholly at ease. Unlike the clerk, though, he was not playing at being professional but declaring himself as nothing of the kind with lobe-distorting ear discs and tattoos that climbed from his hands into the armholes of his tank top. Eli was aware of his own age, the generational difference that had opened between him and the young while he'd been away. When he'd gone in, he'd still been young, a sense that had ended immediately but that he had thought—erroneously—might return when he was released.

Ted had scheduled two appointments for Eli—that afternoon with the cop who'd caught the murder case and the following day with the woman who ran the auction galleries. But Eli hoped the dead man had chosen this part of the city for a reason, that there was something to be learned in the Lower Quarter. He smirked at himself as he imagined asking the kid behind the counter whether he'd ever heard anything about any Eugeen van Mieghem paintings circulating in the neighborhood. He took the sketch he'd made from the newspaper clipping out of his pocket—the one showing the dead man but, Eli hoped, not necessarily as a dead man.

"Buddy of mine disappeared right before the storm. He was staying down here."

To his surprise the young guy took the picture and looked closely. When he said, "Sorry, man," he seemed to mean it. "Thing about the storm is that a lot of people won't be found. Some of them 'cause there's no one to look for them. Some of them 'cause they don't want to be found. Some just because they're gone." He took Eli's cup without asking and added a single shot from the hissing machine. "What's weird is that when a place becomes known for being a place where people disappear, then people who want to disappear start showing up. We'll be lousy with gutter punks soon enough." He grinned. "Yeah, you're thinking I look like one, but I wash my hair. I've got a job. I don't have five dogs, and I can feed the two I do have."

What Eli had been thinking was that he didn't know what gutter punks were, but now, it seemed, he more or less did. This was how he felt a lot—not just because he'd been in prison but because he'd largely withdrawn from popular culture even before he had gone in. Inside he'd stepped back into himself, chosen books over movies, weights and meditation classes over television. He'd given up politics altogether. It was a way to survive without going crazy. So often he found himself like a kid learning a second language, picking up meanings and connotations from context. He'd recognize a gutter punk if he saw one now.

He left some coins on the counter and walked along Decatur Street toward the Cathedral, still with only a vague idea of what he could do on his own. What he decided was this: Poke around enough to be able to write up a daily report, dutifully try to make contact with a few local collectors and fences, keep collecting the paycheck, stay paroled.

What surprised him was how comfortable he felt in this city. He knew any sense of familiarity was false. He'd never been here, and the resemblances he noticed between this place and cities he did know—San Juan, Paris, Madrid, Seville, Guadalajara—were superficial. Perhaps it was just the humidity level, but something put him at ease here when usually he lived his life feeling out of place wherever he was, out of step from whomever he was with.

He started with a shop on Chartres that sold a strange mix of old and new paintings, prints from rare books, and miscellaneous antiques and junk. Then he hit three more just like it: one on Royal and two on Dauphine. The shops varied in their degree of clutter and dust and in the relative proportion of junk to antiques, but it was hard to tell the proprietors apart on sight. Each was a sixty-year-old bald man who wore the kind of pants that teachers do, paired with a vaguely ancient cardigan over a nondescript, dingy button-down. It seemed to Eli that usually people look and dress differently but act the same. In this case it was the other way around. The owner of the shop on Royal was fastidious and suspicious, while the first on Dauphine was loose in his speech and gestures as well as gregarious. The final proprietor, of the second shop on Dauphine, performed an exaggerated sexuality and touched Eli's arm each time he spoke, leaving Eli with the impression that the man was not actually hitting on him but only pretending to, thereby acting out some psychology too complex for Eli to parse. As Eli left the store, he turned and asked the man, "Anyone around here do art shipping or art restoration or even just cleaning?"

"We ship ourselves, *cher,*" the man said, "so I wouldn't really know. As for repair, pretty much everyone goes to that Polack looker on Decatur."

"What's her place called?" Eli asked.

The man shrugged. "I doubt anyone knows that—no sign, no business cards—but I can tell you where it's at."

No sign most likely meant the place was a tax dodge or a front for some kind of business entirely other, but it could mean forger or fence. At the very least, it probably meant somebody who knew people in the lower echelons of the local art world. When he saw the cross street the proprietor had written down, Eli was even more certain he was on to something; the shop was pretty much right around the corner from the Hotel Richelieu.

It would have to wait, though. Eli didn't have much more time than it would take to grab a sandwich before the meeting with the cop that Ted had arranged. He stopped at a small oyster bar on the way and ate fried oyster po'boy standing up, finding it perfect despite the crappy bread.

The detective he had the meeting with had asked Eli whether or not he had an expense account and named a hotel bar in the Central Business District when he said that he did. "But let's meet at three. If you order a Ramos Gin Fizz when they're too busy, the bartender'll spit in it."

The man already sitting at a small table in the dark, cool room was surprisingly slight, his face and neck above his collar the nutty color of a gardener's. He was fifty, maybe even toward sixty, but it seemed that the lines on his face had chosen the same grooves, for his face was mostly smooth but occasionally crossed by a deep crevice: two across his forehead, one on either side of his nose, pointing down toward his chin. Rivers instead of streams.

He shook Eli's hand without standing.

"Detective," Eli said.

"Mouton," the detective said.

A waiter in a white jacket arrived immediately, and Mouton ordered a pair of gin fizzes without consulting Eli. "It's what you order here."

While they waited for the drinks, the cop made fairly aggressive small talk, asking Eli question after question about Los Angeles, about what he thought of New Orleans, about the quality of his accommodations. Too many years interrogating people, Eli decided, or maybe the urgent need for answers—any answers—was what had brought this man to his job in the first place.

Eli disliked the drink on first sip—like a child's beverage spiked with gin—but the second was better. He liked the foaminess of it, at least, the effort that had gone into making something that would disappear so quickly.

The detective put away nearly half of his and then launched a defense against an accusation that had not been spoken. "Look, I don't know where you come from originally or what's going on there, but parts of New Orleans are a fucking war zone. There's no way we're going to solve all the murders that will happen today much less something that happened before the storm. Nearly half the cops who left never came back, and don't even get me started about the cops indicted or in jail for the shit that went down during the storm. Sure, a lot of the dead is just drug dealers shot by drug dealers—nobody cares. But I also got a state senator's son shot up, and I got a nice white lady killed right front of her nice husband and kid in the front door of her nice house, for Christ's sake. These are crimes people want solved. Your guy? Your guy doesn't even have a name."

"But someone does want him found," Eli said, "or at least the painting he might have. Someone hired me. Someone paid real money for that."

"Then I'd suggest you try to find the painting and collect your paycheck. This isn't a case the New Orleans PD is going to give a rat's ass about. Not trying to be an asshole here—just telling you how it is. Better than false promises is what I figure."

When he'd started the job, one of the training lectures had been on jurisdiction. "It's generally not like what you see on a TV cop show," Ted had told him. "Most law enforcement agencies are happy for you to take any crime off their books."

But Eli figured that was mostly with old thefts, nonviolent crime, and not messing around in someone's homicide case. "So you don't mind my asking around some?"

Mouton polished off his drink in one long draw, tenderly touching the foam mustache it left before wiping his upper lip clean. "Look, what I'm going to do is tell you if I come across anything that'll help you. And I'll ask you to do the same, and if you find something, I'll look into it. But the best thing I can do for your case—the only thing likely to make any difference at all—is when I'm kneeling at the Cathedral on Sunday morning, hoping Aaron Neville comes back and sings us some more 'Ave Maria' or whatever—you know he's Catholic, right?"

Eli kind of shrugged and kind of nodded, as though he knew who Aaron Neville was and might even have guessed he was Catholic.

"So I'm going to kneel during Mass and pray that whoever offed your guy gets what's coming to him in the afterlife if not here on this disastrous planet." He paused as the waiter delivered the check, and longer to let Eli reach for it first. "Speaking of which, you know that whoever killed your guy may well have already gone to meet his maker. Sounds like he may not have got out of town before the storm hit, right? And if he did leave, there's probably only a small chance he's around here. Plenty of people aren't ever coming back. Hell, my wife evacuated to some Buddhist monastery up in Mississippi—some New Age friend of hers told her about it or something—and now she won't come home. She says she likes being in a place where people don't talk to her. Says she'll need the rest of her life just to figure out all the shit people've already said to her."

Johanna

T H E artists' house was in the Garden District on a much more modest street than Clay's, on the Magazine side of St. Charles and not so far up as Audubon Place. The house on the corner of the block and one across the street looked wrecked, but the exterior of this one appeared undamaged, save for the roof shingles tiled across the yard in lines that looked almost intentionally patterned.

The couple had left their art and their pet under the protection of a house sitter and air conditioning, both of which had failed when the storm had hit. Johanna knew it was bad as soon as she opened the door. Bad for the art, at least; she did not smell a decomposing animal.

Though there was no pooled water, the wool rugs squished under her feet, and the floor surrounding them was surely ruined. Pervasive dampness, felt and smelled. The light switch produced nothing. Johanna opened the living room blinds and in the added light could sense the double leaving that had occurred: the first a carefully

planned and temporary relocation that had left the place
tidy and the more recent haphazard one, a hasty departure motivated by fear rather than desire. Or perhaps she
could read what had happened simply because she already
knew—the narrative in her mind informing her percep-
tions. After all, it was just a wet living room: furniture,
books, objects, a few paintings.

Darkness is less dangerous than light, but not always.
What might have been a good idea in better circumstances
or a drier climate—closing the blinds to reduce ultraviolet
exposure—might prove disastrous here. Less so for drawings on paper, more so for paint on any surface. It was the
husband who drew, if Johanna remembered correctly.

Johanna climbed upstairs to where the couple had said
their shared studio was. The studio was singular, yes, but
divided by color and relative clutter almost as though someone had drawn a line down the middle. Not quite the middle: The painter's side was smaller as well as more spare and,
paints and paintings aside, less colorful.

She spotted signs of professional care: humidity and
acidity strips, carpeted risers to lift wall-stacked paintings
from the ground, good-quality storage units made of poly-
urethane-covered plywood to keep the plywood's acidity
from migrating to the artworks within, ample sheets of tis-
sue between works on paper and yupo horizontally stacked
on a large drafting table. These artists—one or both of
them—had some eye on the future. They labored with at
least a hope that how they spent their days would be of

interest to another generation or maybe just to some person with money at a later date.

As she looked closer, though, she saw that it was the husband more than the wife who believed in the value of his work, whether to posterity or an investor. There was very little inherent vice on his side of the room, while the wife had created much of her art with cheaper materials. Given her academic position, this choice must have been willful rather than ignorant. Perhaps there was some artist's statement explaining a preference for making works that would degrade.

Johanna had agreed to talk to an artist once who wanted his work to have a temporal quality—to create art that would age as he desired. He'd stood in her studio—she kept no chairs on the first floor except her work stool—and gone through his list of twenty-four questions. She hadn't thought about the conversation for a year or so and then remembered, wondering if he'd made use of what she'd told him and whether his idea of using paper and paint that would degrade on radically different timelines if exposed to heat had worked. Probably just a gimmick, she'd decided: Who besides Buddhist monks and lunatics would want to make a beautiful thing but not have it last?

She wasn't sure why, but she set to work on the paintings first. Several of the canvases would need to be dried as much as possible before transporting, and she began as she always did: lightly. *First, do no harm.* She blotted the backs with the paper towels she had brought. On some of the paintings, she would have next used a handheld hair dryer set on low.

She considered finding the breaker box and seeing if the lack of electricity was an easy fix, but that wasn't her job. She would transport what she could move most safely and most easily and work in her own studio. The artists could hire someone to tend to the house and perhaps another restorer willing to work on location. Johanna had already broken her own rules of work by being in the house at all. This was an unusual time, yes, but that was all the more reason to restore the order of her life, to right the lines that defined its grid.

Two hours later she had made some decisions about what should be moved first, what should be moved later, and what should stay in situ. When she reentered the house from her second trip to the van, she was greeted by the wagging stump tail of a tiny black dog. Unlike many small dogs, this one was proportioned like a large dog. Indeed, it was a miniature replica of a large dog, as though it had been reduced in a copier. It looked up at her, ears flattened back in friendliness, eyes expectant.

Johanna was sure that the couple had said a cat, but perhaps she hadn't listened carefully enough. Her reaction was relief; a dog is more legible and so more trustworthy than a cat. She looked around downstairs, just in case. In the kitchen was a small twin pet bowl, she presumed one side for water and one for food. Both were empty except for the crusted silt left behind by flooding that had since receded. The dog seemed a healthy weight for its small size, and its coat looked glossy. It must have managed by going in and out—through a dog door or a broken window—perhaps scavenging or being fed by neighbors. She would call the couple, and they would make arrangements for their dog; given its miniature size she could put up with it for a day or two. Maybe the neighbor who'd been feeding it could be persuaded to take it in. Or maybe the couple would realize they should return. The house smelled of rot. People often think it doesn't matter when you get to repairs, but Johanna knew from her work that it is always best to respond immediately. Most things do get worse if ignored.

She drove the van downtown with several of the wife's paintings plus the husband's works on yupo in the back. The little dog sat alert in the passenger's seat, its ears looking much larger now that they were at attention. Johanna could name each animal at the Audubon Zoo and several dozen kinds of bird, but she did not know the names of any but the most common dog breeds. A terrier mongrel was the closest she could come to fitting the dog into language.

The open parking space directly in front of her workshop indicated that the city was still half empty or more. When she saw a dark-haired man knocking on the door, her first instinct was to pull the van back into the street. But again her newer, more normal self filled in the most obvious logical explanation: another customer. She lived in a city of wet art, so she should probably get used to strangers at her door. New Orleans was a city that operated by word of mouth, a fact that had served her business well.

The man was tallish and thin, with wavy, very dark hair covering a nicely shaped but slightly large head. He wore a dress shirt tucked into old jeans and European-looking men's sandals. He was empty-handed. She swallowed and put her hand on the little dog's head, holding it there, hoping the man would walk on. Then she remembered hearing from Peter about a guy combing the neighborhoods along the river seeking to buy up property. Realtors were already calling the areas that hadn't seen much flooding *the sliver by the river*. Those who rented their places and only weeks ago talked of reductions were already worried that prices would go up. She relaxed her arm; this was something she could say no to easily.

The dog had a collar but no leash, so Johanna tied a piece of twine to the collar before opening the van door, and he—his small penis was made obvious by long tufts of soft black hair furling it—jumped down to the street after her, using the floorboard to halve the distance.

"Can I help you?" she said to the man, who turned, startled. "You are knocking on my door."

He stood aside and let her open the door, which she propped open with a wedge so she could carry in the works she'd brought down from the Garden District. He stepped inside after her.

"I'm not selling it," she said, watching him look over her studio.

"It," he said. The word implied a question, but his inflection didn't rise. He kneeled a few feet away from her, holding out his palm for the dog to smell. The dog, cautious at first, sniffed his fingers. The man scratched the dog behind the ears, holding his face close to the dog's, and the dog wagged his ridiculous stump of a tail.

"Nice animal," the man said, returning to his full height, which was greater than Johanna's, though not by much. His skin was smooth, darker than hers and even in tone, and his neck had nice lines to it, broken only by a pointed Adam's apple that made him seem vulnerable in a way that might well have been a false impression. Gray hairs, though not many of them, poked through the black hair, their coarser, curlier texture making them seem longer than the rest. Some force pulled at the corner of his eyes, perhaps sadness or maybe only the ordinary fatigue of a poor night's sleep.

"This property," she said. "It is not for sale." She wanted to tell him that she'd bought it not as an investment but as a place to live and work, but the truth was that she hadn't bought it at all, though her name was on the deed and the place was hers to keep or sell.

"I'm not a Realtor."

She tied the dog to the leg of one of her worktables, where he seemed oddly content to stand and look up at her. "It is not my intention to be rude, but I have things to unload and work to do. A lot of work."

"I just have a couple of questions about art restoration. At least let me help you unload your van. It needn't take more time than that. I assume this is a very busy time for someone in your line of work."

She felt herself bristle at the way he said "your line of

work," as though she were something other than what she presented herself to be or as though her profession were somehow dishonorable. She had chosen it, in some part, because it was not at all dishonorable. Maybe there were restorers whose work veered into forgery, but she had never been one of them. "It is a very busy time," she said. "Best to act very fast when trying to save water-damaged art."

She stood in the back of the van and passed the works to him, telling him how to hold and carry each. Though he seemed to have this expertise already, which struck her as peculiar, he didn't claim the skill and accepted her terse instructions with a neutral expression.

Once all the works were inside—the paintings vertical against the walls on risers under her worktables and the drawings properly stacked—she thanked him. "You said you had some questions."

He pointed at an oil still life she'd just finished work on. "Who painted that?"

She shrugged. "A customer's mother or father or aunt, I forgot which. Nobody you would ever have heard of, I'm sure."

"Do you ever clean paintings by well-known artists?" He had stayed very still since they'd come back inside, not taking a step in any direction or even shifting his weight or moving his hands to his pockets. His arms hung at his sides in a way that might have seemed casual at first glance but ultimately seemed awkward: a man who didn't know what to do with his body. This softened her opinion of him as a person, but his question made her more wary of his intentions in whatever capacity he stood before her.

"No Rembrandts," she said, "but I sometimes do some work for the auction galleries—mostly cleaning a painting ahead of an auction, though now there will be more work, as people will want to sell paintings that have been damaged. And maybe also buy replacements for others."

"What's the most-well-known artist you've worked on?"

Johanna tried to read his face but could not. He struck her as a man who was not so much dishonest as accustomed to hiding—a man who could evacuate his own face, a man whose soul could never be stolen by a camera. This they had in common, which was another cause for worry. She said, "May I ask why you're asking? Are you looking for a restorer for an important work?"

He continued to stand still, arms hanging uncomfortably, and it took him a long time to answer. Finally he said, "I might be."

"Then I'd be happy to go over my credentials with you if you would like to make an appointment, and I can recommend people in the region with more expertise in highly valuable works if I'm not what you are looking for." She nearly said that she needed to walk the dog, but since he had helped her unload the van, she worried that he might offer to go with her. "Right now I must get to work," she said. "Good luck." She wrote down her phone number but not her name on a piece of scrap paper. "I never got around to business cards."

At the door he turned back, his hand on the knob, and held eye contact. "Your accent, is it Polish?"

She nearly said that it wasn't, but she stuck to her policy of offering only necessary or directly requested information and shook her head. The trip to the artists' house had her worried that she was giving too much of herself away when all she wanted was to be self-contained and do her work and abide by the routines that were the life of her making.

He nodded, patient, and asked her if not Polish, then what.

"I'm from the Balkans," she said quietly, wondering if he knew that no one from that region would use the generality except to evade other questions.

From the slight squint of his eye, she figured he did indeed know that, but he let it go in a gesture or omission that felt like human respect.

"But I don't really believe in nationality," she said in case he was about to change his mind. "We are all the same, or at least different in the same ways."

He laughed at this, genuinely it seemed, and she saw his white teeth, that his tongue was smaller and more pointed than most men's. "The problem, of course, is that most other people do believe in nationality. Makes it a little hard to hold out, but of course if you're from the Balkans, you would know that."

She nodded and lifted a few fingers as a sort of good-bye. The string of bells fell against the doorjamb as he stepped out, a small collapse of sound.

Just because she hadn't chosen a life that included romance didn't mean she was impervious to attraction. And so what she felt when the man left her studio was relief—even more than her usual relief at returning to solitude after having to talk to someone—but there was another feeling mixed in. He was a handsome man, and it was probably just that: a simple formula of the molecular, of pheromones, of genetic distance. Pop psychology might predict that she would be averse to sex, but she liked the physical act well enough—even very well—when it was on her own terms.

She had read a novel once in which the middle-aged male narrator had solved what he called the "problem of sex" with regular but not terribly frequent visits to a prostitute he found pleasant enough. Knowing that prostitution is rarely genuinely voluntary, Johanna distrusted the author's easy assumption that this was satisfactory. Yet her solution was similar in some of its terms, including frequency and level of intimacy. Over her years in New Orleans, she had had a few lovers, men she liked well enough so long as she did not see them more than once every week or few.

In the novel she had read, the protagonist had ruined his calibrated solution by falling in love—not with his prostitute but with a younger woman when he least expected it. Johanna was never so careless, and the day one of her lovers pushed for more—to see her the next day, to hear of her childhood, to introduce her to his friends—was the day she severed the relationship. Some would attribute this trait to her past, but she saw it more as an inheritance, as likely biological as not, from her father, who had dragged his feet into a late marriage in order to have the child he wanted and to placate his family but who experienced his wife's doting as sandpaper and his wife's intellect as inferior.

Johanna had understood immediately that Clay was to be rebuffed, not only because he was soon enough in love with her but because, despite his brief heroism, he was not a good person. Not that she would have tolerated love and adoration from a good man, either. Pedestals are for museums and brothels.

Unless the man who had visited—Elizam was the too-pretty name he had given—turned out to have a painting she very much wanted to work on, she would avoid him in the future. If he did turn out to possess such a painting, she would be careful about what she allowed herself to feel. Most likely, she decided, she would never see him again. If there was any disappointment in this recognition, then that was only more proof that never seeing him again was a good thing.

Later, though, as she walked the little dog along the river, she recognized again her first impression: that the man might pose a different kind of threat. If he knew Ladislav, then he was a threat. But if that were true, he also represented an opportunity: If he knew Ladislav, then he likely knew people whom Ladislav had known. While she thought of it less and less frequently, allowing it to disappear in the darkened part of her mind that was *during Belgium*, she had never given up completely on the idea that revenge was possible or the faith that it would be worth anything she had to give up for it.

Clay

H E had put in a good morning's work. The drawing
came easily after he pushed through the initial resistance, the desire for distraction. This new book would be
different from the three that had come before—more social
in its comment yet also more personal in vision. That's what
a reviewer would say, and he could be that reviewer if need
be. He'd even thought of a name for her. But he pressed
thoughts of reception from his mind and tried to work for
work's sake.

For a little more than three hours, he produced drawings
of the discovery of the child/protagonist in a cave of recently departed wolves. He sketched several studies of the child,
some close-ups and others at removed angles. His favorite
drawing of the morning was a landscape with a single wolf
looking back over its shoulder in a way that might suggest
longing or sadness. After he completed it, he recognized the
signs of psychic exhaustion. He'd never been able to work
more than several hours at a stretch, and often not that.

His stamina was down, too, having spent most of his time during and after the storm concentrating on his other projects. His computers blinked for attention in his peripheral vision, but now he felt bored by them.

He thought instead of the girl who'd come. He'd hurt her, he knew. Left long horizontal welts striping her thighs, oblong bruises mapping her ass, mild rope burns braceleting her wrists. She'd be back for more—soon, he hoped. He'd never seen anything like her for sheer ability. She could take the pain, but she wasn't a masochist. Not a masochist but a true submissive, who took the pain because it was given to her. Her welts would subside. Her bruises would fade to an ugly yellow and then altogether. She would hide the marks on her arms with long-sleeved shirts despite the warmth and humidity. And then she'd be back to let him do whatever he wanted, to hand over her fate to him because she didn't want the responsibility—or had no idea what to do with it.

What he wanted wasn't what the girl thought he was looking for when she recognized his desire to be punished. He did want to be punished, but only to the extent that he deserved it, just to even the deck. She couldn't give him that—he'd have to find it elsewhere or create it for himself or, best of all, trick Johanna into doing it—but this new girl could give him the other thing he wanted. She thought he needed to explore empathy, compassion, and he'd read this theory before. Maybe that was true of those doughy morons with leather costumes and soft hearts, playing dungeon while hoping to fall in love. That wasn't him.

What he'd enjoyed about the afternoon with the girl was nothing more complicated than control. Having it. Using it. Knowing he could take more of it if and when he wanted to. Find her lines and cross them, the girl whose name he'd forgotten because he'd identified it as fake the moment she'd said it. Next time, the next time, she'd tell him her real name and he would use it against her. And if she thought she wanted to be free from making decisions, then next time he would show her that she didn't understand things at all by making her choose between unpleasant alternatives.

Johanna had agreed to meet him at the park, though the zoo was still closed and flashed no sign of reopening. Since moving to the city, Johanna had visited the zoo every few weeks, sometimes meeting him afterward outside the zoo, across from Ochsner Island. Once—no, twice—he'd met her in the zoo. That second time, she had talked wistfully about the animals living outside their element, removed from the lives that would have been theirs in a better world.

"As if there's such a thing as a better world," Clay had sneered before softening and saying, "That's why zoos are depressing. How can you stand coming here all the time?"

"To witness, I suppose." Then she shrugged, shook her hair from her face. "No, that should be the reason, but that is not quite it. What I do is pay my respects. I don't feel sorry for these animals; I admire them. They sit straight, they eat, they make do with this small life they are allowed. Maybe they wait for the next one, or maybe they are too animal dumb to know any difference. But I think they sense it. The breeze blows, and they smell something else, know the world is larger." She paused, and Clay imagined her trying to pick up a scent in the air. She continued, just a little louder: "Who knows what their life would have been like in the wild? Maybe they would be dead from some suffering disease or be murdered by poachers or probably would not be born at all."

Whether she believed this or was just trying it out or was simply trying to be her version of nice, Clay didn't know. As always, he left feeling blunted.

After that conversation they met only after her trips to the zoo, on the bank of the little canal around Ochsner Island, gazing on the small oval of land that served as a rookery for herons, egrets, and birds whose names Clay had been taught in childhood but hadn't tried to remember. It worked better for both of them to observe only free animals while they talked around the subjects they talked around.

Clay could see her now from a distance as he walked across the park, still unspotted. She was sitting directly on the grass, under a tree, legs stretched straight in front of her, her gaze on the Isle of Birds. He slowed, stopped, seeing her unnoticed, lingering for the moment in which her knowledge of his gaze didn't influence what she did. No impact of the observer on the experiment.

What happened every time he saw her happened now: a tightening of the chest, blood to the groin, the specific small throb of the carotid, a vague sickness. *Perhaps this is enough punishment,* he thought before moving toward her again, *to experience these unwanted sensations every time.* The only missing element was restitution.

Though she didn't turn her head, he knew from the slightly changed angle of the clean line of her hair that she sensed his approach. She was telling herself that it was he, no longer a threat, not a reason to startle but still a reason to steel. He thought he could see her shoulder blades pull back, more than slightly, into a spot between them. The line of her hair returned to a perfect horizontal, and in the sunlight her hair seemed one shimmering pale blond. As he drew closer he saw its thousand subtle shades.

"How bad is the damage?" he asked as he sat down next to her, though she'd already reported the condition of her place to him over the phone.

"Still waiting to see if the floors buckle, but I have no right to complain."

She asked him no question in return, and they watched the birds for several minutes. He'd never known anyone worse at small talk than Johanna, which of course only contributed to his complicated, unrequited attraction. To his surprise, she broke their silence.

"I had a dream about this place a couple of nights ago, that one day all the birds just flew away and stayed away for a whole year. The newspaper was full of theories about construction noise and pollution and changed weather patterns, but nobody really knew why they flew away. The birds were just gone—all the species—and Bird Island was empty. No one knew if they would come back or not."

Clay glanced sideways at her. Whenever he looked at her he felt like he was stealing something, and the shame of that now stopped him from analyzing her dream, from revealing to her the obviousness of it.

"I had a strange dream recently, too," he said. "I dreamed that a child was found in a cave. Apparently it had been raised by wolves, but for some reason the wolves had left it in the cave alone. I woke up that day and started a new book about people who find the child and bring it back to the world of humans. I plan to call it *Raised by Wolves.*"

"Boy or girl?" Johanna asked.

Clay shrugged.

Her gaze stayed on the isle. "You do not think it matters, or you haven't decided?"

"I guess it's a boy, but the book isn't really about the child. It's about the society that finds the child."

Johanna nodded, but she seemed uninterested. "Is the work going well?"

He told her that it was but that he needed to reclaim his stamina. "Not a problem you seem to ever have."

"I think the key is never to lose your stamina in the first place."

This would have been unfair of her if she knew how much he really accomplished, but she didn't know about his other projects—how hard he worked when he added it all up. He knew he would hate the tone in his voice when he said it, but he said it anyway: "How nice for you." Clay forced himself to notice the birds. He pointed toward a white bird that was smaller and more elegant than the great egrets, which always looked to him, when standing and tucked, like curmudgeonly old men incapable of flight. "What kind of egret is that?"

"Snowy," said Johanna, who had learned the birds' names in English right away and always seemed to remember them. "You can tell it is a snowy egret because of the black legs and yellow feet—very at odds with the pretty white feathers."

They fell silent again, and again he was surprised when it was Johanna who spoke first.

"What do you know about Ladislav?" she asked.

His carotid artery throbbed hard, and a salt taste moved from his throat to the front of his mouth. "I know that he's a dirtbag."

Johanna turned her face toward him now, and he interpreted her look as accusatory.

"And yes," he said, knowing he had to give her something, "I saw the paper."

"Did you know he was in New Orleans before the storm? Did you see him?"

The detachment was gone; her voice was urgent. There was fear in the urgency, and he remembered the smell of her that day in Belgium—the day he'd committed himself to getting her from one life to another, taking her on as a responsibility because she was his responsibility after what he had done to her.

He shook his head. "Not until I saw his picture and read that he was dead."

"Promise it. What do you say? Swear to God that you did not know he was here."

"I swear to God," Clay said, and it felt like truth in his mouth. After all, he hadn't known in advance that Ladislav was coming to New Orleans. He had been as surprised to hear the Czech's voice on the phone as Johanna must have been to see his face in the paper—probably more since it was possible that Johanna woke every day of her life wondering if it would be the day she saw him again. "I swear on my mother's grave. That's another thing we say."

She pulled her legs into her chest and wrapped her arms around them, tightening into an egg. "A man came to my studio yesterday, and he acted like he might be a potential client, but it didn't feel right."

"And that's why you agreed to see me again at last?"

"Why would Ladislav have been here unless it was connected to me? But then, if it was, why did he not contact me?"

"Maybe he was afraid you'd kill him, which of course is what you should have done if you saw him." He wiped his hands on his jeans and leaned back on them, hyperextending his elbows. "But maybe it's a coincidence and he was here for the reasons people usually come to New Orleans. The world isn't that big a place. You can run into someone you know on a street in Shanghai—happens all the time."

She looked at him and said no.

"Then I don't know, Johanna, and if the paper's right we can't ask him. But I can ask around." He watched another snowy egret arrive, wings spread, yellow feet stretching for the low branch it landed on.

Johanna nodded twice, very slowly, and described the man who had visited her studio. "I thought he was a Realtor, and then a customer, but I'm pretty sure he is something else than that. He had an accent, too—not from here."

"Belgian?" Clay asked.

Johanna's hair shimmied as she shook her head. "I don't think so, not Czech, either, but maybe Europe somewhere. He had a deliberate way of speaking, kind of distanced or practiced, which made it hard to tell." She turned her legs to the side and pushed off the ground, rising to her glorious full height. "I have to go now," she said. "I'm taking care of a dog."

Johanna fascinated Clay, but she rarely surprised him. Today she was full of surprises.

"A dog?"

"Long story. Another thing you say."

"You should have brought it to the park. Dogs like parks."

She nodded very slowly. "Yes, you're right, but this is not my dog, and I don't want to be responsible for losing him or him getting hurt in a fight. He is a very small dog."

Before the storm, Johanna had always ridden the streetcar up St. Charles, but now Clay walked her to her van. Once she was in, she rolled down her window. "You said I should have killed him. How do you know I didn't?"

"It's not in your nature, Johanna."

"You don't know that," she said and rolled up the window as he tried to tell her that he did. Then she lowered it and gave him just more than her profile. "You could call the boy in your new book Romulus."

After she drove off, he crossed St. Charles and walked the very short walk home, relieved that Johanna hadn't asked him the obvious question. Now he was keen to troll.

Two hours later, he had flagged and removed self-promotional text for two graphic novelists who had obviously written their own Wikipedia pages, inserted the title of his second book into a list of graphic novels that experiment with form, and added a rape accusation to the comments section of the page of a local restaurant owner who'd refused Clay an additional bottle of wine and asked him to leave, even though he knew full well what his last name was. Though the incident had occurred before the storm, Clay had waited until now, when the restaurant had just announced its reopening. Feeling better, perhaps the release a cutter feels when she draws a line of blood from her arm, Clay typed "Romulus and Remus" into a search engine. Maybe Johanna's comment would lead to something more: archetypes at his disposal and an underlying myth for his new book.

Against his better judgment, he swiveled from the computer when the rarely used landline rang.

His father's voice through the receiver: "I arrive a week from Friday. Prepare the house."

Their conversation was even shorter than usual but left Clay feeling wobbly. The near-constant small pain in his left lower back, a result of his small but defining affliction, felt sharper after he hung up. If Johanna was right about the man who had visited, then his father's visit was likely not a coincidence any more than Ladislav's. But it was natural for Johanna to be suspicious; maybe the man she had seen signified nothing. His father had yet to visit the house since the storm, and it was only natural that he would check in eventually, if only to enumerate faults in how Clay had handled the situation.

Clay picked up the phone again and called the house-cleaner and the yard guy he had not phoned in weeks. The housecleaner seemed glad enough for the work and agreed to come the next day, but the yard guy's number was disconnected. For all Clay knew, the guy had been killed in the storm. He would have to get another recommendation from a neighbor, which was easy enough to do but would require him to speak to one of them.

Marion

AFTER her shift behind the bar, Marion walked her bike the block to the tattoo shop and relocked it. The guy had painted the door with a thick, dark green paint and put up a dark green screen between the store's entryway and main room, creating a reception area that hid the actual tattoo parlor. This struck Marion as a throwback to a time when getting a tattoo was more private act than public performance. She approved.

The man came around the screen when she entered and smiled upon recognizing her.

"I didn't have to ask you your name," she told him. "It's Eddie."

He was wearing what seemed to be his uniform: subtly plaid pants, black boots, white sleeveless T-shirt. If someone else were wearing it, Marion might have accused him of trying to look like a badass or a cholo—of posing of some kind—but on him they were just clothes. His movements were natural inside them, his face intelligent above them. She connected the mole by his eye with its geometric partner.

"Small neighborhood," he said.

"Smaller than it used to be, apparently. Show me around?"

The main room surprised her, too. She'd expected it to be cluttered with tools and ink bottles and cartoon images, she supposed, not spare and serene. There was little by way of visual distraction, and most everything in the room was black, white, gray, or green. The music playing was quiet and nondescript.

"You giving massages or tattoos back here?"

"I told you I was a professional," he said, demonstrating the working of a chair that reclined and moved up and down like one at a dentist's office. When he finished he stood straight and found her eyes with his, waiting first in silence as she continued to look around the room. "Can I ask you something?"

"In my experience, if you need to ask permission to ask a question, it's not a question the person wants to be asked. Plus, I can't really say okay until I know what you're going to ask, right, so I can't really give you permission to ask what you're going to ask until it's too late."

He looked amused: head slightly tilted, mouth just starting to smile.

She suppressed her own small smile. "But go ahead."

"You're already a bunch of things, right? I mean you wear a lot of hats. An artist and a massage therapist and a bartender."

Not telling him there was yet another job, she simply nodded.

"So why would you want to add a new hat? But that's not really my question. My question is this—which thing are you most? You don't have to tell me, but my advice, if you were to ask for it, would be to concentrate on that thing. If you have to do one of the others for money, then you do that but think of it as a day job. Put your real time and energy into the thing you most are. For me, this is what I wanted, to have my own tattoo place and give people beautiful images. I think of it as a vocation."

"You mean to tell me that when you were a little boy, you looked up at your mama and said, 'I want to be a tattoo artist and move to New Orleans and have a tattoo parlor'?"

He laughed without smiling. "Not quite like that, no. When I was four, five, and six, I wanted to be a baseball player. Then I read too much *National Geographic*—my aunt gave me a subscription—and I wanted to be an archaeologist or an anthropologist and go to Olduvai Gorge or discover a place like that that no one knew about yet. That was middle school or thereabouts, which is when I started drawing a lot. And in high school I thought briefly about comics or even going into fine art, but when I thought about materials, I kept thinking about skin."

"You were at that age."

"Impressionable, yes, and it's true that there was this very pretty older girl that lived near us, and who I sometimes saw at the community pool, who had a dolphin drawn on the back of her calf. I would watch her swim laps under the water, and she could make the dolphin on her leg look like it was swimming."

"So you chose your career based on a hard-on?"

This time he smiled when he laughed and said, "Don't we all? But, seriously, what I started thinking was that an artist's work is usually only seen by a few people. Whoever comes to the gallery or the museum. Please don't take offense, because that's a very cool thing, but it didn't fit with my vision of my life. Books and comics, they reach more people because they can be reproduced, but then people aren't seeing the original. With skin, it's different. When I give someone a tattoo, my original work goes everywhere they go and is seen by everyone who sees that person. All them tatted-up girls you work with? Every tourist in this city sees their ink. Even better, though, is the motion, like you seemed to understand when I met you and you drew that squid. I get to see my work in motion. It becomes something more than what I drew because of that. It goes into another dimension."

Marion began to feel self-conscious because of the sincerity of his observations, which she would have otherwise dismissed as deluded or at least cheesy. His intense eye contact also made her more aware of herself and the position of her body than she was comfortable with. It seemed aggressive to stare at someone's eyes the way he did, at least outside scripted scene, but she liked him anyway.

"I hope this place works out for you," she said. "I used

to think I was an artist who worked as a massage therapist to make money. Now I seem to be a massage therapist who works as a bartender for money. Mostly I'm just
a bartender." Again she didn't mention her other source of
income, though she wanted to, perhaps because she thought
he might tell her something that would help her understand
why she did it. For the money, she reminded herself, at least
on the lucrative end of the belt.

"Nothing wrong with being a bartender by vocation, but
if you're an artist, that's where you should be putting your
time and your passion."

She looked down at her flat canvas shoes, which were
relatively new but already filthy from walking and biking
everywhere she went. "So you're telling me you aren't going
to give me a job."

"That's not the only thing I'm telling you." He reached
across the reclining chair for her, settling his hand lightly
on her shoulder. "I think you should go out with me instead
of work for me. Like I said, you're a weird girl. I like weird
girls."

Now she looked back at Eddie and tried to hold his gaze
the way he'd held hers, though it was not a natural gesture
for her. "I'm seeing someone," she said, "but I don't know
if it will work out, if it can work out. I'll let you know if it
doesn't?"

"You aren't supposed to be thinking that way going in,
right? If you are thinking it won't work out, then it won't
work out."

"This is an unusual relationship."

"Fair enough." He withdrew his hand and smiled at her again. "The offer stands for now."

"Got it," Marion said. "So I'll have to let you know about a date later, when I see how things go, but meanwhile I might let you ink me. If you had carte blanche, what would you do?"

"I would ask to see your paintings and maybe take something from that, or at least inspired from it. Otherwise I would turn your back into part of a tree, half the trunk disappearing around your waist and one branch reaching across the back of your shoulder. I would call it 'Druid' or something like that."

Marion liked the idea that he titled his work. "What if you were on a smaller budget?"

"Then I'd show you a book of choices and make you choose your own image and location."

She pulled her lips to one side and nodded slowly. "Okay, then, let me count my money and think about it."

A gutter-punk couple who didn't look like they had room on their bodies for any more ink—much less money to pay for more—peeked around the screen from the foyer, and Marion broke away, waving to Eddie as she left.

At home, her bike parked safely in her living room, Marion flipped through the small stacks of paintings leaning against the walls, at once surveying the damage and looking for an image that might transfer to skin. Most of her paintings were of scenes from the Gulf Coast, from around

Biloxi. Occasionally a human figure, most often some local character, such as the old man who'd chewed tobacco all day long on a bench outside the Biloxi Diner, regardless of the weather.

The idea came to her that she need not start completely over if some of her paintings could be saved. If even a few could be restored, she might be brave enough to pick up her brushes and mix a palette. Then she'd be building on an existing foundation instead of starting from scratch with no promise that she wouldn't have to do so again and again and again. Eddie was right: She was floundering around looking for something new to do instead of doing what she'd always wanted.

Another idea seeped in, one that made the space around her solar plexus quiver, almost as if with an electric current. Most of what she had painted—the trees and houses and commercial buildings and perhaps even the people— no longer existed. She had made a record of them, maybe not one as useful as photographs, but at least her vision of the place she'd grown up in, which she now understood was a place where most people had never been and never would go.

At the computer she typed "art restoration" into a search window and wrote down several numbers, putting a star by one on lower Decatur and wondering why she hadn't noticed the place, given how close it must be to the bar. There was no web page, just a phone-book listing. She started to stand, but the mouse held her hand as thought it were magnetic, and she went to the site—*the* site—to see if Clay's advertisements were still posted. Only one was; his experiment on the bottom seemed to be failed and over. His ad as a submissive was gone. She read the other one twice, slowly, feeling blood rush between her legs and the thing inside her chest unlatch. What she felt in her mind, though, was very close to jealousy. She didn't care if he had a girlfriend or a fiancée or a wife, but she wanted what they did together for herself. Otherwise she might as well date a nice guy, someone like Eddie, which was not something she could do with bruises all over her body.

Eli

ᴛᴇᴅ had arranged this meeting, too, and the woman he was meeting had named the time and place: one o'clock at a newly reopened Caribbean restaurant on Magazine Street. He'd expected one of two clichés: a heavy-breasted woman with a deep, friendly laugh or a thin and beautiful descendent of multigenerational *plaçage*, which Ted had signified when he'd used the horrible phrase *high yellow* to describe the Pontalba family. But Felicia Pontalba was more Vassar girl than anything else. A different cliché altogether—one not specific to this place. Her prettiness veered hard from beauty toward the amiable. Her face was wide and affable, her eyes more round than deep, her mouth more flat than sensual. Had he not known she was from a Creole family, he might have taken her for third-generation Italian American or half Lebanese. *Vaguely ethnic* was the term a prison buddy had used to describe the type of leading lady he preferred to star in the movies he watched and the fantasies he indulged in. "I like brunette girls," he'd said, and at the time Eli had agreed with enthusiasm.

Felicia Pontalba was smart, or at the least had studied well for her graduate degree in art history—Brown had followed Vassar on her vita—and she showed the practical good sense that someone holding her job should have. She might have been hired through nepotism, or whatever it's called when you're connected but not necessarily related, but she could have been hired on merit.

"It wasn't clear what would happen for several weeks, but then we got busier than we've ever been," she told him after they'd ordered their food and been delivered cold glasses of pale beer. "It's way, way too early to call the future of the city, but I'm optimistic. It will be different—a lot of people who left won't come back. I think new people will move here, younger people, creatives. We're already seeing it. Some neighborhoods are never coming back. Others will swing up. A friend of mine who just reopened his restaurant is having to pay well over minimum wage just to the dishwashers, when he can get them. A client of mine who is in real estate told me that some of the people moving here are renting or even buying in the Bywater. White kids. In the *Bywater*. Speculators are already there snapping up shotguns and painting them all kinds of colors. Painted ladies they're not, but painted somethings."

One of the casualties of his time in prison was Eli's conversational adeptness. Not knowing what to say, he pulled out a platitude: "Change can be a good thing."

"Don't get me wrong," Felicia said, animating with her frequent sips of beer. "I'm not one of those fools who thinks that 'things happen for a reason,' and I'm not saying the storm was a good thing. It was an awful thing. An awful, awful, awful thing. People died. Lots of people had to start all over, and the ones who will come off the worst are those who started with the least anyway. Now they'll be just as poor but living in some horrible place that's not New Orleans. Can you imagine having to live in Houston? All the heat and none of the joie de vivre. That's where a lot of them landed. Also Atlanta. And some just stopped wherever the money ran out, God help them wherever they are."

The clichés seemed to be working, so Eli stayed close to them. "But you're also looking at the half-full part of the glass."

"Well, of course I want to. I love this city. Love, love, *love* it. Naturally I'm also glad to see my business not just returning to baseline but booming."

Eli realized it was his turn to say something so stalled with a question: "Are more people buying or selling?"

"There are sellers, of course—there are always people who need money or who overextended or can't wait out appreciation or guessed wrong in the first place. But a lot of people are actually buying. In many cases, insurance money is coming in, and people are looking to rebuild their collections. Southern art especially is flying out of the houses, and textiles, but really *everything* is doing well."

"Speaks to your skills, too, I'm sure."

"The key to success in the auction world is to have things other people want—or at least to matchmake people who want things with the people who have them."

"So are you better at acquiring the valuables or making introductions?"

"I guess if I had to start over, I'd establish one of those dating services they advertise in in-flight magazines."

Eli shrugged, his expressed ignorance authentic.

"You know, I'd match 'successful' people with each other over lunch."

Eli took a slow sip of his beer, less of a stall than a settling into Felicia's pace, which punctuated the languor of the place with her more rapid enthusiasms. "You said Southern art is hot, but what about European paintings lately? Belgian?"

"Ted told me you're looking for a small painting by Eugeen van Mieghem." She lifted her eyebrows, her taste for obvious communication extending from words to gestures.

The waiter interrupted with their plates: shrimp with garlic, black beans with yellow rice, fried plantains, green salad.

"Any whiff of it?"

"We're extremely cautious about due diligence. More than most houses, even. We have to be, given the city's general reputation for corruption. So it wouldn't surprise me at all if the painting were here, or came through here, but I didn't hear about it. Not a whiff, and I do hear at least some things I shouldn't." She gave another eyebrow raise and a smile that felt stock to him—something she'd learned from a movie or perhaps an imitation of someone she knew and wanted to be more like but wasn't.

The food was better than it looked, which was beginning to seem like a citywide truth. "People know how to cook here," he said.

"From way back." Felicia's wide smile transformed into something more authentic, tilting her back toward beautiful without getting her all the way there. She was attractive, but affable was indeed the word. He decided he liked her a lot.

"Ted said you might be able to help me with some contacts, or at least some names. I'd be interested in knowing about any collectors of European painting, particularly interwar, but also any known questionable dealers. And of course full-on fences. There may be names you have that we don't."

"When I get back to the office I'll type you up a list and email it, assuming you have access."

"I'd appreciate it. It would also be good to have the names of any appraisers and, given the hurricane, restorers. It's probable that the painting was in the city when Katrina hit."

Felicia ate with energy, relishing the large bites she washed down with the golden lager. "Two more," she told the waiter, though Eli had finished only half of his beer.

"One thing," she said to Eli. "I'm going to put an asterisk by the name of one of the appraisers. Prejean is his last name. Go gently if at all with him."

Eli borrowed her gesture, raising his eyebrows.

"What I mean," Felicia said, "is that I wouldn't tell him who you work for. He's out on his own now, but a couple of years ago he was working for one of our excellent local institutions. The Lost Art Register got in touch with him—I don't think it was Ted but someone else—because there was a lead on a painting that had been stolen from the museum—a Pissarro or Sisley, I believe it was. The LAR offered to pursue it for a fee. The museum couldn't really afford it, or didn't think it had to, and went to the police instead. I don't know exactly what happened, but the painting still has never been recovered, and folks at the museum harbor some hard feelings."

Eli set down his fork, lifted it again. "I'm sorry to hear that."

"Well, it's not like Ted pretends your outfit is a law-enforcement agency or a nonprofit. You guys find a lot of stuff that would never been found if it was left up to local police or even the national enforcement agencies, but do go gently with Prejean if you talk to him. My impression of his impression is that he thinks the LAR knew where the painting was or could have put your hands on it but didn't and then, because you weren't getting paid, refused to cooperate with the police."

Eli started to say something apologetic, but Felicia hushed him.

"It was before your time. Anyway, as for restorers, there's a woman who works for us sometimes. She's excellent but a bit of an odd bird. Has a shop in the Lower Quarter, on Decatur."

The woman's face came to him, almost as though she had just walked into the restaurant, and he sat up straight, recognizing the feeling as attraction. He'd never in his life—not once—chosen a blond over a brunette or light eyes over brown. But here he was, almost paralyzed by the thought of the absent blond even as he sat across the table from an attractive and thoroughly present brunette.

"I met her," he said as plainly as possible. "Do you know where she's from?"

Felicia shook her head, took a sip of the new beer. "Eastern or Central Europe. Some people refer to her as Polish—*Polack* is the word they use, I'm sorry to say—but I don't think that's right. I'm pretty sure she's not from Belgium, though, if that's what you were thinking, given the artist."

When they were done, Eli paid the bill using the company credit card Ted had told him to live it up with.

"I'll email that list this evening," Felicia said and thanked him, a bit too exuberantly relative to the price of the meal.

He told her that it was he who was indebted for her time, feeling more confident about his ability to deliver his expected lines than he had been before lunch.

"Just let me know the outcome," she said, her voice slightly huskier than it had been at the beginning of lunch. "I like mysteries."

They hugged on the sidewalk—she initiating the contact

and Eli accepting it awkwardly, not knowing whether to go first to the left or the right for the double-air kiss.

"Speaking of Belgium," she said, turning back, "there's a man in town from an old New Orleans family—his father and his great-grandfather were mayors. He actually served as ambassador to Belgium back a ways. At least I think it was Belgium, though it might have been the Netherlands or Liechtenstein or something. I can't imagine he'd be mixed up with a stolen painting—if only because he's a man who can buy whatever he wants—but he is a collector, paintings especially. I'll include his name in the list."

Eli had taken a cab to the restaurant, in part so that he could find it, but he decided to make the long walk back to the Lower Quarter. The humidity that had assaulted him on his arrival remained, but some of the heat had fallen away. Also, he was getting used to humidity again. Growing up, he'd never thought about heat or humidity or even mosquitoes, but he knew how quickly a person could get used to comfort. It was an embarrassing fact about the human species, really. He worried that if he stayed in Los Angeles much longer, he wouldn't be able to tolerate winter or summer anywhere else. Even though it seemed as likely as not that he would live there for a long time—even after he was off parole, no one else would hire him at the kind of salary he was pulling, if at all—it still didn't seem real to him. At any moment, his life could change. It wasn't simply that he needed to believe this; he did believe it.

As he walked down Magazine Street and around Lee

Circle, he knew he was walking not to his hotel but to the art-restoration studio on Decatur Street. That the two were in the same direction allowed him to pretend that this was not what he was doing—or at least not to think about it much. A good thing, because he had no idea what he was going to say to her when he got there.

He walked most of the Quarter's length on Decatur, passing by a pair of tourist bars occupying spaces that had housed some of the first gay bars in the country before stopping in the Louisiana Music Factory. The owner had thinning long hair collected in a ponytail, the kind of look Eli associated with bad taste in music, or good taste in jazz only. Still, Eli bought some CDs on the man's recommendation and arranged for them to be mailed to his office in Los Angeles: a funk album from Galactic with an assortment of local celebrity guest singers, a zydeco band he'd heard of, a female singer he'd never heard of, and an up-and-coming local band called the Resurrectionists. He continued along Decatur, skirting Jackson Square, where he turned down a solicitation for a horse-and-carriage ride and reminded himself to cross over later to look at the river.

A half block short of the restorer's studio, he entered a bar and bought a beer so that he could use the bathroom and choose an approach. The bartender was short and thin— early twenties, probably—with long, almost black hair. She was very pretty, almost delicate except for the leathery toughness of her expression. She looked angry, or maybe just hardened in a way she seemed too young for. A large group of men entered just after Eli, and she worked quickly, her movements efficient, to fill their complicated orders and match person to drink. All she said to Eli and to the other men was "What'll it be?" and the price of their drinks when she delivered them. As soon as she made change or returned a credit card, she moved on to someone else.

On the door of the bathroom was a sign that read, "One customer per bathroom or you will be asked to leave." Eli remembered seeing, long ago in a San Juan nightclub, a couple having sex on a chair, the woman's panties around one ankle as she straddled her seated man, the skirt of her dress partially covering his thighs their only effort to conceal what they were doing. Just over a year later he'd found out what it meant to want someone that intensely. *Te quiero*. Now, and for the first time, this memory did not trigger the usual image of dark hair on a white shoulder, the stab to his solar plexus.

From the sidewalk, he watched the blond woman working through the windows of her studio. Her movements were as deliberate as the bartender's but slower, responding not to the demands of people but to the rhythms of her own work with the inanimate objects she treated as though they might be breathed to life yet. When he'd seen her before, when he'd helped her carry in canvases from her van, she'd seemed uncomfortable, self-conscious and almost cautious or at least restrained in her gestures. Now that she was alone—or thought she was—she seemed at ease in her body. She stood as she cleaned a painting that lay flat on her worktable, her feet planted but her body making small twists back and forth in response to the movements of her hands. She wore faded slim jeans and a white T-shirt. Her hair hung long and straight on her back, and her feet were bare on the old wooden floor. He imagined how the direct contact with the old wood floor felt—felt to her, would feel to him if he were in her place.

He wanted to stay still, just as he was, to watch her for hours or forever, but he was afraid she would turn and catch him, would misunderstand and think he was something he wasn't. Or that he would attract attention from neighboring establishments in an area where it was fine to stumble around drunk but possibly suspicious to stand sober in one place.

The bells jangled as he pushed the door open, but she'd startled even before the sound. In the moment in which she turned toward him, he saw her face momentarily unguarded, sensed something essential about her in her unpracticed expression. But she recovered quickly, her eyes shuttering, her lips closing. Either way, unguarded or posed, she was beautiful. Genuinely beautiful and undeniably so. It was not a matter of taste, he understood; no one would say that she was not beautiful.

"You've come back." Her words were toneless, presumably also a practiced occlusion.

On the walk over and then again at the bar where he'd used the restroom, he'd meant to figure out what he was going to say to her, but he'd failed and then just forgotten.

Forgotten, he knew from experience, was a word that glossed a wide set of shortcomings that included avoidance and denial and parts of himself he didn't have names for. Perhaps one of them was noble: He didn't like to lie to people and so wasn't very good at it.

At this point, the truth seemed like the best option, which might well have been his mind's unconscious plan. Yet he knew also that truth was dangerous, knew that Johanna might well be a murderer as well as a thief—or at least know people who were these things. He forced himself to acknowledge that her beauty made this more likely rather than less, and he reminded himself that this wouldn't mean they were of a feather. He was a thief but only a certain kind of thief. He had never injured anyone, except for a few guys back in grade school and later in prison, but even then never badly and never except as a response to a punch that had sailed his way first.

He chose a condensed version of the truth: "I should have just asked you the other day. I don't really know why I didn't, but I'm looking for a missing painting and thought it might have crossed your path."

She stared at him, cleaning cloth loose in one hand, an utter cipher.

It didn't seem that she planned to speak at all, so he continued, "I'm asking people in your line of work, among others, whether they've seen the painting or heard of it coming through town. It's possible that the person who has it wanted it worked on."

"Was it damaged during the storm?" she asked flatly. "A lot of paintings have come through here since then."

"It's possible that it needed to be cleaned."

"If you don't know, then it is not yours." She leaned back against the table she'd been working on, lifted her chin. "If it is not yours, then why are you looking for it?"

He had a fantasy, brief as in a dream that happens in two seconds even if it takes ten minutes to explain, of her as damsel in possession of stolen goods through no fault of her own, with him as her savior. He'd return the painting but keep her name out of it.

"I've been asked to help return it to its rightful owner," he said, his stomach twitching slightly at the word *rightful* even as he hoped it was the correct term.

"'Rightful owner,'" she repeated, and for a second he thought he heard something bitter in her voice, confirming his suspicions—both the one about her and the one about whoever had hired him through Ted. A second later he determined that he'd imagined it. Most likely she had nothing to do with any of it, and her shop's location was a coincidence. But then there was her obviously European accent, on top of his personal conviction that coincidences are rare, that things appear to be coincidences only because you don't have enough information to know that they aren't.

"Do you speak French?" he asked.

"Not very well, not that I see what that would have to do with anything. All the paintings I'm working on now are in here. Everything is out but some works on yupo—the ones you helped to carry in—and those were in the house of the artist. Have a look for your painting if you want, but then please let me return to work."

He made a small show of skirting the tall worktables that lined the room's three windowless walls, though he knew he would not find the Van Mieghem. He turned back to her with the idea of describing the missing painting while measuring her reaction, but he was startled by the bells hanging on the door. Across the threshold stepped the petite, pissed-off bartender from down the street.

"You'll excuse me, please," the restorer said to him. "I seem to have a client."

He nodded and awkwardly moved for her hand, grabbing her left hand with his left instead of reaching across for a proper handshake. He squeezed her fingers lightly and gave a little shake. "I can't remember if I introduced myself correctly," he lied. "My name is Elizam, though most people just call me Eli."

She didn't offer her name this time, either, and so he asked. Her look was suspicious enough that he didn't know whether to believe her when she said, "Johanna," pronouncing it as "Yohanna." Later he would look at Felicia Pontalba's list and see if there was a Johanna on it and so perhaps learn her last name. For now he resigned himself to having failed again and was surprised when she stopped him.

"I'm working all day today, but I have some time tomorrow. I have lunch across the street every day at half past noon. You could find me there then or here after. I don't know if I can help you, but maybe you could show me a picture of the painting you are looking for, or at least tell me about it, just in case it did come through here. I could even ask around some."

He wanted to hear what the bartender said—he felt a momentary paranoia that she had followed him from the bar—but there was no excuse to linger.

"*À demain*," he said. Regretting his choice of language, he tried again with "*Hasta mañana*," but by then no one was listening to him.

PART TWO

Water Damage

Johanna

DURING her first weeks in New Orleans, Johanna had bristled when Clay had spoken of the city's history, of his great-grandfather, who had been mayor until ousted by Long family fiat. She'd thought of herself then as a person without a real history, at least not one that she wanted to claim, and she didn't need to be reminded of that fact through negative comparison. The old buildings she walked by held no particular interest for her, and she thought often, in those early days, of choosing a newer city as soon as she could free herself of her dependence on Clay. She would perfect her English, finalize her legal status, save her money, and start over out west, perhaps in a planned community whose apartment buildings and houses had all been built in the last twenty years, whose stores showed identical facades. She and everyone she encountered would live in an eternal present, every day new and unconnected to the days that preceded it.

How the change had occurred she could not have articulated if pressed, but across time, mostly gradually and unconsciously but occasionally with moments of leap and clarity, she began to feel as if she was part of the city—an anonymous part and so perhaps an even more integral one. This nourished an understanding that a history can be adopted, that the history of the city could be her history and that she could become part of its history, regardless of where she'd been born or how recently she'd arrived. After all, that was what New Orleans had always been: a receiver of outsiders and immigrants, a blender, a granter of new identities, a place where you could disappear and then resurface under new terms. There were people like the Fontenots, yes, but there were many more like her.

Once she found the location for her shop, she made herself of it. "I live in the Lower Quarter," she would say when potential clients called her. She'd think it to herself when Clay talked about *the Garden District* or referred to himself as an *uptown degenerate*—that sliver of wealthy old New Orleans that could think of nothing better to do with its money than spend it on vices and watch the world go by, often in bars and rather early in the day, or else all night long, or both.

As Johanna learned the general history of the place, she began to populate it with individuals. Not actual historical persons but people who were at least a little more than types—vague-faced but specific individuals representing history's larger tides. She imagined these people living not quite in her studio and apartment but at least in the neighborhood—on lower Decatur or around the corner on Barracks or Governor Nicholls. One person she imagined inhabiting her apartment, or one much like it, was a dapper man: one of the last of the well-to-do Frenchmen living in the neighborhood, dealing in sugar, minding his store, dressing carefully for opening night at the French Opera, whose former site was now a hotel she often walked by, preferring to look straight ahead so she would not see that it was no longer the Opera House, decades ago burned to the ground, a place she felt nostalgia for though she had never seen it except as a photograph in a book.

Down the street, a block or so toward Jackson Square, there still stood an Italian market, which until the storm had been busy all year long, the noontime line for sandwiches out the door for half a block. The former inhabitants there were easy to imagine; she was face to face with their direct descendants, some of whom she guessed still made a prickly wine from oranges, though that product you could not buy from their store, which sold imported pastas, cheeses, olives, and meats.

She imagined, too, though in less detail, other representatives of the Quarter's history: a black family whose children played *boules* on the street, the short-haired women of the 1920s literary circle that formed around Lyle Saxon and Sherwood Anderson (such good American names), gay men almost out in the open in the 1960s and '70s, the nuns of the Ursuline Convent with the heron pond in the back, the famed musician James Booker, eventually one-eyed but still bedding dozens of men and women singly or multiply. *Mud if it moved*, people said of his libido. *Lighter fluid if it would get him high*, people said of his addictions.

She was working in types and clichés, and no doubt she had some of her facts wrong, but having her own place gave her a history. If it was a faulty one, or even unoriginal, that mattered little because it was a rich and good one, much better than the one she'd shed and considerably better than having none at all.

And this belief in progression on the part of someone who believed in very little, and certainly not in human goodness, gave Johanna an unlikely optimism that she knew was not universal in the months following the storm. When she thought this way, there was only *after Belgium* and then her imaginary *before* nestled in the history of New Orleans. There were waves of good lives here before, and there would be waves of good lives here again. The city could give that to people, at least to those who were willing to see it. The city could give this to her.

This way of thinking had something to do with her work, too. She understood that her vocation made her, by choice, a person who believed that at least some damage can be undone, that original states can be recovered or at least approximated, that life can go on as though some things never happened. She knew, too, that you could also simply paint over a canvas, change the picture for good, so that without an x-ray machine it looked like the former story had never even existed.

Perhaps this was why she felt sympathetic to the young woman in her studio. The girl had an unanchored quality exacerbated by the fact that she looked as though the wind could knock her down, the determined expression on her face be damned. She would curse and shake her fist as she fell, but fall she would.

When the girl spoke, she wanted to know first about prices. Most restorers would not even hint at a price until they saw the work, but for this girl money was crucial, as it is for most people in the world but not for most people seeking to have art restored, not even in Johanna's world of lesser works, where she encountered plenty of uptown degenerates with bottomless bank accounts and sentimental attachments.

"I cannot tell you for sure without seeing, but if you can tell me about the paintings—sizes, materials, degree of impasto, kind of damage and how much—I can come close. The most important thing is probably going to be what has happened since they got wet—how they were stored, whether they were moved, how soon."

Johanna kept her studio nearly free of furniture on purpose. She preferred to work standing and did not like clients to linger. Drop off, go away, pick up, go away for good. Her business was with people's canvases, not with them. Now, though, she wished she had a chair to offer this girl who looked like she had been on her feet all day. What she told Johanna was not good, and she was obviously talking about paintings she had done herself and not without aspirations.

Most artists know something about how to care for the works they make; this girl was what Peter would call a *disaster*.

Johanna willed her face to be kind and said the truth that she knew was cruel: "Sometimes you just have to cut your losses and start over."

One thing Johanna had learned after the storm that she should have known before but had not is that you cannot predict who is the crying kind and who is not. People she had barely known from the neighborhood broke down upon seeing her again for the first time, as though she were some long-lost child or lover or dear, dear friend. Others at the Mojo Lounge could describe incredible loss with no emotion at all. She was thinking particularly of a woman whose elderly father had made her swim away from the home they shared, leaving him to drown in the attic that contained all their family pictures because she understood that he really did prefer that she save herself. From that woman, not one public tear.

At first glance Johanna would have pegged this girl—Marion, she said her name was—as a crier despite the toughness, or because of it, but she would have been wrong. Marion simply nodded at the bad news, and Johanna admired her for it. Some people know when to try to change their luck and when to get used to things as they are. This was the trait Johanna most admired in herself: the proper timing of effort. Far too many people either give up too soon and permanently or else waste their energy and luck by ramming their heads against the wrong wall or by not waiting for the wall to weaken.

"Look," she said to the girl, "why don't you bring in one or two? Either the ones that have the least damage or the ones that are the most important to you. I can at least assess them for you." She watched the girl for a moment and then said, "For free. That way you can make an informed decision." She wrote down her phone number. "Call before you come—make an appointment, but most times are fine."

When the girl left, Johanna found herself unsettled by the double interruption. The first one bothered her more, but the second one also pricked at her memory in a way that didn't quite make sense. Upstairs she topped off the food and water for the little dog, brewed half a pot of coffee, and took inventory of what was wrong. What was wrong, of course, was that her whole life could be undone, her false but necessary history ripped away and replaced with the real one, the one she thought she had escaped. She wondered if it would be a slow unraveling—a loose thread that eventually unweaves the whole fabric—or a fast tearing away. She wondered which would be worse, knowing that every bad fate is its own strange bag of torments.

But she started her inventory small—another survival skill. First was the little dog. When she had called, the uptown artists had sworn that their pet was feline and not canine and that they had never seen a small black dog like the one Johanna described. Johanna broke the news to them: Their cat was gone. "Cats are strong," she said. "It might be fine." That was true—it might be fine—but it would never again be their cat. Despite her own feelings about cats, she could understand that this would cause them pain and worry.

There were things she could do about the problem of the dog, actions she could take. She could post "found dog" flyers in their neighborhood, call animal shelters, knock on doors. But she knew the score for pets after the storm. Many were lost, but many found went unclaimed. She would take the steps required to make sure she was not stealing someone's beloved companion—the calls, the flyers—but in the end the dog would be hers. This was a responsibility she wanted to want but did not, even as fond as she was of the small body, the alert eyes and ears. On the other hand, she couldn't very well condemn the creature, which had shown her nothing but trust and affection, to an overflowing animal shelter or mistreatment on the street or the bottom of the Mississippi. She looked at him now as he rested heavy in the crack formed by her crossed ankles and outstretched legs.

The girl's visit was trickier to parse, but what Johanna came up with was straightforward enough: The girl reminded her of being younger, of the way her life had been turned by others, of the very bad route she had taken to arrive in the life she wanted to keep.

This brought her back around to the big thing: She wanted to keep her life. She wanted to keep her apartment, her studio, her work, her quotidian routines. She had paid for these comforts in advance. Even if she had needed Clay's help to start, she had paid for that up front, too.

Ladislav's picture in the paper and now this man, Elizam—she refused to think of him as an innocuous three-letter nickname—meant that everything she valued, every simple and perfect thing, was endangered. She tried to order it in her mind: Ladislav had been around the corner from her. Someone had killed him, and that someone might have been Clay or might have been someone else from *during Belgium*. Soon after, a stranger appeared looking for a painting, which had to be the painting she had kept close for more than a decade. This could not be a coincidence. Maybe the man, Elizam, was looking for Ladislav. Or maybe Ladislav had told him to look for her. If he knew where the painting came from and why she had it, he was both a bad person and the person who could lead her to the one person in the world she wanted to kill.

Clay thought she should have wanted to kill Ladislav, and maybe she should have, but it was the other man—the one who had paid him—whom she wanted to watch die slowly, knowing his demise was by her hand. A man she should never have had to remember but would always, even when she most believed in her place in the imagined history of a city far away from everything she had known before leaving Belgium. If she was going to lose everything, had she not earned at least that? Did not both she and the man deserve that?

She nudged the dog from her legs. He sprang awake and

leaped down, watching her from the floor as she took out the painting, still wrapped in brown paper, and loosened the strings. As she looked at it, she decided she could part with it. In her mind, the girl who was its subject had crossed the ocean and made a new life. That girl's ending was a happy one. Johanna knew this because she had cleaned her colors, renewed the red of her collar, cleared her eyes. She could let that girl go to some anonymous new home and trust that she would be all right. What Johanna could not bear, though, was the thought that the painting might be returned to the man Ladislav had stolen it from before she had stolen it from Ladislav. She would burn the painting before she let that happen.

That first time she had seen the painting, her head twisted, trying to find the human figures in the dirty brushstrokes, first wondering how a painting might be cleaned, its colors restored, her voice had been trapped stale in her mouth because the man who had paid for her virginity had paid a few Euros more for the wide strip of duct tape across her mouth.

Not all men who prefer the clarity of rape to the grayer territory of coerced or merely purchased consent want to hear the screams, Ladislav had told her later, when that territory was known to her in all its hues. This man, this first man, had paid extra for his silent joy. He paid most of all, of course, for her virginity. Every day for several years—but not in a long while—she had wondered why he had prized that above all. Perhaps he thought that the first violation would hold unique physical pleasure, or perhaps he merely wanted to guard against the possibility of unpleasant disease. It was months before she surmised a deeper motive: He wanted to be remembered. There were many other men she remembered in pieces: a beard here, a voice there, the fast thrusting of one, another's grunting, the odd smell, whether rank or pleasant. Other than Clay, though, whom she remembered for other reasons, that first man was the only one from *during Belgium* that she remembered fully and to this day.

So he had got what he had paid for, and perhaps he could be made to wish that he had not.

She called Clay to ask directly whether he had killed Ladislav or knew who had. Usually he took her calls, often on the first or second ring, but this time he didn't answer. She rewrapped the painting and took the dog for a walk, realizing that it would still be unwise to give it a name.

Eli

THOUGH he held no faith in his approach, Eli decided
to start on the list Felicia Pontalba had provided because
he was being paid to do so. Many of those listed, including the Prejean whom Felicia had warned him to be careful
with, had left the city and not yet returned. They could be
followed up later, if necessary, though most had departed
before the mysterious resident of the Hotel Richelieu had
been killed, making them less likely suspects than someone
who'd stuck out the storm.

The list included one couple who had refused to evacuate and had come through the hurricane just fine: Lafayette and Mignon Broussard. "Don't call him Lafayette,"
Felicia had instructed. "Call him Fatty." Before he'd come
to this city, he would have assumed their names were
self-authored, or at least nicknames stuck to them by others. Now the names just made it sound like they fit in, like
they were from here.

"Biggest pink house in the Marigny," a man had told him

when he'd inquired about the address, and now Eli saw that he was exactly right. It wasn't just pink but all that pink implied, with strings of Mardi Gras beads festooning the balcony jutting out over the small side street near Frenchmen and a ridiculous number of concrete lawn ornaments populating the small square of front yard.

Ways of thinking groove deep, and Eli found himself casing the house like the person he used to be. It was a game, an approach to the world he'd taken even as a kid: plotting the secret moving or removal of objects. It had been a game before it had become something else; the game had led him to his illegal occupation. As a kid, he'd figured out how he might unburden a convenience store of an entire shelf of candy, but he'd never pocketed so much as a stick of gum or twist of caramel.

The very first thing he had ever stolen had been a painting. Every object he had ever stolen had been a painting or drawing. The last thing he'd ever stolen had been a painting. A painting by his own hand, hung in a small museum in Brooklyn. Like the others, it was meant to be returned to a person or a place, most often Puerto Rico.

He was good at his work; he'd never been caught in the act. Yet, that last time, he'd underestimated the exposure of motive. Some smart young detective had thought carefully about what had been taken and what had not been taken and sought to make sense of it when it didn't make sense at a glance. In the absence of proof, though, or at least a greater accumulation of circumstantial evidence, Eli would have stayed out of jail. What did him in was something that he thought of for many years as chivalry, but the simple truth was that he had been incapacitatingly infatuated. The woman whose portrait he had painted before he had stolen it went unscathed despite her additional roles in the crime, such as it was. With his confession, he might have been brushed rather than slammed by the law in another context, but a couple of nationalists were playing at a more violent game, and the government was not smiling benevolently on their antics. At the plea table—a literal table, which had been a long oval of compressed wood stained to look like red maple—the prosecutors had chosen to interpret the knife Eli had used as a tool as an intended weapon should he have been interrupted, as though Eli hadn't done his research and wasn't sure the marijuana-addicted minimum-wage security guard wasn't at his girlfriend's flat. And so there had been jail, a lot of it, and would have been even more if Ted hadn't heard about him and seen an opportunity.

That his ongoing freedom was substantially up to Ted's discretion was something Eli understood but preferred not to dwell on. He used his fist to knock rather than touching the enormous mermaid knocker whose large breasts sat right at eye level.

"You're just exactly on time," Fatty Broussard told him as he pulled him into the house. "Any later and your ice would have melted."

Fatty was a rotund man wearing a safari getup, minus the hat. His wife was an even greater spectacle: an enormous woman in a floor-length garment whose floral print was dominated by large red roses. Her face was powdered white, and she'd drawn sharp eyebrows and a scarlet mouth onto that canvas. Eli figured the pair to be in their sixties, but it was possible they were significantly younger or older.

"Have a seat, have a seat," Fatty said, but a long-haired cat seemed to occupy each piece of furniture intended for sitting. Mignon displaced a pair of them from a sofa that nearly matched her dress or robe or whatever it might be called, and Eli sat, accepting the sweating glass her husband offered.

"Eleven o'clock," Fatty said, "means old-fashioned time in this household."

Eli thanked him and assessed the room as quickly as he could given its incredible clutter. Surprisingly, everything was clean, save for the cat hair on the furniture, and Eli couldn't imagine how much they would have to pay someone to dust the place. Every surface was studded by small statues and pieces of pottery and knickknacks, ranging in value, as best as Eli could tell, from none to quite a bit. The walls were equally obscured, nearly floor to ceiling, with prints and paintings in a mix-and-matched assortment of frames. Again, they ranged in value from high-print-run lithographs by popular mediocre artists to paintings worth thousands if they were originals, which at first glance they seemed to be. What struck Eli most, though, was the complete lack of discrimination not only in worth but in style or subject matter. So often when he saw a cluttered, price-variable collection—as he had done several times on both sides of his art game—it was the hoard of someone attached to a theme, usually some particular animal, most often a domesticated one—a pet or farm animal.

"You're looking at our collection," Mignon said, her voice beaded, presumably from the household's manner of observing the passage of late morning or perhaps from a former history of smoking. "As you might have guessed from looking at us, we're gourmands as well as gourmets."

Not smoking, Eli decided, since the house did not smell like cigarettes and Mignon did not strike him as a woman who would ever give up a bad habit once acquired. He sipped the bitters-heavy cocktail, which, surprisingly, exactly matched the time of day as promised.

"That's right," Fatty picked up from her. "I'll eat and enjoy the hell out of a fast-food hamburger, but I also have a taste for ortolan."

"Ortolan?"

Fatty, having made very fast work of his old-fashioned, was mixing another small pitcher of them on a small cart that had been wheeled into the living room.

"The little French songbird. It's illegal to eat them now, but for enough money you can buy anything you want." Fatty smiled and traded Eli's half-full drink for a fresh replacement.

"You might have read about it," Mignon said, "in the press accounts of François Mitterrand's last meal."

"Also a gourmand as well as a gourmet," Fatty said. "The key is to pop the whole bird in your mouth at once and bite down. Blood, bones, like the best consommé you've ever tasted, except, you know, not soup."

Continuing their conversational pattern of trading interjections, Mignon spoke up: "But you're supposed to eat it with a napkin over your head. So that God won't see you, because it's a sin to eat a songbird."

Fatty laughed, spraying whiskey. "Now, dear, that's just a good story. The truth of the matter is that you tent your head so you can get the most of the aroma. God can see through cloth."

"But you, my dear man," Mignon said, turning toward Eli as a cat leaped onto her enormous lap, "you wanted to ask us some questions, Miss Felicia told me."

Eli gave them the short version: He was inquiring into a misplaced painting—it had been Felicia's idea to use the word *misplaced* with the lower echelons of the local art aristocracy—that had apparently been seen in New Orleans shortly before the storm. He offered a few identifying details and said he'd appreciate it mightily if they happened to remember seeing it, or hearing it mentioned, as well as if they would keep an eye and ear open in the future if they had not.

"Prior to this very moment," Mignon said, "we'd neither seen nor heard of it. But now that we've shared a drink, we'll be lifelong friends, and so of course—of course!—we'll be listening closely and calling you with any news whatsoever."

"Indeed!" Fatty concurred in his deepest bass. "Indeed."

Shortly thereafter, Eli stood on Frenchmen Street, drunk half an hour before what anyone would call lunchtime.

Marion

MARION had been going uptown twice a week since that first time, each time looking forward to it, thinking only two more days, eighteen hours, four hours, time to check the air in the bike tires. Some days she went uptown seeking physical pain to be given only embarrassment. Some days she readied for petty humiliations and experienced true fear. One night, home alone, she dreamed she was staked to a bed while a venomous snake crawled the room. She understood, in the logic of the dream, that it would finally sense the heat of her body and make its way to her. This was not a variation that was in the actual mix, though it felt like it almost could have been.

Her mind knew to wake up just as the snake approached. Her brother had once told her that you always wake up before you hit the ground when you dream you're falling from the sky but that you'll die if you don't. She had no idea whether this was true—her brother had always spouted an unpredictable mix of truth and lie—but she wondered now what would have happened to her real body if she hadn't wakened before the snake had reached her, if she would have felt its fangs sink into her skin, been made ill by its venom, experienced a slow death creep through her veins.

There were days that she pedaled home disappointed, still anxious, still craving. Usually this happened because she could not suspend her disbelief, could not experience Clay's power as real and unchallengeable. Once it was because the narrative was one of infantilization, which she found comic and nonsexual. But most often she could believe in the stories he told, or that they plotted together, and so got what she came for.

There were days on which things went too far and left her rearranged, put back together after the taking apart but not quite in the right order. She would notice the next day an extra piece, happen upon an unrecognizable shard of herself. Like those common dreams of a long-known house revealed to hold a corridor to a secret room, the discovery was unsettling but not unpleasant. Yet she worried, often, that the opposite process was occurring unnoticed, that she would on some day reach for some necessary part of her psyche—some defense mechanism or piece of knowledge—and find it missing.

Yet when things went too far she never stopped them, never used the word they agreed would break the scene or even the yellow-light word, and she held to the idea that Clay would not abide by it if she did. She needed to believe that events were not in her hands, that she couldn't stop things even if she really tried. It was part of the suspension of disbelief necessary for real release. It was a point of pride, too. She was stronger than Clay was, and he could not make her say the word. He had met his match.

At the end of one visit, as she dressed and took stock of the damage, estimating the longevity of her new marks, she told him she was considering a tattoo.

"Do you want to know what I think?" he asked, his voice now soft.

She waited, nodded. "That's why I mentioned it."

"I think that my opinion matters only in this room. Here you do what I tell you or else. Out there, you shouldn't think of me at all. Make your own decisions."

"I wasn't agreeing to do what you said." Marion's voice hardened in her throat, leaving her mouth holding something solid. "I only wanted to know what you thought."

"I think that you should do whatever you want. But if you do get one, I would like to watch."

Her jaw relaxed a little. "So you can see me in pain."

He smiled at her—a rarity. "Another kind of pain, yes, for me. As a voyeur. I would like to witness it, but it's not the same thing when I'm not causing it. It would be a diversion. Or maybe I should say a delicacy—something you don't really like that much but is enjoyable because rare."

She told him she'd think about it, but she'd already decided that she would visit Eddie and not invite Clay to watch. He would discover the tattoo later and know that he'd missed out, that another man had been alone with her pain. The idea of what might follow already formed a small thrill.

She had a dilemma, then, and she weighed the cost of paying Eddie for his work and having the blond woman—Johanna—restore some of her paintings. She thought that Eddie would tell her to choose art, against his own interests. Or maybe he would tell her to cut her losses and start over. That was what Johanna had told her before pity had made her generous. It's what Johanna would surely repeat after she evaluated the two canvases that Marion had brought her to assess: a small, angled oil of a pawnshop that had once been her parents' furniture shop and a horizontal seascape darkened by the shadow of the Beau Rivage casino over the Gulf—the original building and not the new casino so quickly built in its place after the storm.

Her doubled desire for money, on top of her habitual need for it, made it all the more strange that she said no when a call came in one afternoon while she was sitting at home, idle. Nothing she did paid more than strapping herself in black and putting some man in his place, and she didn't have a shift at Molly's that night. Still, she said no.

She was seized by the idea that surfaced from time to time: Eventually her number would come up. A scene would turn unpleasant, get out of her control, and she'd be hurt in ways she didn't want to be by someone she didn't want to be hurt by—either on the job or on the way home, alone on her bike at night. She'd declined calls on instinct before, the same way that some people, once in a while, give up their seat on a flight whose number doesn't sound quite right or whose pilot looks tipsy, only to feel foolish when they arrive at their destination ten hours late to discover that no airline crash made the news that day.

Of course in her line of work, she never knew if she had dodged tragedy or not. Maybe a girl had gone missing and no one had noticed, or maybe a potential killer had struck out on the phone across the board and been forced to wait for another day. Maybe she'd saved her life, or maybe she'd just missed a nice paycheck. What bothered her most on these occasions was that she'd never get to know which way it was.

Still, she felt the relief of potential escape when she declined this particular call. Yet fear of losing the lottery was not the only reason she turned down the gig, because what she did next was take an inventory of her supplies, check the freshness of her paints, count how many new canvases she had and how many she owned that she could paint over without regret.

When the phone rang again, she prepared a more vehement no, but the offer was different this time. The Ritz-Carlton had recently approved her résumé for its waiting list. There was a room massage booked and a sick therapist. "Yes," she said, "I'll be there." She'd been trying to get in at that hotel for weeks, and perhaps the single session would lead to something more permanent. She didn't have time to prepare properly, but she switched her cutoffs for cargo pants that hid the marks on the backs of her thighs, changed T-shirts, and pulled her hair back into a bun she hoped looked more sanitary than it was.

There was rigmarole accessing the club level of the hotel—more than if she'd been dressed for her seedier line of work—but everything was easy after that. The portable table was already set up in the room, and the man—tall and thin and the blackest man she'd ever seen—answered the door as soon as she knocked.

"I'm sorry I'm late," she said. "I was just asked to fill in."

"No worries, no worries. Just tell me how this goes." His voice was deep, the accent the Queen's English after being transported to some part of the world being colonized.

It struck her how the beginning of sessions wasn't much different whether she was present as massage therapist or dominatrix.

"I'll step into the bathroom. Disrobe to your comfort level and get under the sheet, on your stomach, your face in the face cradle. I'll knock before I come back out to make sure you're ready."

When she returned, she placed her hand on his back through the sheet, establishing the physical connection that she would maintain for the entire hour. She swallowed tension from her throat and mentally prepared her gentle voice, slightly husky. "Before we start, I'll ask if there are any areas that are talking to you, that need special attention."

"It's all good and all bad, so proceed with your usual approach. I am going to warn you, though, before you lower the sheet, that I have some bad scars on my back. Don't be frightened of hurting them—they are old and long healed. I just don't want to startle you."

Marion felt a flutter in her throat, which she swallowed as quietly as she could. She started, as she usually did, by massaging through the sheet. Easing into intimacy, they called it in school, though it was also intended to warm the client before uncovering him. Even through the thick, high-thread-count cotton, she could feel the webbing: a woven mat across most of his back down to his waist. To hide her surprise required concentration, so she focused on delivering the massage as though the grooves and pocks were not there, reaching for the muscle below. She went a bit harder than usual, even, proving to him or at least to herself that she was nonchalant, that she was a girl who'd seen everything and was moved by nothing.

When she finally rolled down the sheet, her hands froze for several seconds. His back was crisscrossed by dozens of white-pink lines, as though his pigmentation had been removed by whip or martinet or blade or whatever weapon had been used to do this to him. Some of the lines were fine and shallow, as if etched. Others seemed cut right through his skin. She'd once read, because it was the kind of story she couldn't stop herself from clicking on, that torture makes a person unnaturally sensitive to pain his whole life, including through constant anticipation.

She was unsure if she could continue, if she should, but eventually she moved into the experience, finding pleasure in giving pleasure where there had once been extreme pain.

His response was ordinary in her experience: relaxation. In moments her thumbs lingered in the small rivers, reaching in for the past, but she made sure to do her job, finding the knots—unrelated to the old scars but rather the product of recent hunching over computers that she found in all clients—pressing into them, making him breathe against the pain, relax around it, until the kinks submitted and then were gone.

When it was time to cover his back and move to his feet and legs, she did so reluctantly and by reminding herself that here, for this brief time, she was not an artist or a bartender or a provider of adult niche services or a submissive. She was a bodyworker, a therapist, someone whose job was to make things better.

Thirty minutes later her client lay on his back, legs and arms done, and Marion finished by manipulating his neck, taking away the final traces of too many hours on a computer. She reached down under him, her last touch of his scars, and worked her way up. Hot towel over the face, light touch down the arms, squeeze of the covered foot.

"We're all done. Feel free to relax for a few minutes before I go," she said softly, hoping he would rise and give her a cash gratuity instead of running it through the hotel spa—something her nonmassage clients seemed to understand was the best way to do business.

As though she had willed it, he did sit up. He asked her to hand him his wallet, pulling from it a hundred-dollar bill, which was generous in the extreme and usually meant that he was about to ask her to "finish the massage." She weighed the pros and cons of giving him a hand job and decided she didn't want to. She wanted to be an artist who was a massage therapist on the side. Only that. But if the money was contingent on the extra service, then she needed the money. She wondered how long he would take.

But he just thanked her and gave her the hundred. "A most excellent massage. I'm going to ask for you by name next time I'm in town."

"Marion," she said and thanked him. "I know I shouldn't, but can I ask how you got those scars?"

"An aficionado of scars? But you asked me a question and not for my opinion of your question. My scars were legally sanctioned, or at least delivered by the state."

"But here you are in the Ritz-Carlton."

He laughed, deep and throaty, as though genuinely amused. "You see, in my country they will torture you even if you are very rich. In fact, the more money you have, the greater risk you might pose. Of course, if you are as rich as my father is, then they can't hold your son forever." He smiled at her, but his eyes looked sad and tired. "They can just make him feel as though it would be, as though it was."

She looked at him, and it seemed in that moment that they shared something authentic, though almost immediately she realized that they didn't know each other at all and perhaps had nothing in common. Choosing moderate pain and having severe pain inflicted against your will are not the same thing at all, and she felt slightly sick about herself for linking them momentarily. She vowed to return to the unexamined life, starting immediately.

"Marion," she repeated, feeling certain that she would never see him again but that, years later, she would remember him, this man who now told her his name was Samuel.

Clay

HE'D scheduled one more assignation with Marion before his father was due to return. His father never indicated how long he was staying, which could be anywhere from a couple of nights to several weeks. Clay knew he might not see the girl again anytime soon.

Hooking up with Marion about twice a week, which was what they had worked up to, seemed to fit well for both of them. He did not want to see her more often than that, but after a few days since he'd last seen her he would find that he almost missed her—and that he was ready to do more of what they did together. Between visits he would work, mostly, but still he thought too much about Johanna. Designing scenarios and scripts for Marion gave his mind another destination. He and Marion were compatible; he and Johanna were not. Yet he was in love with Johanna—it was as simple as that—so after a few hours with the girl he found her increasingly unpalatable and wanted her to leave. Two or three days later, though, he would smile when she came to mind, and he would plan their next encounter. Then he would call her if she didn't call him first.

Sometimes she would still be marked from her last visit, and he would hesitate. "It's okay, it's okay," she always said, often insisted. She never used the safe word, even when he felt he'd gone too far. He admired her for that, he really did, even if it was the product of nothing more impressive than stubbornness, or pride that manifested as stubbornness. Eventually she would have to use the word he'd given her, her key to unlock the door Johanna had been unable to unlock—the way out of pain. He planned to make sure that Marion would eventually give in. It would disappoint him when it happened, in both of them, but he was who he was and couldn't help it. When she said the word—screamed it or whispered it—he would, of course, stop. It would be their last encounter, not because he would necessarily end it there but simply because they would be done with each other then and would have to realize that sooner or later.

Marion arrived wet, having ridden her bicycle in the rain. He could have picked her up or paid for a taxi to fetch her, but he liked the idea that she worked for it, that she suffered even on the way and would have to make her way home on quivering legs.

He was feeling affectionate, though, and drew for her a hot bath with expensive bubbles and opened a bottle of one of his father's purchased-at-auction burgundies. His father boasted about his frugality—and about not being a snob—because he bid for burgundies rather than wines from Bordeaux. But Clay had a close idea of just how much of his mother's fortune was sunk into the wine cellar. It was an amount that would set someone like Marion up for life.

Marion emerged from the bath dewy and naked, holding a glass of the ruby-colored wine. Her body was a reduction of a perfect one—right in its proportions but of unsatisfactory substance because she was so short. She stood waiting for him to pounce in some way, if only with instructions, and he could see she worried about spilling the wine.

"Sit down and enjoy it," he told her, and sat in one of the room's two wing chairs. She sat in the other, pulling her knees to her chest.

"No," he told her. "Put your legs down and cross them. Sit up straight. Pretend you're at a cocktail party, only naked. Then relax."

She did as he said, except that she did not relax. He could see it in the tension between her small ankles, in the unnaturally even way she lifted her glass to her mouth, in her darting glances. Really he didn't know anything about her outside their shared interest except what he'd gathered from her speech, which was that she came from a lower-middle-class background, probably in the region but definitely not the city. Partially educated—probably more than her parents but not by a lot. He sensed that she was isolated, though whether by circumstance or choice he wasn't sure. If he had to guess, he would pick circumstance. There was an abandoned quality to her, but perhaps she was just picking up the smell of the city she inhabited.

"Today why don't we try something different?" He waited for her to look him in the eye. "Let's have sex like normal people. I'll go down on you nicely and then you can get on top and make yourself happy."

"Are you telling me to?"

He shook his head. "No, Marion, merely suggesting today."

She seemed disappointed. Remembering her long bike ride, he said, "But there's a catch. You're not allowed to come while I go down on you. If you do, there will be consequences."

She looked down—she typically showed her submissiveness with slight abjection—but she was smiling a little.

He gave her what she'd come for and, after she left, wondered why he'd almost gone the other route. But what he felt most was vague disappointment, then a sense of aggravation that moved from her to himself before landing on his father.

He'd washed the sheets in the master suite before Marion's visit but now only pulled them taut and aired them dry before making the bed. He wanted his father to sleep on what had happened there. If his father noticed—Clay had no idea whether he would or not—it would only confirm his opinion of his only offspring. If he didn't, Clay would enjoy the joke privately, which was the way he enjoyed everything that he enjoyed.

His father's flight was very late, no doubt infuriating the traveler, so it wasn't until morning that Clay sat across from him. Just like the good old days: coffee, his father's newspaper, and silence broken only by his father's occasional comment on whatever objectionable story he was reading about politics or economics. And as always his father looking like a picture staged in some catalog trying to sell unnecessary products to people who already own everything else. The clothes always correct for the occasion and falling just right (even this morning's smoking robe and pajama pants), leaning alternately back or forward at an angle posed to look natural, full hair brushed back from his forehead, handsome if bland when he looked at you straight on but hawkish in profile—more interesting and more dangerous.

Gerard Fontenot came from an old New Orleans family, founded by the arrival from Paris by way of Malta of a Civil War–era merchant who profited from both the war and the New World's craving for sweets. He quickly married a local girl, and soon the family had consolidated and then diluted and squandered great sugar, lumber, and other forms of wealth. Their political power—mostly municipal, though the Fontenots were not without friends in Baton Rouge and Washington—had fared more steadily.

Gerard, realizing that power cannot be fully substantiated without access to wealth, had married for money much more than love—an Episcopalian from a good Atlanta family who was considerably less attractive to her opposite sex than he was to his. He'd insisted on her formal conversion to Roman Catholicism and implicit permission to conduct numerous but mostly discreet affairs with more attractive women, but he'd allowed her to set almost all the other terms of their merger. In her final decade—she'd died young, though, because she had never been beautiful, not tragically so—she'd encouraged him to pursue diplomacy. His long stints abroad provided her with several advantages, not least the higher level of discretion it afforded his extramarital adventures and the fact that she was left mostly alone with her son.

It seemed to Clay that he had been blamed for all of it, but especially his mother's inferior gene pool and superior financial situation, both of which his father resented. Most of Clay's money depended on his father's goodwill for a few more months, but his mother had seen to his temporary comfort and eventual freedom so long as his requirements were not too extravagant. This—and the impending thirtieth birthday that would mark his economic emancipation—made Clay increasingly reckless with his father, whose only good turn to him had been helping with Johanna. And that had been something more owed than given, more extracted than offered.

Never one with a taste for a pound of flesh, his father preferred to destroy the soul rather than the body. Clay had delayed his financial emancipation by five full years, which likely had cost him tens if not hundreds of thousands of dollars at the hands of his father's accountants, who seemed to be quite good at what his father called "moving things around for best advantage." Clay knew to whose advantage these movements were. He could have tried blackmail instead—he had at least some goods on his father that day—

but stupid as he was, he was smart enough to know that he couldn't win any kind of long game that way. He didn't so much mind the financial losses even he could read from the spreadsheets the accountants sent—he would still have more money than he could ever figure out how to spend— but the additional five years of his father's shadow, now nearly endured, had been a genuine punishment. So perhaps he had been punished, and it was only reparations he had left to pay.

Clay excused himself to wash his hands and returned with a paper of his own. He opened it, folded it inside out and in half, and pushed it toward his father. He watched his father's eyes move from his *Wall Street Journal* to the rectangle Clay had put under his nose: the sketch of the dead Ladislav in the *Times-Picayune*.

"Friend of yours?" asked his father without even a pause.

Clay looked over his father's shoulder into the kitchen, holding his nerve. "Funny thing is that I met him at one of your parties. In Brussels."

"One of the biggest challenges of *that* job," his father said in his chatting-up-a-stranger-in-an-airport-bar tone, "was that one could never control the guest list. All kinds of people coming and going just because they were someone's nephew or had slept with someone's wife. One of the reasons I returned to private life, truth be told."

The lie was so fluid and clean that Clay wondered if his father really did not recognize Ladislav or if he didn't remember him—the catastrophe of his son's adult life just a slight brush with something vaguely unpleasant in his own.

Clay replayed the party that night he had first met the vile Czech, his father saying, "My son could stand to get laid, truth be told," and turning to Clay, saying, "My friend here caters to a variety of tastes." For a moment Clay thought his father knew about his particular proclivities, but then he understood that his father still thought he was gay, a suspicion he'd developed when Clay had announced a dislike for football at the age of eleven and a suspicion that his father—a man not given to doubt his own beliefs—had never released despite bountiful contradictory evidence.

"He was acquainted with my friend Johanna." Clay emphasized the word acquainted, trying to make it sound ominous, which of course it was.

"Ah, yes, the lovely blond girl you helped study for her citizenship test. How is she? Did her little place fare the storm all right?"

"She's fine," Clay whispered, staggered by his father's tidy repackaging of history and recognizing the necessity of tactical retreat.

Johanna

H ER eyes, straining to focus from the bright day to
the darker bar, settled on a boy sitting before a bottle
of beer. She lifted her gaze to Peter, walking toward him,
wanting to ask him what the hell he thought he was doing
serving alcohol to a child.

Peter greeted her with a large smile. "Johanna!"

She glanced at the seated figure, seeing the adult clothes,
the lined face. Not a child but a very short man, a midget.
She sat a few stools away and nodded to Peter's raised eyebrows, which brought the pencil from behind his ear, caused
the scrawl on the paper that would yield her sandwich and
a taste of beer. *Cause and effect*, she thought; at least people
like her could trigger small effects in the world, predict triv-
ial aspects of the future.

"I'm a midget," said the man down the bar, his tone neither belligerent nor playful, "not a dwarf."

"I didn't ask," Johanna said.

"I just like to get that straight because people have a lot

of ideas about dwarves from the way they're represented in movies. A professor at the University of Maryland wrote a whole book: *The Cultural History of Dwarves* or *The Representation of Dwarves in Film and Fiction.* Something like that. But I don't have dwarfism. I'm not 'a little person.' I'm just very short."

Johanna hoped the man wasn't about to become a regular. Chatty people made her uncomfortable, but at least the man was talking about himself and not asking about her. She gave his face a fraction of her attention: the early lines of middle age, the milky skin of the Irish, blue eyes, long brows. She could leave without eating, but Elizam might come to find her here, and she wanted to see him for interwoven reasons that she did not care to pull apart just now.

"Disaster tourist?" she asked, her tone slightly rude on purpose.

"I'm with the Red Cross. I train the new volunteers as they arrive."

"Very noble."

"Wrong." His smile looked nearly triumphant. "I do it for the paycheck and the retirement benefits. I train volunteers, but I'm not one."

Peter brought the sandwich, and Johanna lifted one of the halves from its plastic basket.

"Know what the hardest part of my job is?"

She finished chewing her bite, and he waited for her answer, expected one. She considered it and said, "I would guess dealing with the volunteers when their naive idealism meets with real people. Most people who need help are not happy about needing help and don't always appreciate it when it comes." She dabbed her mouth with the thin paper napkin. "Or who brings it."

He laughed a sad snort. "That's another problem, but I'm good at that part of my job. Having been born into the wrong body—some other guy got the tall, good-looking corpus that was supposed to be mine—I understand what it feels like to believe the world is getting it wrong. Hell, I can actually help with that part of it. That's a lot of what I do: get the volunteers to stay after it gets hard, to keep working even if they don't get the kind of immediate reward they're hoping for. A challenge, yes, but a good one—and definitely not the hardest part."

Johanna shrugged. "Then I don't know." She took another familiar bite, chewing more slowly than usual because she was being watched and also because she was conscious of the door behind her right shoulder, the feeling that it might push open, that Elizam might walk through it.

"The hardest part is that first presentation to a group—and I make one almost every day sometimes—when I have to come out and make a midget joke. You know, be the happy, funny guy, put everyone at ease. I become 'the cool midget,' the guy who can laugh at himself. Self-deprecation is a rare enough thing that people really like it."

"Like you just did with me. The 'good-looking corpus' line. And if you don't like doing it, then you were practicing." Johanna sipped her beer. "But unless it is your job to make people comfortable, maybe you could skip the joke."

"It kind of *is* my job to make them comfortable. But even if it weren't, it makes things easier later."

"I never learned that," Johanna said, but she trained her thoughts on the present, thinking how nice it was to work mostly alone, limiting her conversations with people to the necessary arrangements and requests, the scheduling of pickups, the acceptance of their compliments or, on rare occasion, a complaint, usually that the restored picture just was not that good. To those, Johanna simply shrugged and said, "That is between you and the artist. All I did was restore it to itself." She felt no compulsion to make her clients comfortable, and she never felt at ease in their company. This was not just because of what had happened to her; she had always been that way, as far back as she could remember, except perhaps with her father, though most of that was behind the veil of memory and so not accessible to her in any direct or useful way.

When the man finished his lunch and his drink he laid down some money and hopped off the bar stool, nodding good-bye.

Johanna finished her sandwich alone, watching Peter make a slow advance through the tall, uneven stack that remained in the corner, sorting the merely water-damaged games from the ruined magazines, separating what could be salvaged from what must be classified as destroyed. "I keep putting this off and then putting it off some more, but today is the day."

"Don't you want to just throw it all out, start over?"

Peter turned his head, his torso following only a second later, his expression confused. "Why wouldn't I want to save whatever I could?"

Having no answer, she took a ten-dollar bill from her pocket and set it on the counter. "I will probably see you tomorrow."

He nodded. "Hope so, hope so."

Before crossing Decatur, she looked both ways multiple times—not for cars but for Elizam.

It had been years since she had thought about what she could do with the name that Eli might have, that she might be able to elicit from him. She had been happy finally to let go of her desire for retribution, which she knew was incompatible with the life she wanted, which was the life she had, and which contaminated her fictional history as a resident of this city with her real story. Yet even though she had given it up, and even though she had been relieved to give it up, she had felt robbed when she'd seen Ladislav's picture in the newspaper—bereft of the possibility of revenge, which as long as Ladislav was out there had at least a faint existence. Having it snatched away had rekindled the desire, and now the means to satisfy that desire might yet be grasped.

She had read about a popular book in which a woman rapes, with a brutal object, the man who had raped her. The symmetry was appealing, it was true, but she knew enough of the art side of her job to know that a balanced composition is rarely created by such straightforward symmetry. No, she wanted the man fully clothed but dead, and she wanted him to know before he died that his death held her signature. Whatever else Eli might have been to her in some other circumstances—in another life, which could only ever be fiction—in these circumstances, he could only be the means to that end.

Her lunch break had coincided with the completion of a project, and it took her some time to decide what to start on next. The unusual sense that she might be interrupted complicated the choice—a realization she found unpleasant. Concentration was generally not a problem for her, which was yet another thing that Clay resented her for, another representation to him of the big thing he resented her for, which was that she did not want to be with him and could not love him.

She told herself to choose something and was surprised by her choice: Marion's paintings. Then again, it made sense that she would choose an assessment, and a nonpaying one, when she expected to be interrupted.

The paintings were more subtle than she would have guessed from her short interactions with their young maker, but she was not surprised—given the girl's youth—by their noticeably different styles.

One was a good but imperfect attempt at photorealism: a meticulous painting of a pawnshop on a sunny day. The painting was devoid of human forms, but people were suggested through their absence, particularly by objects in the shop's windows, and so the sense was that the pawnshop was closed rather than abandoned, though of course the objects in the window had been at least temporarily abandoned as possessions. The overall effect was eerie, but this effect was controlled by discipline in the lines, restraint in the palette. The water damage to the painting was extreme, particularly in the lower right quadrant, where the paint swelled in blisters. Paint loss also looked significant in the far-right lower corner.

The second painting was somewhat larger, more technically accomplished, and less damaged. Though the wistful but energetic sweeps of sky and sea hinted at an unprocessed Turner influence, the painting as a whole did not strike Johanna as derivative. The shadow across the water cast by a large box of a building made the work ominous. There was abrasion in places, but Johanna thought that a basic cleaning might be enough to save the painting, at least for Marion's purposes, which she assumed were both personal and modest even if her ultimate aspirations reached higher.

Johanna lowered the blackout shades and began by photographing the works in three different light configurations. This was mostly to have a record, though sometimes she found she could see things in photographs that she couldn't see when paintings were staring her in the face.

She let the natural light back into her studio and set to work on simple cleaning. It took a while, but eventually she lost herself in the labor, where she was unconscious of the stream of time. She jumped at the sound of the door bells but composed herself—a quick reflex. When she turned, she was confident that she knew whose face she would see.

What she was unprepared for was how that face made her feel. She told herself to remember that he was a means to an end, that what she wanted from him was a simple piece of information. Well, a piece of information that was far from simple, but still only a fact. A name, perhaps with a location. Simple for him if not for her.

She considered taking the unique step of inviting him upstairs—she could make coffee or tea, see if the little dog again warmed to him or not. But the painting was in her flat. Even though she had wrapped it again in thick butcher paper, she would worry about it calling attention to itself like some telltale heart, the decades-old paint undrying and soaking through the brown paper, the deep red becoming the color of blood as the paper absorbed it. She didn't have enough information to predict which bad thing might happen to her if Elizam knew she had the painting, if he found it. The revelation might mean jail for her or her death or, worst of all, the return of the painting to the person Ladislav had stolen it from before she had stolen it from Ladislav.

There was also a small practical reason for not taking Elizam upstairs. She'd learned soon after her arrival in this country that if you want to get an American to talk, alcohol is better than coffee. She suggested a drink.

He walked her to Molly's. "Your new client works here."

Marion was not behind the bar but rather a young woman with a girlish top only partially covering what appeared to be a full-body tattoo, or perhaps a series of tattoos that ran into each other, having run out of space. The bartender wore pin bangs and had made a bright coral heart of her small mouth. The effect was a strange mix of the tough and the vulnerable. Marion, despite the absence of visible tattoos, had not managed to make visible any vulnerability beyond her lack of height. Johanna suspected that this meant she was more rather than less vulnerable than the young woman now opening a beer for Elizam and squeezing lemon into her club soda.

"A cultivated anachronism," Elizam said, and Johanna smiled, understanding that he was talking about the bartender and agreeing.

Eli

THERE were more likely candidates on the list Felicia Pontalba had emailed him. Usually he would start with a local fence or two or meet with a collector of questionable reputation. Though Felicia had said he was likely not involved, the man called Fontenot stuck in Eli's mind because he'd once been the American ambassador to Belgium. It was probably just the sort of weird coincidence that was nothing but a weird coincidence, but the name caught, and Eli had emailed Ted to ask him to set up an appointment. Calls from Ted opened doors that were otherwise shut for people like Eli.

Waiting for Ted's answer gave Eli the excuse he needed to move Johanna to the top of his talk-to list. It was a hunch, he told himself, and not something else, and his was a line of work in which hunches were necessary and to be trusted. Yet he had no idea how to go about getting information from Johanna, now occupying the next bar stool at Molly's. The more he thought about it, the less sense it made that Ted had not just hired him but had gone out of his way to do so. He did indeed have what Ted called a skill set, but it came in handy for only small slices of the job.

Johanna let him off the hook by starting. When she asked him to describe the painting he was looking for, Eli told her the old joke about the long-winded man who told you where he'd bought his watch when you asked him for the time of day. It was a warning, as he started his tale, because in that moment he decided to tell her everything. He told himself it was a strategy.

He wasn't a detective, he told her, not really. He was a painter, a thief, a guy with a new job. "I've been in prison," he said. "Quite recently, in fact."

She sipped her drink but didn't look away. She tucked and retucked an errant strand of hair behind her ear, and it looked so smooth that Eli imagined it felt like satin sheets between her fingers. "Is this going to be one of those exchanges where you tell me a secret about yourself, and then I'm supposed to tell you one of my secrets?"

"Not at all," he said. "For one thing, what I just told you isn't a secret. I don't really care who knows, not that anyone would necessarily even understand what it meant. Not many people know what it is to waste the biggest chunk of your adult life on a cause that's already obsolete."

"That's what you did? Were you some kind of Robin Hood?" She paused, then posed a question that sounded less rote: "Was it worth it?"

He ignored the last question. Even though it sounded

like the one she wanted an answer to, it wasn't a question he wanted to hear the answer to. "Except for me it was more like give back to the poor. Return what was taken. The funny thing is that the thing I got caught for was stealing a painting that I myself painted, that bears my signature."

"They put you in jail for stealing your own painting?"

"It didn't belong to me legally, you see. That's what I got caught doing. I got sent to prison because they knew there was more and because some of my, let's call them compatriots, were into some more serious stuff, which they also knew about." He drew from the beer. "Anyway, idealism isn't the whole story. I threw away more than a decade for more than a cause. I also kept someone else out of jail, and that was worth it even if I never talk to her now. But it's not really a question of worth, anyway. Like I said, the cause is obsolete—to me and to most people."

"So you have been robbed of time. Or you have martyred yourself of time for a cause and for a woman."

"There's another way to think about it, because those twelve years weren't quite gone. Even incarcerated, the mind and body live on. They think, sleep, read, draw, exercise, plan a future. I lived those years, too."

The corner of Johanna's mouth ticked down as though tugged by some tiny, seldom-used muscle. The effect was one of sadness, loss, but Eli felt it was too late to change the direction of what he was saying.

"So my time in prison, that was life, too. Sometimes people's lives are changed by great tragedy, like Katrina here, or by really good luck, but your life can also change tack due to some small accident."

"Such as?" Johanna asked, looking at her drink, her mouth now an even curve.

"Say one day a man with a history as an art thief bumps elbows in a prison cafeteria with a man with a mouthful of mashed potatoes and a connection to a man who wants to hire an art thief to reverse his old ways. Right there, his life is already about to change again."

Johanna inhaled, a sharp intake that she tried to hide as a normal breath. He watched her gaze sift over, down—the two directions distinct movements, first to the side, then down. Her forearm tensed against the bar, yet her grip remained open, her hand almost relaxed. A piece of her hair moved in front of her ear, swishing back and forth with the ceiling fan's oscillation. It must have tickled her face, but now her tic was gone. The strip of hair stayed free, her hand still at rest. He saw in her now a control that frightened him: She was a person who could commit violence in passion and later hide it. Or almost hide it.

He regretted his openness with her, though it had felt good to talk. Despite everything she might be, despite his own attraction-caused awkwardness, he felt a level of comfort with her built on the simple fact that she seemed to understand what he said. So often he was asked to explain what he meant, though sometimes the person who clearly didn't understand didn't care enough for the explanation. People told jokes he didn't get and failed to laugh on those infrequent occasions when he said something he was certain was funny. In most company, he didn't just feel like he was from another world; he was from another world.

The bartender took Johanna's glass and shot in carbonated water with a hissing soda gun. She replaced the lemon with a fresh slice and set it back down on the bar. "Here," she said, grabbing a flyer from under the bar. "Trying to let everyone know that the Halloween parade is on this year."

"It's always a good one," Johanna said, her flat tone making her response sound like an answer you repeat in a foreign-language class, scripted and not what you would actually say if you found yourself in that particular conversation in your native language.

The bartender didn't seem to notice, though, and grinned. "It's the best, and we're not going to let a little thing like a hurricane shut it down. I'm working on my costume—going as a Thinly Veiled Threat. Got boxing shorts and gloves and a pink hat with a little veil attached."

Eli guessed that Johanna wouldn't understand the bartender's use of the word threat, so he spoke up to give her cover. "Very clever."

"At the very least," the bartender said, her pitch ticking up at the end of every phrase, "I expect you two there to watch. But you should consider parading. Life's more fun from the inside."

When she left to attend to some new arrivals, Eli turned back to Johanna, who was obviously studying him.

"I'm guessing you're more of a watcher," Eli said.

She smiled, just a little. "No costumes for me. The opposite, really, because I wear pretty much the same clothes every day."

It was true. He'd never seen her wearing anything other than faded jeans and a solid-colored shirt, either a plain T-shirt or a nondescript shirt with a collar. Her effort not to stand out only made her more beautiful, of course. Whether that was calculated or not, he couldn't guess without knowing her better, but if he had to now he'd say it was unintentional, that she was unaware of the effect, that she genuinely wanted to go unnoticed.

"Back to where I bought my watch," he said. "I used to steal things, mostly works of art. Not for the money, not mostly, though sometimes I made some, but to give them back to the people they really belonged to. Or the place— Puerto Rico. So I never really thought of it as stealing. But legally it was stealing because the definition of *belong* can be tricky, and some of what I stole had been paid for by the people I took it from. People who thought they owned it, who *believed* they owned it."

"And then you got caught and went to prison, and I would guess that you stayed there longer than you had to in order to keep the woman's name out of it."

Eli suppressed a flinch. "The weird thing about prison is that even if you didn't do anything so very wrong, even if you are completely innocent—I saw this in a man who became my friend—after a while you believe, or at least half believe, that you belong there. You see a hair shirt hanging on a nail and think, *It's yours; put it on.*"

"I understand this." She was nodding slowly.

He tried smiling at her. "I thought you might."

She straightened, turned her head toward him sharply. "Why would you say that to me?"

"I'm sorry," he said. "I didn't mean to make assumptions. I just—I just thought you might understand. You seem like an understanding person. Wise. Maybe because you listen more than you talk. I've seen your way in the world—there's something tentative about how you interact with people. Not shy or insecure, but something."

"I don't like to be watched that closely." Her face was utterly blank, though her voice held a tight anger.

"I'm sorry." He cursed himself. "I'm really sorry. Please. I overstated that. You know the way that happens when you try to put something subtle into words, and then you make it into something not subtle at all?"

She remained unreadable, but her shoulders seemed to soften a little.

"Anyway, since I might as well finish my tale. I got let out to take a job at the Lost Art Register, the thinking being that if I could steal paintings, I could think like people who steal paintings."

"Can you?"

"Sometimes. But not always, maybe not even often. Because why you're doing something matters a lot. If someone steals a painting to sell for money, I can guess how they stole it but not necessarily what they're going to do with it next. What I think I might be good at—at least I have been so far—is guessing who did the stealing. But only if they're involved, inside somehow and not some expensive gun for hire. Those kinds of thefts only get solved by the likes of Interpol or because someone in the know gets mad later about something and picks up the phone. If a professional was hired to put a painting on a boat to Qatar, I'm obviously the wrong man for the job, except that I can probably tell that's what happened, and then at least they'll know they're looking for a professional." He paused, hoping she wasn't about to ask him if they thought he was the right man for this job.

"So the painting you're looking for now," she said, "tell me what it's like."

Eli closed his eyes and pulled up his memory of the photograph of the painting—a twice-removed version of the original he had never seen. He described the young woman at the Antwerp docks, the browns and reds, the mood of the painting—its mix of something like sadness or bleakness and hope. When he looked back up, Johanna was again studying him.

"It sounds very beautiful from the way you describe it."

He waited, hoping the discomfort of silence would lead her to give something away, but she simply sat, not touching her drink or tucking her hair. No tics or tells, either because she had something to hide or because she had nothing to hide.

Finally she spoke: "You said you used to steal paintings

to give them to the person, or the country, they really belong to. Does the painting you are looking for belong to the person you will give it to if you find it?"

Eli sipped his beer as though she had not just named his greatest worry about his job, as though he did not find her instincts uncanny. "Are you asking me to consider that whoever stole this painting might have done so because it really belonged to them?" His tongue tripped just a moment before *them*, intentionally avoiding saying *him* or *her*.

Johanna shrugged, another movement that seemed rote rather than instinctual—a gesture consciously acquired. "I would have no idea, of course, but I guess I would answer you by agreeing with you that there are a lot of different ways to define belong. So maybe the first question is about the person you are searching on behalf of. Who is that person?"

He felt a small shame that he didn't know the answer to her question. "I typically don't meet my clients directly. I work for the Register and report to a boss. He's usually the one to meet with clients."

Johanna leaned forward now, which was something he'd never seen her do before. Usually she maintained distance, either sitting erect or even pulling her carriage back slightly. "So maybe your boss can tell you who hired him." She pulled back now, enough to notice. "I only mean, so that you can judge for yourself. Since this is an important consideration for you."

Eli's intuition failed him—not because he was wrong

about something but because he had no idea at all. All he knew for sure was that he wanted Johanna to be innocent, because she was either unconnected to the whole business or just not at fault. But she couldn't possibly be interested enough in his personal integrity to push such a statement if she weren't connected at all. His best hope was that she was connected but innocent. The beer expanded in his stomach, and he felt a circle of nausea in the middle of his forehead.

"So you'll let me know if you hear of the painting? If someone brings it in to be worked on?" he asked, knowing that he was failing, that there was some question he could ask that would move everything forward instead of backward.

Her beautiful face was a cloak now, again. And again he experienced her as a person capable of violence, either in her past or her future—a distinction that unsettled him. She nodded but did not answer.

He hesitated before signaling to the bartender for the bill, which he paid. As he tucked his wallet into his back pocket, he said, "Maybe I'll see you at the Halloween parade. Or maybe we could even plan to meet there. No costumes."

Her look was placid. "No costumes," she said. "Why don't we meet at my studio? We could even watch through the window."

"I think the noise is part of the appeal," he said as they stood.

"Yes, that makes sense, so then not through the window."

Unable to think of any reason to prolong their conversation, Eli found himself exiting the bar before Johanna, afraid to turn back around to see if she followed. The elation he felt over her suggestion that they meet again collapsed into anxiety over why she had done so. Surely it wasn't for the reason he hoped it was. As his eyes adjusted to the brighter light outside, the broadened peripheral vision that came with stepping out of the narrow bar onto the open street, Eli treaded the understanding that he was part of something larger than he realized. Heavy at the bottom of his stomach was another stone of knowledge: Johanna was part of something larger than he realized. She would not see him again because she liked him. Perhaps that was an emotion even alien to her in a general way; he saw now the abstraction and coldness. She would see him again because she wanted to know who had hired him, quite possibly because she had stolen the missing painting. That this might make her a murderer as well as a thief was a realization he came close to before rearing away.

Marion

MARION gently squeezed her oils, making small indentations in the colored metal. It was something she had always done: make her tubes look used to lower the intimidation factor of brand-new paint. Perhaps it had been easier in the old days, back when artists had to grind their own pigments, mix them with oil. The ritual of it appealed to her: a way to begin that was known before you start. And it had to be repeated every day, though artists had devised ways to save their paints for future use or to carry with them. Glass syringes, sometimes, but the longest-lived method was to store the paint in a pig's bladder. So maybe the old days weren't better, but there was an appeal to starting each day and working to finish before the colors you mixed were gone and could never be perfectly duplicated.

Yet she knew that people always think other people have it easier or better. "I wouldn't want to be really poor," her mother had once said, "but there are people who are good at it. It's better for them. They prefer a simple life." Her brother had stormed out of the house yet again—indignation being the only form of energy he could ever seem to muster after he'd discovered video games and pot.

She'd heard customers at Molly's say that some of those living in FEMA trailers preferred them, which she doubted, and one say that most black people have a more utilitarian relationship with their pets and so don't suffer as much when they have to leave behind a dog. Marion remembered a television image of a National Guardsman taking a fluffy white dog away from a nearly hysterical child before allowing the boy to board an evacuation bus. She hadn't said anything to the customer who'd stated the offending falsehood, but she had walked away and been slow to serve him for the rest of the evening. Everyone at the bar knew how to do that: discourage unwanted repeat business. She could see its usefulness in all her lines of work.

Probably it had sucked to be a painter in the seventeenth century, and she wouldn't have made it for five minutes. She wouldn't have even got to try, most likely, being a girl.

She squeezed the sides of the tube of titanium white symmetrically at the middle, pushing past indentation to distortion, wondering at what point the tube would give, spew small, thick streams of white. She raised her sight to the new canvas. Also white.

She set down the paint, deciding to feel satisfied that she was now ready to start, that she would start tomorrow, or maybe even in a few hours. Twenty minutes later she was locking her bike to a street-sign pole in front of Eddie's place.

Eddie's look had changed. He'd shaved off miscellaneous bits of facial hair, and the hair on his head had grown a bit longer, a bit shaggier. The semi–cholo uniform was gone except for the black boots, which he now wore with plain faded jeans and a thick white T-shirt. She saw him almost as a silhouette against the dark green screen separating his entryway from his work space. He found her eyes and held them, which to her surprise did not make her uncomfortable.

He stuck his hands in his pockets, a gesture that expanded his chest, spread his T-shirt taut. "Come to ask me out?"

She shook her head but did not look down or away. "Draw on me," she said. "Whatever you want."

He looked at her for what felt like a long time and then cocked his head. "Follow me."

In the back he gave her a glass of orange juice and a thick spoonful of peanut butter. "A precaution against fainting."

Mildly insulted, she told him that she wasn't a fainter.

"I suspect that's right, but I still have to insist."

She made the mistake of putting all the peanut butter in her mouth at once and then had to work through it, finally washing it down with the sour juice in one go.

"You have a new look," she called from behind the screen as she changed from her shirt into the smock he'd given her.

"Every time you move somewhere, you evolve into something, right? But it seems this is a place where you get to be yourself. More yourself."

She stepped around the screen and looked at him again. "So this is you?"

"Maybe," he said, palming his clean-shaven face. "Time will tell."

He chose the back of her shoulder blade as the beginning location, and she lay on her stomach, the smock open.

She'd told him her pain threshold was high and believed this to be true. A week earlier she'd typed "what does getting a tattoo feel like" into a search engine. The answers ranged from "annoying" to "like the corner of a hot razor blade cutting through your skin." One thread she'd read quickly deteriorated into false bragging: the fifteen-year-old girl who claimed her first tattoo, on her neck, hurt not at all, while the second, her daughter's name on her arm, hurt like hell; the nineteen-year-old who warned potential military recruits that the navy wouldn't admit him because he had tats the uniform wouldn't cover, including one that said. "Fuck the navy"; the guy who said he was addicted to the feeling but out of skin to mark. "Poor, poor pitiful you," Marion had typed into a comment box, meaning it for all of them.

"The long cut lines come first and hurt the most. Then it's just fun for kids. You know, coloring, which should barely even bother you. Just in case, though, we're going to go short. Even if the pain is not bad for you, it's still trauma to the body's energy. Stamina is something you build."

"Don't leave me half finished."

He pressed his hand into her lower back, a technique she recognized as intended to calm and create a connection between worker and client, noting also that it worked. "I'm going to give you a complete image but something we can build on if you want more later."

"No cartoons," she said.

"You already know me better than that." He turned on music. The high volume didn't surprise her; the Mozart did. "Now I need you to be quiet and to relax."

The sound bothered her more than the anticipation. Then came the scratching, as though on sunburn, but just one thin drag at a time. It was fine at first, but the pain accumulated. It was different than the kind of pain Clay gave her: smaller but closer to the bone, bizarre in its localness, completely nonsexual.

Several times she thought she might not be able to continue. She exhaled and concentrated on breathing air back into her lungs, pressing it out again, something she'd picked up somewhere along the way to her massage certification. And then she felt good—not sexually charged like with the other kind of pain but the ordinary elation that comes with the release of endorphins. And then the long lines were done. Eddie changed tools and worked on small pieces of skin. Nothing worse than patches of chafing. The coloring, she assumed.

Several hours later, she looked at the back of her shoulder in the mirror while Eddie gave her instructions for caring for the tattoo as she healed. He'd worked perfectly with the lines of her shoulder blade to create an elaborately colored hybrid of fin and wing. At some angles the red and purple and blue and green ovals looked like feathers, but when she squinted they looked like scales. She was beautiful.

"I changed my mind about the tree." Eddie's voice was deep and felt soft around her. "I thought that living here, it's a good idea to be able to swim and to fly."

Clay

CLAY forced himself to work on sketches for what he
now thought of as the wolf-boy book for a full hour
before fortifying himself with strong coffee and turning to
his new project.

Clay's campaign of indirect investigation began with
information gathering, and he was surprised by just how
easy his father's computer was to access. He could never be
an ambassador now, not in any country with more American concerns at stake than Belgium. Clay could have ac-
cessed his father's email accounts without the password, but
he started there and found it to be a variation on the third
theme he'd tried: the name of his father's last favorite mis-
tress. He'd started with the first, pegging his father as a closet sentimentalist, and then tried GeauxSaints, given that his
father had an economic as well as a municipal interest in the
local football team.

Making Clay's work even easier, most of his father's accounts (three email accounts and an invitation-only social

media site calling itself Un Petit Monde) used either the same password or a close variation, and his father seemingly never cleared his browsing history. He was embarrassed by his father's idiocy, incongruent as it was with the man's passion for wielding power. Clay knew that power is given as well as claimed, and soon enough he would have full access to his inheritance, depriving his father of his final strong weapon against his son. Without the power of money over him, his father would have no power left.

The email was boring on initial inspection, though Clay planned a more thorough scouring later, when he would look for obscure financial irregularities and the like—situations hard to measure at first glance. People are often taken down by the most boring parts of their lives, by money rather than sex, by the illegal rather than the salacious.

The social site was at least entertaining, more or less a Facebook for people who thought of themselves as rich, well connected, and culturally elite. An old guy in Cannes whom Clay had never heard of but who had to be connected to the film festival given the number of photographs of himself with women who looked like models and who were too young to give him the time of day if he couldn't help them in fairly astounding ways. A few guys posing in front of their helicopters or private jets, a Turkish woman who'd had herself photographed in a red living room wearing lots of real or fake diamonds and holding an absurdly long-haired cat. And so on. The boards on the site ranged from a forum to arrange travel-assisted hookups to a discussion of high-end watches, which explained his father's recent upgrade to a timepiece that cost more than any one of his cars alone.

He traced his father's history of recent posts and found one short, peculiar entry titled "exotic leather." Some man teetering past middle age had asked what the finest leather on earth was, a question mostly ignored by the otherwise eagerly materialistic site users, though one or two had dropped a comment on snakeskin shoes that don't look like snakeskin. His father, though, had written simply, "Human leather," followed by a sourcing query, which someone had answered with a URL for a site based in the United Kingdom.

Clay clicked and was taken to what he first assumed was a parody site advertising products made from human leather for a discerning clientele. Clients were assured that the families of "providers" were handsomely rewarded and that, yes, only high-quality stomach leather from attractively hided providers was used. Costs were available by serious inquiry only. Due to the special nature of the product and the scarcity of supply, there was a long waiting list. Though skinny friendship bracelets made from scrap leather could be procured more or less immediately, special-order belts and wallets were another matter. Indeed, all orders were temporarily on hold.

Clay read through each page of the site, including one describing the tanning process and one assuring the acquisitively minded of the fully legal nature of the fine goods being offered. The deeper he read, the more he was unsure whether the site was a parody or the commercial presence of a purveyor of leather goods made from the skin of human beings.

Next he researched human leather generally, finding the height of its popularity in the nineteenth century, when many people requested that their memoirs be bound in their skin after their death. Due to the wide availability of relatively young human skin during the French Revolution, anthropodermic bibliopegy surged, and skin was used to bind books as diverse as poetry and household management instructional texts.

What interested Clay the most were the British execution books, in which the trial transcript of a murderer was bound in the skin of the subsequently hanged convict and presented to the victim's family. A skin for a skin. *Let the punishment fit the crime.*

The usefulness to Clay of his father's interest in human leather was questionable. There were a few people in his circle, the ones he might call *Garden District ladies,* whose stomachs would turn at the very idea. They would say it just that way: "The very idea!" But mostly Clay's father associated with his own kind.

Clay had observed that large wealth and power didn't merely allow but caused men to pursue rare, often obscene tastes. Clay had witnessed his own fetish develop, after all, the thought of which reminded him to phone Marion. He suspected his father would choose shoes, would like the idea of walking on another man so literally. But even if his father had ordered and paid for such an item, unless he'd sourced the leather himself, it did Clay little good. It wasn't information that could be used to cause his father any real harm. Even the Garden District ladies would be titillated as much as horrified if Clay exposed this pursuit. Even so, he was glad to know this thing about his father and added it easily to the collage of assholery that had accreted in Clay's mind through years of exposure.

Another idea angled in: If a wealthy man did have unusual and expensive tastes, who better than the vile Czech to put you in touch with the people whom you wanted to know, such as someone who could shorten the wait for an unusual product, move you to the top of the list, assist your supplier in increasing his supply of materials? Perhaps the interest in human leather spoke of an ongoing connection between his father and Ladislav or had sparked a renewal of an old friendship of convenience.

Expecting his father home soon, at least potentially, Clay returned appearances to what they had been. An hour later, in the guest suite, in the bathroom where Marion had first changed into her absurd dominatrix costume, already looking more like someone who should be taken over his knee than someone who should be wearing leather, Clay stripped off his shirt. Standing before the mirror, he ran his hands up the smooth skin of his abdomen. Yes, he had to agree: it was the most beautiful skin on the human body. On someone like him, it was his only unblemished beauty. He wanted to show it to Johanna, to have her gaze upon it outside a moment of terror.

He felt his stomach harden, a defense against the nausea of memory. He'd visited the place Ladislav had managed before, naively thinking it was simply an establishment of high-end hookers—good-looking and clean and well paid. Twice he'd visited just to get laid before explaining to the vile Czech his particular interests, inquiring whether there might be some girl in town into that sort of thing and how much an hour or two with her might cost.

He wept now, first over his own stupidity and then over his guilt, for which he knew he had to make reparation.

Eli

THE phone conversation he'd had with Ted left Eli smarting. What at first felt like anger, Eli recognized as injured pride. He'd learned that distinction even before prison: People often show hurt as anger. It was important to tease out those feelings, to know which came first and yielded the other, to be honest with yourself even when that meant embarrassment, meant acknowledging shame. Ted had put him in his place, and it was a low place indeed.

To Eli's question about whom they were seeking the missing Van Mieghem for, Ted had just said, "The collector it belongs to." When Eli pushed, Ted said, "There are no provenance issues. The three paintings have been in the man's family since well before the war. Ownership is clean."

"Have the two found been returned to him?" Eli ventured.

Ted gave him an unelaborated yes. "And he'd like the third one returned to him as well."

Eli pushed once more, hinting for a name or some piece of identifying information.

"Look, Eli, you're paid to do the finding. Your job description ends there."

The tone of voice stung Eli, if only because Ted had previously always talked as though they were partners or buddies, even though they both knew that wasn't the case at all.

So now Eli acknowledged the sting to his pride, reminded himself of his place in this particular hierarchy, told himself he was lucky to have what he had. Ted had more power than he did, including the power to return him to jail to serve out the final two years of his sentence. That was how things had always stood behind the friendly demeanor, so maybe it was better to keep that fact in plain sight. To lose sight of it could be to make a mistake; Eli did not want to go back to jail, ever.

What mattered to his investigation was to determine whether Ted was simply pulling rank (maybe he was tired and didn't want to have the conversation Eli was trying to have) or whether there was some more nefarious reason Ted wouldn't reveal any information about their client. Probably it came down to confidentiality, Eli decided, which was fair enough, even something he could respect.

Still, his last conversation with Johanna nagged at him. More disturbing, he knew that he had to investigate Johanna more thoroughly. What he hoped most was that his investigation would prove that she had nothing to do with the missing painting or the dead man. He even admitted to himself that he hoped this was true in part because then he could ask her to dinner, see what might be between them outside his current quest. If she had no interest in the painting, then her interest in him—however faint it might be— was personal. He stared at this unlikelihood and began the work he at least had to scratch at.

Even armed with her unusual full name and also searching alternative spellings and common typing errors, Eli could find scant digital evidence of Johanna's life. Nothing from Croatia or Poland—the two countries people had told him she was from. Nothing from the rest of the Balkans, as far as he could tell, or from Belgium. And only a handful of items from Louisiana. One was a passing mention in an auction report, naming her as the restorer of a work that had sold through Felicia Pontalba's outfit. Three were standard, incomplete listings of local businesses.

There was one more: a photograph taken at a society party called Sazeracs in September. In the sprawling backyard of a fancy Garden District home stood a semicircle of people—all smiling save the tall blond wearing a dark green dress, who glared just under the camera with what appeared to be contempt. Though a search of her name had yielded the pre-Katrina photograph from the *Times-Picayune* society page, and though several others in the semicircle were named, Johanna's name did not appear in the caption. One name did strike Eli as familiar: Fontenot.

It took him a moment to place it: the last name of one of the collectors on the list Felicia had sent him. The former

ambassador to Belgium. It was not Gerard Fontenot identified in the photograph but rather a Clayton Fontenot, a
thin young man with fine light hair, angular in a pale gray
suit that wasn't properly tailored. Unlike the other men in
the picture, young and old, he wore a thin, straight tie rather than the bow tie that had apparently been obligatory at
this particular function. He and Johanna stood next to each
other, but, unlike the arm-wrapping merrymakers on either
side of them, they did not touch.

Eli experienced a sensation very much like nausea, except that it settled in his throat and again, as it had with
Johanna at the bar, in the center of his forehead, a couple of
inches over the bridge of his nose. He moved the meeting
with Gerard Fontenot to the top of his list.

One of his tasks would be to assess Fontenot as a collector. In personality tests, a majority of collectors—but by no
means all—score in ways similar to artists themselves. They
are more likely to act on intuition than empirical knowledge, for instance, and more likely to be open-minded and
to engage in novelty-seeking, even risky behaviors.

Of course people collect art out of a variety of moti-
vations, from a simple calculation to diversify investment
types to a desire to possess what no one else does or can.
For some, collecting is a lifestyle, an all-consuming subcul-
ture. Other collectors simply use their acquisitions for social
access or to show off. Many—an encouraging number, really—collect out of love. But Eli had seen enough of life to
know that love can be perverted as well as altruistic.

Most legal collectors in Fontenot's economic bracket were "show-ers"—people who wanted to own a piece of cultural history but were willing to share it. But Eli could turn up no evidence that Fontenot had ever opened a museum wing or anything of the kind and only two instances when he had lent a painting to a museum for show. It was possible he had done so anonymously on other occasions, but Eli had noticed that people either sign their names or they don't. That Fontenot had taken credit twice suggested that he would always take credit, unless he'd experienced some sort of negative result from that, such as a spike in loan requests. A possibility, though Eli—being yet another intuition-reliant artist—discounted it. *Former artist,* he corrected himself.

Illegal collectors tend to be motivated by money or covetousness. The first kind acquires stolen works to trade or sell. The second enjoys the onanistic pleasure of having a painting all to himself. Most collectors were a mix of all of this, and many legal collectors were also illegal collectors—an easy ethical blur.

Eli would need to meet with Fontenot and place him somewhere in this messy chart. The queasy place in his forehead reasserted itself when he thought about another line of inquiry he would have to follow: How was Johanna connected to Gerard Fontenot? He again brought up on his computer the photograph of her, glaring in her emerald dress.

Johanna

WHEN the phone rang, Johanna was waiting for the coffee machine to fall silent. She'd awakened very early in order to get some work done before Elizam arrived to watch the Halloween parade, and a call at this time was a surprise.

The voice on the other end was female and older. "I'm calling about Maxwell," it said.

Johanna started to tell the woman that she had the wrong number, but then she remembered a painting she'd cleaned about two years ago and assumed she'd been referred as a client. "Do you mean the Maxfield Parrish?"

"Maxwell," the woman said. "I'm calling about my dog."

Shivers climbed Johanna's arms in lines.

"I saw your flyer. I think you might have my little Maxwell. I'm desperate to find him."

Several ideas passed through Johanna's mind, including telling the woman that the dog's owner had already been found or even that the dog had died, cruel as she knew that might be. "Yes," she said after what she knew was much too long a pause. "I found a small dog in the Garden District." She agreed to let the woman stop by later that morning to identify the dog. "I have somewhere to go later," Johanna said, perhaps simply because it was so rarely the situation that this would be a true statement. "So come by in the late morning."

The little dog watched her pour her cup of coffee, waiting for her to sit and stretch out her legs for him to lie on. She remained standing; they would have to get used to not being part of each other's day. Unless this dog was not the caller's Maxwell. Finally Johanna sat on the sofa with her legs outstretched and crossed at the ankle. The dog jumped up, settled into the crevice between them, the ridiculous stump of a tail pointing toward her and his chin facing away, snout buried between her knees. They fit each other perfectly.

Perhaps the woman who called was not merely a mistaken owner but a liar—a hoarder of animals working out of some dark psychology or a person who made her living stealing pets and selling them to pharmaceutical or cosmetic laboratories needing animals to test their products. Johanna vowed not to take the woman's word for it that the dog was hers. She would let the dog tell her whether the woman was his rightful owner, whether he wanted to go with her or stay with Johanna.

As she walked the dog up Elysian Fields and back, wondering if this would be their last stroll together, she let him stop and smell whatever he wanted for as long as he wanted.

She wondered what a dog's memory was like, if he would remember her as she remembered her father or even less than that. She hoped that she would at least be a smell in a dream during some afternoon nap. Back at the workshop, she considered taking a picture of him but instead went to work on a small oil painting.

Before noon the door bells jangled. The woman was in her fifties, stout and dark, well dressed in a slightly flamboyant print blouse and black slacks. The dog ran to her, stretched in front of her like a bull, his front paws tapping a dance. He leaped as high as her knees several times, turned three circles, and then leaped again. This time she leaned over and caught him in midair. She held him to her face, which he licked energetically. "Maxy, Maxy, Maxy," she said.

Johanna stood there, useless.

"Thank you so much," the woman said. "I've been beside myself, going from shelter to shelter. When I saw your notice I was afraid to even hope."

Johanna shrugged.

"You must let me give you a reward," the woman said, shifting to hold the dog in one arm so she could reach the large purse hanging from her shoulder.

Johanna shook her head.

"At least to cover his food."

"He doesn't eat much," Johanna said, thinking of the almost full bag of dog food upstairs. She should go get it, she thought, give it to the woman to take away with the dog, but her body didn't move.

"Well, then, thank you for taking good care of him. If you ever need anything ..."

"If you ever decide you cannot keep him for any reason," Johanna started to say, but the woman smiled a feeling-sorry-for-you smile that told Johanna that was never going to happen, not in a million years.

When the woman asked her if she wanted to hold the dog, say good-bye, Johanna shook her head again but walked across the room and held her hand on the dog's small head for a moment. The woman left with the dog, disappearing down Decatur out of Johanna's view. Johanna stood alone before one of her windows, watching ornamented people walk by, all moving to the right, toward the bar where the parade would begin in several hours.

She returned to the oil she had been working on: a mediocre still life whose theme of the transitory nature of life on Earth was made too obvious by the unskilled foregrounding of a rotting fish. Tears came into her eyes, a stinging ring, but they retreated before they fell.

It was not often that Johanna experienced the impulse to revise. The history of art restoration is splattered with revision, some acts of erasure or reinvention done for practical reasons and others for some combination of the aesthetic and the ideological. The example Johanna had studied in the most detail was Sassoferrato's *Virgin and Child Embracing* because her mentor had been a student in the 1980s, when the painting was cleaned and the revision discovered and investigated.

Charles Eastlake, who had been Keeper of the National
Gallery in the mid–nineteenth century, had been stung by
controversy after freeing several old Italian paintings from
varnishes that had browned with age, violating London
museumgoers' notions that old masterpieces used somber
palettes. When he acquired the already-cleaned Sassoferrato, he bowed to those notions by having the virgin's elec-
tric-blue robes painted over in cobalt (a color painters would
not have had access to until a hundred years or so after Sassoferrato's death) and the lighter portions of the painting,
including the pale faces of mother and child, darkened with
what his notes referred to as a *patina*. She knew, too, of a
case in which a restorer had painted over an ox's head on
the grounds that the snout was too close to the infant Jesus.

In her own work, the stakes were not so high, but there
were times when she warned clients that a real cleaning to
remove old varnishes might leave them with a painting that
no longer matched their sofa. Occasionally someone requested small "improvements" in the works they left in her
care, and she was not above granting such requests if they
fell plainly within the boundaries of her abilities.

She looked now at the rotting fish on the canvas before
her with an eye toward toning it down to compensate for
the fact that it had been painted too large for its position on
the canvas in a violation of perspective and, it seemed to her
now, decency. In the end, though, she left it as it was and did
only the work she had been contracted to do.

Eli's arrival startled her, and she was pleased to see that

she had not been watching the clock, nor thinking about the dog she would never again see.

"It was nice to see you like that," Eli said when she turned. "Engrossed in your work like that. Like I told you, being able to concentrate on something else made prison bearable for me."

Johanna tried to hide the depth of her breath. In Belgium she had not been allowed books or paper and pen. It had not been twelve years—she knew that she had been luckier than some, luckier than Eli in this way—but there had been no freedom at all, no future to plan. She had been suspended as a person, except inasmuch as she could feel pain and frustration and fear and boredom. Sometimes the accumulation of the three became something else: despair. There was nothing bearable about captivity; it was only that you could not actually die of it, even when you wanted to. And maybe she would have died of it, eventually, had not the possibility of freedom punctured her despair, arriving unexpectedly through the man who had, after the first, hurt her the most.

Marion

THEY'D enacted a prisoner scene, a variation of their play that Marion particularly liked. At first she'd hoped that her tattoo would rile Clay, would be the trigger for what followed. She suspected this had something to do with a desire to connect what happened in Clay's house with her life outside it. Yet when the time came, she was more relieved than disappointed that Clay barely took note of her flaking shoulder. "Nice work," he'd said, and he'd avoided the still-tender skin in their scene, landing his blows elsewhere on her body.

Usually Clay pushed her to leave almost as soon as they were finished—not actually throwing her out but letting her know through gestures of boredom and irritation, punctuated by small, insincere compliments. He'd ignore her—either not listening or pretending not to—when she told him some detail about herself, her past, her parents' death.

Sometimes he would do more than ignore her; he would bring up on a laptop an online dating site so she could see him reading women's profiles. "Hmm," he would murmur, as though trying to follow her stories and failing through no fault of his own but simply because she was uninteresting and inconsequential. Then quickly, without sensible pause, he'd tell her that he admired the fact that her purse was small, as though that were some essential fact about her, as though it were more important than what she was trying to tell him. She would leave, sometimes angry and sometimes hurt, often but not always vowing to herself that she would not return, that the next day she'd stop by the tattoo parlor and ask Eddie if his other offer was still good. She and Eddie would go on dates, like a real boyfriend and girlfriend. They'd go hear live music and take walks on the levee, and she'd slip him free drinks at Molly's, and he'd continue his work on her back in exchange. Maybe when her bruises faded so that she would not have to explain them, these things would prove additive, would become something more, though the simple relationship she imagined was just plenty. What she imagined was more than she had ever had.

But on this day—the first in a while that they'd seen each other, the first, in fact, since his father had arrived in town—Clay indicated that he wanted her to linger. She'd slipped back into her panties but was otherwise undressed, and they were talking like normal people, and she was running her finger along the top of the books on one of the many bookcases.

She stopped at the one whose title read *Damsel in Distress* and pulled it out, expecting it to be just the sort of book that she'd read too young, her first erotic exposure setting her sexual bent even before she'd noticed a boy as anything other than an inconvenient brother or a playground rival. But *Damsel in Distress* was a graphic novel, and he was the author: Clayton Fontenot. The drawing on the cover was of a woman with long blond hair, visible through the floor-length window of a tower. Though the woman's features were merely suggested, there was something familiar about her, perhaps the angle of her limbs, her erect carriage, her long neck.

"Like me, an hour ago." Marion tried out a smile but, as always, felt insecure around Clay in a way she never did in real life.

Clay looked at her for an unnervingly long time. "Except the opposite because we're all pretend. The consent is in the frame of what we do. A real damsel in distress, that's someone who has no choice, someone you have to sacrifice yourself to save."

Yet again he'd managed to hurt her feelings despite the fact that she didn't really care about him outside this place, not anymore, if she ever had. Again she thought of Eddie, or someone like him.

She didn't hear the noise, not at first, but Clay's ears picked up something downstairs. "Get in the closet," he said, "and don't make a sound or come out until I say so. Do you understand?" More emphatically, his voice hard and ugly: "Do you understand?"

Though he delivered the words as an order, almost as

though he were starting a new scene, there was something foreign in his tone. It was fear. She did as he said, for a moment worried that burglars had entered the house, that the danger was real. But she figured it out even before she had confirmation: His father had come home earlier than expected, and Clay did not want him to see her.

She considered her options, trying to play each out to one of its possible endings, but her imagination failed because she didn't know enough about Clay's father to make an educated guess. Clay feared him, obviously, but whether his fear was necessary she didn't know or, if it was, in what way it made sense. It could have been any of a hundred things.

The closet she stood in was fairly small and held Clay's clothes. Not the T-shirt and old corduroys he usually wore when she saw him but slacks and button-up shirts and a few jackets. She made a space for herself amid the shirts, their smell a mix of starch and Clay's cloistered odor. Clay tapped on one of the many keyboards in his room in a fast but irregular pace.

His father's voice sounded from the direction of the room door, deep and loud, with the drawl of a rich man: "I am going to ask you a question, and it is imperative—imperative, mind you—that you answer honestly. No games, no omissions."

"Can we please do this later?" she heard Clay ask. "I'm working."

"Interesting choice of verb for a man with no job." There

was triumph in the tone, and Marion understood more about Clay than she had a minute earlier.

"I have a book contract and a deadline. It *is* a job."

"Drawing pictures for your little stories? Fine, fine, but this can't wait. You asked me if I knew our Central European friend was coming to town. What I need to know from you is whether you did, or—and this is the important part—whether *you* talked to him or saw him while he was here."

"I'd rather talk to Jack the Ripper," Clay said, just loud enough for Marion to discern. "He would at least provide an interesting topic for discussion."

Marion shifted her weight to her left foot and felt the oxford cloth of a shirt against her left cheek.

"I seem to recall I said no games and no omissions. If you saw him, then fine, but tell me now. How did you know he was here?"

"Don't you have somewhere to be? A fund-raiser, wasn't it? I'll drive you, and we can talk on the way."

"Well, your little offer of help, while much appreciated, I assure you, is so completely out of character that it makes me quite certain there's something you're still not telling me. I've got the Fontenot name to protect, which I can do, no matter what, but only if you'll give me accurate information. How did you know he was deceased?"

"I just don't want to be having this conversation here and now."

Marion understood that he hadn't forgotten she was

there. She wanted to be quiet for him, but her feet were tingling, one nearly asleep. The next time Clay's father spoke—something to the effect of here and now being exactly how and when the conversation was going to happen—she lowered herself carefully and sat on a pair of shoes, knees bent to her nose, and wiggled blood into her toes.

To his father's reiterated question, Clay answered, "I saw his picture in the paper. If he was in New Orleans to see a Fontenot, it certainly wasn't me."

"Swear on your mother's grave that you did not see that man while he was here."

"I swear on my lovely mother's grave that I have not seen the vile Czech in this decade or in this country with the single exception of seeing his dead ugly mug in the *Times-Picayune*."

"Your lovely blond friend—if I recall correctly, she and Monsieur Ladislav were acquainted previously. Perhaps they had an occasion to talk on his recent visit to our fair city."

Marion couldn't make out Clay's response, which sounded like a series of spits, as though he were trying to get a bitter taste out of his mouth.

"And you would not be in possession of anything that may have been in his possession? Or perhaps your friend took possession of something that you know about?"

"I have no idea what you're talking about." Clay's typing resumed, slower but the pace now nearly even.

"If that's not true, you tell me now. Hell, I can fix it even if you killed that son of a bitch, but only if I know."

"I understand," Clay said quietly. "None of that was me. I swear on your wife's grave."

"That's all I needed to know, but I think I will take you up on your generous offer to drive me downtown. If nothing else, it will give us a chance to chat a little more."

Marion imagined Clay's face, which she felt sure would be grimacing. She wondered less about what they were talking about and more about whether Clay's answers would have been the same had she not been in earshot. His father's questions, she was sure, would never have been asked in front of her knowingly. It occurred to her in a way that didn't feel quite real that this might put her in danger, but she didn't think that Clay would ever breathe her name aloud to anyone—not to protect her but to cover himself.

What disappointed her was to find out that rich people were exactly like she expected: unhappy but none the nicer for it. Just because they had troubles of their own didn't mean they empathized with yours. This man's annual cigar bill could probably have bailed out her family's furniture store, but this was a man who would never give up those cigars.

"Father," Clay hissed just as his father seemed at last to be leaving him alone, "you leave Johanna out of whatever business this is, or I swear—I swear not just on my mother's grave but on every burial plot and mausoleum in this city— that I'll put you in the ground next to her at my earliest opportunity."

Even Marion could tell that Clay couldn't make good

on this threat, and that was her greatest disappointment: Clay himself. Her relationship with him required that he have power, real as well as the kind their fictions bestowed on him—the imagined derived from the real—and now she had seen him stripped of it. She had seen him weak and feeble.

Her initial angry fantasy of bursting from the closet, punishing Clay for putting her in there, for being that ashamed of her, evaporated and left behind only the saltier desire to leave quietly and not come back. In this arid space she felt something else: her aloneness.

She didn't have family. She didn't have anything with Clay. She didn't have any career worth having. She didn't have friends. Everything she had was borrowed or rented or otherwise temporary, and if she ever needed real help, there was no one she could ask and expect to come through for her. Her times with Clay had served to make her forget that—to sever her from her past and her small future—but he was right. They were nothing but pretend, had never been anything but that.

PART THREE

Approaches to Cleaning and Restoration

Johanna

WHEN the man told her he was a police detective, she was not surprised. He was, as Clay might have said, *straight out of central casting*, right down to the rumpled pants and hastily combed hair. He looked like a man who lived alone, a man married to a job that was hard enough that he felt justified in making use of its few privileges. In New Orleans that meant he was probably corrupt. Maybe a little, or maybe through and through.

He strode around her studio as though it were a property he owned but had never seen, switching off her music without asking and putting a hard gaze on Marion's painting of the pawnshop.

"I'm very sorry to bother you," he said in a way that not only wasn't convincing but wasn't even meant to be convincing.

Johanna liked that she knew where she stood with him; she hated false kindness and feared the dangers it represented. This man let her know almost directly that she should never trust him. "But you are interrupting my work," she said, "so perhaps you could get to your point."

He told her things that she already knew or had figured out. He told her that there had been a murder just around the corner, that a painting believed to have been in the deceased's possession had not been found in the deceased's possession, that he was investigating both crimes—the murder and the theft—and was wondering what she knew about either or both. "Given your line of work," he added, which she was starting to think was a lot of people's favorite phrase.

Choosing expediency, she performed one of her rare smiles and told him she didn't know a thing about either, though it was the case that she had seen a lot of paintings since the storm, and he was welcome to look around and leave his card in case she thought of anything. "I've seen the same movies you have," she wanted to tell him, though if she did she would omit that she'd watched those movies just to learn English and not because she cared for them.

"Who was this man, anyway?" she asked, aiming for simple neighborly curiosity. "A tourist?"

"No idea," he said, making a show of going from painting to painting around half the room's circumference. "What's upstairs?" he asked.

She swallowed, controlling the muscles of her throat so the movement would not show. "It's an apartment." She chose the indefinite article carefully, acknowledging no possession. "All the art is down here."

He stood in the center of the room, thrust his hands in his pockets, and glanced around again. He lifted his chin toward the window. "Mojo Lounge. Good place?"

"Great sandwiches." Johanna produced another smile. "I never go in there at night."

"So this fellow who knocked off at the Richelieu. We have reason to believe he might be from your part of the world. I brought a picture in case you might recognize him."

"If you have no idea who he is, why do you think he's from one place rather than another?" This time Johanna held back her smile, knowing it might look smug to offer it as she called this policeman out in a lie. "I only mean, if you found a passport or something, then you would know his name."

"Confidential part of the investigation," he muttered, with no real effort to sell his lie to her, meaning that he did indeed know who the dead man was. *Elizam*, she thought, or *Clay*. Or maybe it was even worse than that.

"Of course." Now she smiled again, slumped a little so she could look up through her eyelashes, an approach that might work on a man who lived alone. "Maybe you could leave your card with me? I could call you if I remember anything suspicious, or if I hear anything around the neighborhood."

He moved his hands from his pockets to his hips, then fingered through his inside coat pocket, extracting a white business card and a scissor-cut rectangle of newspaper. "You didn't ask me about the painting. How do you know you haven't seen it?"

"Since you didn't tell me, I thought maybe that was confidential, too." She willed an innocent face, a face free of sarcasm and ulterior motive, brows lifted just slightly to widen her eyes, barest smile, blank expression.

"Truth is, I don't really know." He shook his head as though remembering something else and left.

She looked down at the pieces of paper in her hand: the card reading "Detective Trey Mouton" with a precinct address and phone number and the photograph of Ladislav she'd seen in the *Times-Picayune* the day she'd returned, cut from its page with careful scissors.

The photo of his death face looked nothing like her memory of the almost handsome man offering her a way out of a dismal Bratislava apartment that smelled always of reused cooking grease, where she'd been forced to move when her father had finally died at the end of his long decline. She'd been taken in begrudgingly by relatives of her mother who had never approved of her mother's choice of husband, whose language she understood only partially, who were misers who figured they would be much better off without an extra mouth at their table, particularly such a pretty mouth when they already had a daughter who shared Johanna's age but not her beauty.

They'd been glad to push her out the door, and—yes—she had been glad to go. "Who lives in a house with no books?" her father had always asked when trying to explain why the happiness of his marriage had been doomed from the beginning, who had tried to explain to Johanna that "Marry your own kind" was not snobbery but just good advice that he should have heeded. "Except," he would always add, "I wouldn't trade you for all the happiness in the world."

Au pair was the term Ladislav had spoken when he'd described the job awaiting her in Belgium, and Johanna had imagined herself reading books to bright children. She could think of no better way to learn new languages that might change her life, might make it more like the life her father had wanted her to inhabit.

To think back to the last time she had had a choice before she had been stripped of her volition was to self-inflict pain, because on that day she had made the wrong one. Each time she thought about the moment she agreed to leave with Ladislav, she remembered it differently, assigned herself a different portion of fault. In some versions Ladislav was a monster and her mother's relatives beyond redemption while she herself could be forgiven on account of her innocence. In others, her innocence itself was the villain.

When Ladislav first tried to touch her, on the train to Brussels, she'd been flattered and mistaken his retreat for respect when she told him she was a virgin. Or at least for consideration, the idea that it was an economic calculation never occurring to her. She had no idea whatsoever of the story line taking over her life.

She knew soon enough that it was an old story that never goes away, one repeated here and there and everywhere, and she was just another girl with the same tired tale to tell. Yet while the plot claimed many, it was her only story, at least on those days when she was unable to believe the fictional history she had imagined for herself. When confronted with her real autobiography, she tried to comfort herself with the fact that at least she'd avoided a few of its clichés.

Perhaps that was why her sentiments toward Ladislav were less murderous than Clay had always wanted them to be. Ladislav had never hit her in the face, never stuck a needle in her arm, never raped her himself. They'd never even kissed after his aborted attempt at railway seduction. Even if his only motivation had been the financial advantage of her status, and later of running an establishment known for girls who were both beautiful and clean, she knew it could have been worse. She heard other variations on the story, too, from girls who told her that Ladislav's house was a big step up. For months she'd believed that she could put in her time, attract no complaints, and at last be rewarded with the return of her passport, a modest wallet, and an open door.

The day before she saw Clay for the first time, Ladislav entered her room after dinner, sat down next to her on the narrow bed, tucked a strand of her hair behind her ear with one finger. "There's a client," he said quietly, "with particular tastes."

As he described what might take place, she knew that she would feel fear, later, probably right when she heard the man at her door. "Ordinarily I would assign a more experienced girl, but there are reasons I need you to do this. I can make it worth your while, grant special privileges."

"Why do you bother asking me this time?"

"I'm not asking, but I'm telling you in advance because he has specifically requested someone who likes this sort of thing."

"Who could possibly like it?" she asked quietly.

"You would be surprised." He looked almost sad, almost apologetic. "If you can manage to be convincing, I'll take two years off your time here." He grinned then, the spaces between his widely spaced square teeth looking black and opaque.

"Two years," she whispered, realizing that her situation was much, much worse than she realized if her sentence could be reduced by that much and yet remain. She vowed to change her story, or at least its ending, and it was a promise to herself that she found a way to honor.

Eli

T H E parade was at once less organized and more cohesive than he'd expected based on his notions of the only holiday he associated with New Orleans: Mardi Gras. Those preconceptions came either from footage he'd seen on a television somewhere or from his own imagination—he wasn't sure which. This parade was less organized because it wasn't a real parade but rather a motley collection of strollers, marching clubs, wagons, and bicycles decked out like floats. Yet it was more cohesive because everyone seemed to be a participant; there were no real spectators save he and Johanna, and even they walked along. Many marchers were close to nude, but no bystanders lifted their shirts and screamed to be thrown beads and trinkets. There was seriousness to this revelry, almost purpose. He figured it was the pride of having survived a great natural disaster, of holding ground or at least quickly reclaiming it.

Johanna was indecipherable, unless she was merely miserable but stoic, which was his best guess. Eli found himself softening, his body giving way to the beats, the steps, the very mood of the place. He'd felt cold when the sun faded but warmed quickly with movement. He liked the ridiculous names and costumes of the marching clubs: the Kazoozie Floozies with their plastic dime-store instruments, the Bearded Oysters, the ornately costumed Muffulettas in their ridiculous ruffled skirts. The near-naked men and women on bicycles, saved from possibility of arrest by the odd strategically placed flower or sequined pasty and saved from the descending temperature by liquor or bravado or sheer hardiness. The women in hoop dresses and parasols with their second-line steps that moved sideways and back almost but not quite as much as forward.

Eli and Johanna moved along with the parade but at its outskirts, the crowd often pushing them together and then apart. Once she took his hand, but it felt precautionary, a necessary way for them to maintain their proximity, and soon she dropped it.

"I like the Katrina costumes," Johanna said as they walked down Conti Street. She gestured to a couple dressed like broken refrigerators, a person walking under a blue tarp, a monstrously colored whirlwind of a man.

"You're perverse," he told her.

When she just nodded, he said, "I like that. It's part of why I like this city—it's perverse."

It was hard to hear, even when they leaned into one another, so mostly they just walked until the parade crashed in on itself back where it started, with new arrivals mixing in with the sore-footed. People milled about talking, some going in and out of the bar, a few drunk off their asses, but most merely happy, smiling at their job well done, reacting to others' small infringements of personal space with generosity. It looked like one kind of freedom.

When Eli asked if he could buy Johanna dinner, she surprised him by agreeing. He'd wanted to take her somewhere nice, and also somewhere quiet where he could hear well across a small table, but she led him down Decatur and up Frenchmen Street to a dingy box whose entry was flanked with poker machines. They sat at the bar and were waited on by a large, bearded young guy with full ink sleeves. Johanna ordered a tofu po'boy and tater tots, which was not what he had imagined them eating, though now he ordered the same with a local beer. Johanna asked for a glass and poured two inches of his beer into it. "If you don't mind," she said, but it was not a question, and he was confused by the change in her personality, the switch from reticence to forwardness, awkwardness to something like social comfort. Perhaps this was simply an alternative strategy for guarding herself, a portion of her repertoire that he hadn't yet seen.

Eli did three things he rarely did: eat too much, talk too much, and drink too much. Johanna drew speech from him without asking direct questions, and he ordered a third and then a fourth Abita and told her about small events from his childhood, about working as a tour guide helping unskilled tourists steer their kayaks to and back from the eerie waters of the bioluminescent bay outside Fajardo, about his early painting days in Spanish Harlem and the place where he'd always taken his morning coffee. It felt good to loosen his tongue and good to talk, connecting his life now with the one across the long, narrow bridge that was prison.

"And now you are here," she told him, refusing his offer of another dram of his beer.

"Which reminds me," he said clumsily, "I'm supposed to ask you how you know the Fontenot family."

He imagined himself watching her carefully, dissecting her gestures and expressions, discerning whether or not her answer was truthful. But with the beer, he simply forgot, though he heard what she said, which was that she had once restored a painting for Gerard Fontenot.

"So that's how you came to be at a party with those people."

She held her head straight, smiled with one corner of her mouth, which carved a small crescent an inch higher on her face, which looked like someone had dug in a fingernail or like a very old scar. "Yes. I met his son there as well." She swirled the last piece of potato on her plate in hot sauce, but did not eat it. "By the way," she said, "there was a policeman also asking about your missing painting."

Eli felt foggy from the beer and could not quite make sense of what she was saying. He'd felt certain that the detective he'd talked to had no interest in investigating the case, which meant he'd been lying or else had changed his mind. Unless it wasn't the same cop, which made no better sense, given the labor shortage in the city for that kind of work. He marked this revelation as important, as something he'd need to figure out when he wasn't drunk.

As they walked back, Johanna cut off Frenchmen a couple of streets before Decatur, walking toward his hotel rather than to her place. "I could come up with you," she said, and he could not imagine a world in which he would have this much luck. Perhaps sensing his disbelief, she added, "That little dog, his owner claimed him today. My apartment will feel too still. It's strange how you can become used to something quickly if you are not being careful."

This made enough sense that Eli discarded his good sense, claimed his key at the desk, and led Johanna up the staircase toward his room. On the landing, he kissed her. He expected it to be clumsy even as he moved toward her, but it was not. They were a good fit—anatomically, chemically, electromagnetically, or whatever it is that makes that happen. He opened his eyes and nodded; she was already looking at him, also approving. In the room, Johanna stood by the armchair and undressed completely, so he did the same, though he would have preferred it if they had moved more slowly, if they'd had undone each other's buttons one at a time rather than their own all at once. He met her at the bed, which she turned down while he watched, again registering that he was a little drunk and so working doubly hard to remember every detail of what was happening.

Since he had given up all the ideas he had previously held of what she would be like, he was not surprised, as he would have been before, that she was not shy and was not quiet. He lay on his back and let her do as she wished, and she knew how to bring them both pleasure. He hoped for imperfections but found none. He loved the sharp jut of her hipbones and collarbones, her small and perfectly shaped breasts, the elongated concave oval in the center of her stomach. Her skin was evenly colored, with no sun lines, no tattoos, no scars—almost as though she were not real. At one point he closed his eyes, but he opened them again quickly; he did not want to miss looking at her, not even for a moment. He was afraid he would wake up, find himself in prison, shaking off the long, vivid dream, moving his hand in case anyone looked into his cell and saw him.

Sometimes she returned his gaze; at other times she closed her eyes, and he wondered if it mattered to her whom she was with, if she even remembered that it was he. During a break she lay on her back and looked around the room. Before he'd made love to her, he had not viewed her as a person of passion. Now he saw her as a person who usually hid her passion. He wanted to ask her if she'd been in the hotel before, but he knew he would not do anything to disrupt or ruin this moment.

He pictured her in this same room, or one adjacent to it or maybe down the hall, bashing in a man's head with a lamp or a rod or whatever had been used to kill the man found with two paintings but not three. "Blunt force" was all he had been told by Detective Mouton. It seemed both possible and impossible all at once that she had killed a man as the winds started to buffet the city, as though both realities were simultaneously real. This was a feeling he'd often had in prison, when he'd imagined an alternate self walking the streets of the Bronx or swimming in the glowing waters off Fajardo or bundled up against the icy wind blowing down off Lake Michigan.

She was capable of murder, he felt sure of it. Though he did not think she meant to harm him, he admitted the possibility, which did not stop him from starting again after their rest. He would serve up his jugular to her if she would let him keep making love to her until it was time for him to die.

And if he had to go to prison to protect her, it wasn't as if he'd never gone to prison to protect a woman before. At least this one had made him no promises, so there would be no promises for her to break. He would know the sacrifice was selfless and not just a long-term strategy.

Clay

JOHANNA had agreed to meet him again after he'd told her it was necessary. It was a little too cold and far too wet to sit on the grass in their usual place across from the birds, so he suggested that he meet her in front of her studio—he never entered her space—and that they walk along the levee. The weather wasn't good for walking, either, but he hoped the greater privacy of open space might make her more open than she would be if they were somewhere they would be interrupted by a server or were seated near potential eavesdroppers.

In her hooded rain slicker, Johanna didn't seem to mind the plan. They ascended the levee across from Jackson Square and looked across the swollen river, their shoulders at the same height, close but not touching. The walkway, which had been neatly laid for tourists, was separated by a sparse but even row of streetlights, now unlit, from the gray rocks that sloped down to the famous river. Up the river, maybe half a mile to their right, sat a useless mostly indoor shopping area and, behind that, spikes of taller corporate hotels desperate for the return of conventioneers. Perhaps the city's best-known bridge to the West Bank crossed the river there. Capable of looking romantic in the right lights, it now looked ugly and functional—its twin peaks nothing but architectural necessity, its gray metal something chosen only by some equation to maximize relative strength against price.

"It seems that you want to tell me something or ask me something," Johanna said, turning a partial profile toward him, the perfect slope of her nose extending just past the crinkled plastic hood of her raincoat.

She stood at Clay's left, between him and what he considered her part of town: rougher but more interesting. On the West Bank in that direction were scaffolds and cranes, sitting in front of long, squat industrial buildings that might never be repaired. The river itself was nearly free of traffic: just a lone tugboat pulling a barge carrying what looked to be lumber, though it was already too far off to tell, heading slowly toward someplace near the river's mouth into the Gulf. *Asshole of the nation.*

Clay stepped around to face Johanna more squarely, memorizing her features in the drab-green halo that obscured her hair, saving the image for later. "Both."

"Tell first, then ask," she said, starting again to walk along the empty walk toward the old Jax Brewery, passing usually full benches made vacant by some combination of hurricane depopulation and current dismal weather.

"When I told you that I didn't know Ladislav was coming to New Orleans, that was true."

She said nothing but walked more slowly.

"But when I told you I didn't see him while he was here, that wasn't true."

Now she stopped and turned back toward the river. Her hood hid her head completely from him, but she seemed to be nodding. What she said was so quiet that he couldn't quite hear it, but he thought she said, "You were the last person to see him."

The memory is vivid, yet more like a memory of seeing a movie than being in one. Like sitting in an old theater, the red and gold of the seats and curtains and carpet once grand and now threadbare, the smells layered and faintly unpleasant, the movie on the screen larger than life but flat, its color washed toward sepia. Close shot of a hotel room, its fabrics old like the theater's. The villain is square-headed and square-jawed. His mouth opens to reveal square teeth, spaced widely to reveal the blackness within him. Underestimating the strength of the hero, who is really an antihero because the best heroes always are, the bad guy taunts his weakness, besmirches the woman he loves, turns his back as his final mistake. The old phone on the nightstand is black and heavy. The audience gasps at the sound it makes, loud but corrugated, not the sound of a heavy object hitting a hard surface but the sound of something man-made crushing through skin, blood, and bone. The impact closes the black mouth. Outside the wind howls down an almost-empty street.

"I was the last person to see him," Clay said, unsure whether he was repeating what Johanna had said or telling her something new. "And I thought that would make us both happy, that you wanted him dead just as much as I did."

He wanted to tell her more, tell her how it both was and wasn't an accident that he'd seen Ladislav. Not an accident, because his father was obviously behind the vile Czech's presence in the city, but a fluke that his trip had immediately preceded the storm, mere chance that his father had been unable to return home as planned for the rendezvous. Unless it was destiny, which Clay had never believed in but was beginning to contemplate, it was sheer luck, good luck and bad luck all twisted together, that Clay had taken the call, recognized the voice, pursued the meeting, and gone to that hotel, perhaps knowing what he would do and certainly knowing what he wanted to do.

"Is that what you brought me here to ask me? You want to know that I am glad he is dead?" Her hands were shoved stiff into the pockets of her jacket, which was slightly too short for her, its waist falling at her rib cage.

"Sort of, yes, but what I want to know is more general. I want to know what you want now, if you could have anything."

"Besides changing the past?"

The mist had turned to drizzle, slanting at them from the river, and Clay faced it, let small drops trickle down his face like cold tears. "Would you change the past?"

"Of course I would, but also I like my life here. But, yes, of course I would. I would probably go all the way back. All the way and then start the clock over."

"It can be implausible but not impossible, what you ask for, so besides changing the past, what do you want?"

Her eyelashes held drops of rain, but her eyes were dry; she was not crying. "I would have to think about it."

"Don't you think about it all the time?" he asked.

She reached for him, held his forearm between both her hands, an initiation of physical contact that shocked him because he knew he repulsed her. "I don't," she said, still looking away at the river. "Hardly ever."

"Then let me ask you the other: *Are* you glad Ladislav is dead?"

"I think so, yes. If he were here, so close to me as he was, then I am glad he is dead. I would not have wanted to ever see him again, not even from a distance. But I have always blamed him less than you did. I was stupid to go with him. He was just playing his part in the world. If not him, then it would have been someone like him. And someone else and someone else."

Clay felt his anger rise, the sides of his neck heating in streaks. "How can you defend him? He's a parasite. No, much worse. And you were a victim."

The hood moved side to side. "Not only that, but I don't blame myself more than a little, and I don't defend him. But Ladislav, people like him, they just try to find a way in the world. Some man in Kenya, his children are starving, and he kills an elephant. Is it his fault, or do we blame the rich people who want ivory? The analogy is not so good, but you know what I mean. Worse to me are the people who pay for the rare and bad things that they want but will not get their hands bloody acquiring them. Demand and supply, as they say."

As Clay listened, his plan both solidified and complicated. "You mean me," he said, spitting the words, but softly.

She looked at him. "I was not thinking of you, no, but I guess that is true, too. But you didn't know, not really."

"I should have. Ignorance is a poor excuse if it's willful. Or I suppose I should say lazy. In my case, it was lazy."

Here, finally, they were talking about the thing that mattered, the most real thing between them, but as he tried to name the truth, the truth was that he couldn't really remember. He'd paid Ladislav for a room and a beautiful girl and permission to do to her whatever he wanted, to finally live out in flesh the scenes he had imagined since he was twelve years old, since years before he had even kissed a girl. And in his euphoria he'd done so without stopping to consider that she didn't want to be there. Or maybe he'd known that—surely he'd known that—but he hadn't considered the gradations of *didn't want to be there*, which ran from the unsympathetic version of some girl cornered by bad choices and an unwillingness to give up an addiction to Johanna's tragic lack of all consent whatsoever. She hadn't made some deal with the devil; she'd been imprisoned by one. The situation wasn't what he'd really wanted at all, but he hadn't stopped to think about that, not for a moment, because all he'd thought about was getting what he did want. He was giddy with fruition.

"Should you have asked more questions, thought about it a little more—why those girls would be there? Why I would be there? Yes, but you can blame that on youth, too, and you should also give yourself some credit for what you did after. Once you did know, you did the right thing. I have not forgotten that you saved me, and you should not forget that, either. Anyway, it wasn't you I was thinking about."

Clay's sternum tightened as it always did when he thought about the other men who had been in that same room, what else she had gone through. He hoped he had been the worst of it, for her sake, and for his own he hoped that he hadn't. Of course he had never asked her, and she had never told him much of anything without him asking first. Even now, he couldn't ask her the obvious next question.

She answered it anyway. "I was thinking of the first person, the biggest money. It is men like that behind all of it, always, for everyone."

Now Clay turned to Johanna, holding her by both shoulders as gently as he could while still holding her in place. "And you took something from him, didn't you? Something he wants back."

She stayed perfectly still yet seemed to shrink inside his hold, reducing the contact between them. "I didn't take it from him. Ladislav did. He sold me to that man and used the access that gave him to rob the house. Paintings, jewelry, money, some guns. And when I left Ladislav, when you came back to get me, I took that one thing." She looked frantic, an expression he had not seen on her face for years. "Only that one thing—I don't know what happened to any of the rest of it; that was all Ladislav. All I can say is that what I took belongs to me. It is mine, and I am going to keep it."

Clay was glad he'd killed Ladislav. He hadn't intended to, not exactly, but he was glad after it happened—had relished it even while it was happening, that delicious sound of the trauma that would take the ugly little life away—and he had decided he'd be glad even if he got caught. But now he worried, because if Ladislav knew that Johanna had taken one of the paintings, then he might have told anyone. What Clay already knew crystallized: Ladislav was in New Orleans because of his father. Perhaps his father had intended to buy the paintings Ladislav had with him, though that seemed too simple.

"The man who Ladislav robbed, that's the man I want dead," Johanna said. "But I want to do it myself, so he will know who and he will know why."

As he looked at her, Clay had no idea how far she'd go or whether she'd have any idea how to go about it. If he let her, even if he helped her, it would end badly for her. Bad was the only way it could end.

"You like your life here," he said, repeating back to her what she had said only a few minutes earlier.

Now Johanna reached again for him, grabbing his forearm with surprising force. "You can find out who he is. You can find out and tell me his name. That is what I want from you."

Later in the day, when he replayed the conversation in his mind, wishing he had asked more questions while understanding that he could not have—not without invading Johanna's sense of privacy and causing her more discomfort and eliciting from her more anger—he realized how calmly she had taken the news that he had killed Ladislav. Perhaps it was because she had known all along, and so there was no surprise to his admission. And perhaps it was because that was what she'd always thought Clay to be: a person who commits violence on others. Or maybe Johanna had expressed no surprise simply because she was beyond surprise; she was a person who expected that anything could happen at any time.

That he was not such a person, not yet anyway, was proved by what she said next: "By the way, you should know that a policeman came to my studio. He's looking for my painting, too, and I suppose he's also looking for you."

Distorted by the distance and the angle and the now almost-full rain, the left peak of the upriver bridge looked higher than the right, as though the trip to the West Bank was an uphill one. Clay imagined pressing the left side down, leveling the road. Maybe he could protect Johanna and give her what she wanted at the same time. Perhaps all his childish pranks and petty acts of revenge had a direction and purpose. Perhaps they had been leading him toward a single act of reparation, of real justice.

Marion

"NOSE to the grindstone," her father had always advised her about school. While she'd known what the phrase meant, if not its origin, it had never made any sense to her. Her parents spoke often of working hard, but when she saw them at work they were strolling the floor of the small furniture showroom, making small talk with customers, or perhaps sitting over a bit of bookkeeping. Now she recognized that their hard work was the boredom of it all. And the worry: The store had paid the family's bills and nothing more. Surely one or both of her parents had held other ambitions, occupational or financial, but she'd never glimpsed them. Her aesthetic life growing up had been a slightly cheaper version of what everyone else in their neighborhood seemed to have: silver tinsel on the Christmas tree, casseroles made with cream-of-something soup, homemade cookies studded with off-label cereal, mustard-yellow kitchen appliances when everyone else was sensibly returning to white. Teachers and electricians bought dinette sets at their store. Doctors and lawyers drove to Mobile or New Orleans for theirs. Even her parents' deaths had been modest: early but not tragically so, closely spaced but not eerily so, and of the most common causes.

Her childhood home had had no influence on Marion's palette—or perhaps only as something to react against. But Biloxi itself was evident on the cardboard rectangle now: the mossy grays and greens of Spanish moss and algae, the many lighter greens and grays of the Gulf, the dirty whites of the frothy small waves, the pinks and blues and transparent blacks of the streaked sky, pelican brown and pelican gray. Maybe that was homesickness: the desire for the colors of your earliest longings for escape.

She was trying to mix one of the colors of Biloxi's sand when she heard the screen door open and a rap on the bolted door behind it. The idea that Eddie had figured out where she lived thrilled her for a moment, but then she realized that it must be a delivery. She'd ordered some new brushes that she couldn't find in New Orleans, at least not until the larger art supplies reopened, if they reopened.

She didn't recognize the guy on her stoop at first look. He was heavier than the last time she'd seen him, his face bready, his eyes deeper set, which made his nose seem longer and more crooked. His look had changed, too: black jeans with chains, gray hoodie with the name of some band, blackened shaggy hair, large black discs deforming his earlobes. Height hadn't been distributed fairly in her family, and he hulked in her doorway, looking down on her even from his slump.

"I know you can't be happy to see me, but I hope you'll hear me out."

"I don't have any money, and I don't have anything worth stealing," she said, turning away from him but leaving the door open for him to follow.

"I'm clean," he told her when they were seated, he on the couch and she on the beanbag chair that constituted the only furniture in the front room of the three shotgunned rooms her rent paid for. "More than clean: I'm straight edge."

"So this is some step for you, then? You're here to make amends?" She heard the resentment in her voice, how it made her sound like his teenage sister and not a storybook orphan.

"Something like that, Marion. I was an addict, and addicts do bad things. Part of my recovery is to set as many of those right as I can."

She remembered the last time she had tried to register for classes, the small anger and large embarrassment of being told by some sorority girl with a work-study job and perfectly straightened hair that there would be no degree in her future if she didn't clear her bills. She didn't have enough to pay her library fines, much less tuition.

"The only amends you can make to me is to give me the money that should have been mine. We didn't have much of a legacy, but we had that. You had that. I've had to work my ass off. You could have gone to college if you'd wanted to. I actually wanted to. I tried."

Henry straightened himself out of his slouch. He looked thinner than he had in her doorway but not junkie skinny, which meant he might be telling partial truth. "Yes, okay," he said, nodding, "I'm working on that. It's going to take a while for me. I'm on my feet now, not much more, but here's a start." He handed her an envelope, clean, white, and sealed. "It's a couple of hundred. It's a start. It's why I came here even though I knew you wouldn't want to see me."

She wondered if he expected her to turn it down. If he did, he was deluded. She tucked the envelope under her thigh. "Okay, then," she said. "Thanks. You can go now."

"Marion, we're the only family each other have. Meager for you, maybe, but it's nice to be connected to something in the world. You can't just pretend you're nobody from no-where."

She resented him for hitting her in the one place she was vulnerable. Of course that one place was everything, was her: She was alone in the world. Her only friends, if they could even be called that, were her tattoo artist and a guy she'd met online and hooked up with for kinky sex. She barely knew either of them, not really, and she hadn't even made a real friend at work. She'd never been an extrovert, never been the life of the party, but she'd had friendships before. If not friendships, then at least people she'd hung out with, a group to be a part of.

She shrugged. "I don't know about that. I think that's what New Orleans is good for. You don't even have to pretend. You can just be nobody from nowhere, and this place will take you."

He palmed his knees, still holding his posture straight, and tried out a smile that didn't quite stick. "Maybe I'll come to see that."

"You're staying in town?"

"For a while, yes. I'm going to try to get some construction work. There's going to be a lot of it, so I don't think they'll be too picky about who does it."

Marion shifted her weight, burrowed into the chair more deeply, hearing the artificial sound of its beads as they rubbed against each other, feeling a sharp corner of the envelope of money in the back of her thigh. "You can't stay here. Even if I was okay with that, I don't have room."

"I'd like to stay here, even sleep on the couch, but I know that I can't even ask that." To his credit, he stood to go. "Anyway, I have a crew of sorts here, and we find places to stay. It's a good town for that these days. Lots of empty buildings."

"Look, you caught me in the middle of trying to work." She found a notepad and a pen and wrote down her phone number. "Give me a call later this week, or even tomorrow, and maybe you could come by for dinner or something."

He moved to hug her, her hand and the paper caught awkwardly between them, before taking the paper with her number. She felt something inside shift and decided not to examine it.

"You have paint on your hands," he said, pointing. "Show me?"

"Sure," she said, and he followed her back through the kitchen to the third and final room of the barrel of her place.

He looked at her landscape-in-progress for a long time without speaking, then said, "See, you aren't nobody from nowhere. You're somebody from somewhere."

Tears welled in her eyes, but she willed them to subside and muttered, "Whatever."

"Not 'whatever,' Marion. It matters."

"No," she said, "because where we're from doesn't even exist anymore."

Now he managed a smile he could hold. "I'm looking at it right now." He punched her lightly on the arm, like he used to when he was in high school and she was in middle school, an affectionate joshing that marked the only moments she could remember him feeling to her like an older brother—the way older brothers were supposed to be.

She tried to count the times it had happened and found that she could, because she only had to get to four. This time made five, but now felt too late.

Johanna

CLAY had wanted to walk her back to her workshop, but she had insisted on saying good-bye in Jackson Square, sending him uptown while she walked the few blocks down. A few blocks wouldn't have made a difference, but she preferred to walk alone. He had asked if she was embarrassed to be seen with him. She wasn't sure if he meant because of the way he walked or because he was obviously rich, even when he tried to dress like everyone else, which he never got quite right. In either case, he was wrong. She didn't care what other people saw, what other people thought of her. She just wanted to be alone.

She passed a gutter-punk couple huddled under an awning with five dogs. The woman thrust a paper cup at her, mumbling something about pet food, and Johanna was happy that the little dog she had cared for had better luck in life than these dogs lying on wet concrete.

Ignoring her studio, Johanna went straight upstairs. It was the first time since the previous winter that she had turned on the heat, and the smell of dust came through the vents after she turned the plastic dial on the thermostat.

She unwrapped the painting and sat cross-legged on the sofa, looking down at the canvas, peering at the face of the young woman waiting to leave Belgium for a better life. Perhaps it was Elizam who had allowed her to say what she always felt: The painting belonged to her. Clay might say that she had earned it, but that idea was disgusting to her. It was simple: The painting belonged to her in a way that did not need to be explained. Unlike the little dog, this small thing had no one else suitable to care for it. She had restored it, she loved it, it was hers.

Her thoughts were interrupted by the bell downstairs, and she was alarmed by the idea that she'd gone upstairs without locking the door—something she had never done before. She descended the steps, pepper-spray canister in her loose fist, to find a couple standing awkwardly in her studio. She knew right away who they were. What surprised her most about this was that she'd had any expectations about them at all, but, then, of course she had: She had heard their voices and had entered their work.

Both were tall, thin, and stylish—the kind of people others looked at when they entered a room or just walked down the street, in part because their bearing and clothing requested attention. The woman was almost a great beauty with her dark hair and fair skin, but her thinness gave her face a drawn quality, her mannerisms were flighty and nervous, and the red coat she had on seemed to wear her. He was more comfortable in his clothes, more certain he was entitled to the space his body occupied. This made sense from their work.

When Johanna showed them what she had done so far, he told her it was more than he'd expected. Only the woman seemed disappointed, but Johanna was not sure if it was due to the incomplete restoration—which Johanna refrained from telling her was due at least in part to her choice of inferior materials—or some sense of her work as less accomplished than she had remembered it.

The painting upstairs interfered with Johanna's concentration—she did not like to leave it out—but she did her best to report on her progress and her plans for additional steps.

"We were overseas, you see, and simply couldn't return in time," the woman said over and over as though seeking absolution for allowing harm to come to her work.

Finally they left, taking a few of the drawings and one painting—those that Johanna had finished with, having either restored them fully or done as much as she could without causing further damage. She understood well that what artists want out of a restorer is not the same as what the owner of a painting by another hand wants and so had left certain things alone.

Back upstairs, Johanna's painting sat on the floor, tilted against the sofa. It struck her that the angle was the same as the day she had seen the painting for the second time, leaning against a wall in Ladislav's office the day she had left with Clay. Though she hadn't been sure what her future would be, she had gone with him, because different was more likely to be better than not. She'd talked to girls who had known worse, but it was hard for her to believe that her own situation could be a series of falls with no recovered altitude at all.

There was also this: Clay himself. She had hated and feared him more than any of the others since the first, but he had changed in a moment. He was genuinely horrified at what he'd done, this she believed, and whatever he felt for her—warped as it surely was—cut him deeply. His father, he had told her, could arrange papers, and he could get her out of Belgium. She didn't have to ask him why he would help her; she knew it was penance. At the same time, she knew he would not have gone so far had she not been beautiful, that her beauty made her more tragic in the eyes of men, because, when it came down to it, it was always their loss and not hers that concerned them most. She did not understand what or why, but Clay had lost something. What he had done to her had come at some personal cost, one that he could repay to himself only through her.

As Ladislav and Clay traded insults in two directions and money in one, Johanna lifted the small painting leaning against the desk and worked it into her duffel bag, which otherwise contained only a few dresses, a hairbrush, a toothbrush, and a pair of high-heeled sandals. The pine-scented incense Ladislav was obsessed with burned in a holder on the desk, and she was conscious that it would be the last time she would ever have to smell the smoke that Ladislav believed contributed to his house's reputation for cleanliness. Though she had taken the painting in plain view, neither man had noticed as they haggled over her passport, a negotiation that Clay finally won by producing more money.

She saw now that the unlikely presence of the painting had been more than auspicious; it had been predictive: She would clean the painting she had so badly wanted to clean the first time she had seen it. And the desire, carried out properly, had led her to everything she now had: her vocation, her place, her fictional history.

On the day she first saw the painting, she decided to become a new person. On the day she took it, she started to become one. And now that work had been completed. Again she wrapped the painting and put it out of sight. Someday she would be able to hang it.

Eli

AFTER standing in front of the Hotel Richelieu for ten minutes and seeing only one cab, whose driver ignored him, Eli walked to and across Jackson Square and tried his luck on Chartres Street. After what seemed like another ten minutes—he was starting to worry about being late when his plan had been to arrive at the bar earlier than Gerard Fontenot in order to have that one small advantage—a black-and-white taxi stopped for him.

"Uptown," Eli said and gave him the name and street address of the bar Fontenot had named.

The driver's expression in the rearview mirror was blank.

"It's off St. Charles," Eli said, concerned because a major reason he'd opted to take a cab was so the driver could find the location for him.

A quarter hour later, at a stoplight on St. Charles, Eli realized the driver had fallen asleep at the wheel when the red light turned to green and the car remained motionless. Eli looked behind them, fearing rear-end impact but also hoping for a loud honk to relieve him of the responsibility of taking action. The street was empty of other cars and divided by the tracks for the streetcar that had not run since the day before the hurricane. The driver was snoring. Eli knocked on the Plexiglas dividing front from back, and the man jostled awake. The light turned red again.

The driver's eyes bulged in the rearview. "Had a cookie after lunch," he said, as though that explained the situation. "I'll take you up a few more blocks. That should be pretty close."

Eli doubted his location but was glad to be out of the narcoleptic taxi. He was pretty sure he needed to go farther up. Most of the houses along St. Charles seemed undamaged, or only mildly damaged, or perhaps already repaired. Down the side streets, though, he saw unrepaired damage: buckled sidewalks, piles of shingles, lots occupied by the crumbled remains of a house that was no more. Pockets of good fortune and bad luck, side by side.

He had passed almost no one since quitting the cab, and he realized he needed to stop the next person he saw. The runner he waved down paused to catch her breath and told him where he needed to go: three more blocks up and two over. He would definitely be late, which was out of character for him and a bad idea under the circumstances. Ted had scheduled a meeting for him with someone unlikely to wait long or give Eli a second chance.

But when Eli arrived, Gerard Fontenot was at the bar watching a very pretty bartender make a martini.

"The same for you?" he asked.

"Just a beer," Eli said to the bartender.

"That simply won't do," the older man said, and Eli was struck by how much like Ted he was. Not his features but his hair, the way his shirt fit him as though tailored, the way he sat with his shoulders slightly pulled back, his chest slightly pushed out. "This place is fast becoming famous for its wonderful concoctions. Make him a Negroni, sweetheart." Turning to Eli, he said, "They make their own campari. Reason enough to come here even if the bartenders weren't gorgeous."

Eli was embarrassed, but the bartender seemed more uninterested than offended. She shook his drink and strained it into a martini glass. It tasted like sweetened alcohol.

"Get started on another round for us, sweetheart."

After the Broussard experience and now this, Eli worried that his liver wouldn't survive a meeting with everyone on Felicia Pontalba's list.

"Ted tells me you're here looking for a little Van Mieghem. I told him I doubted I could be of any real help but that I would be pleased to meet you and offer any assistance that I can."

Eli was pretty sure Fontenot was exaggerating his drawl to downplay his intelligence or his ambition—a man who wanted to be underestimated.

"Perhaps you were thinking that my former national affiliation, with Belgium, I mean, might mean something, but I'm afraid that's just a coincidence. Anyway, the nationality of an artist decades ago isn't likely to be predictive of a painting's location."

"I suppose I was thinking that because of that connection, someone might mention something to you if they came across a painting by a Belgian artist, perhaps someone conducting some presale due diligence—or maybe looking to sell something on the side, not at auction."

"If the latter, then that person would be making a serious error. I'm all about due diligence and proper provenance. There's not a painting in my collection that I don't have crystal-clear title to, and I would do nothing to damage my reputation. Miss Felicia must have told you that."

"Rich enough to buy whatever you want to own is how I remember her putting it." Eli immediately regretted being drawn into the conversation on Fontenot's terms and worried that his words might cost Felicia something. He vowed to stop drinking before what the rest of the world considered cocktail hour, which was about six hours later than it seemed to be in this city.

"That's true; that's true." Fontenot stroked his face and seemed to be thinking about something far away.

"Belgium's beside the point, though, really, because two Van Mieghems were found right here in New Orleans."

"Ted said a missing Van Mieghem."

Eli had no idea how much Ted had told this man or why. He ran his tongue over the front of his top teeth, feeling the smooth film left by the drink. "Three paintings were stolen together a good long while ago. Two of them were recently found in New Orleans." He felt pretty sure he was telling this man something he already knew.

"And you think the third one might have walked off here."

"It's one possibility. Another is that the paintings became separated at some earlier point, shortly after they were stolen or else somewhere on the way here. But if that's the case, it's strange that word of it never got out. Stolen art generally shows up if it's sloppily fenced. These aren't the sort of paintings that would have been whisked straight onto a yacht headed for a Saudi palace or anything."

"Perhaps whoever stole them wanted to hang on to them but needed some money and so had to part with one. But we're just surmising now, aren't we?"

"Well, if you do happen to hear something …" Eli gave him one of the cards the Lost Art Register had made for him. It named him *a consultant* and contained his cell number and email address.

Fontenot pocketed the card without looking at it, and Eli imagined the dry cleaner who would extract it from the pocket and throw it away, also without a glance.

Fontenot smiled, almost as though he were reading and responding to Eli's thought. "Now, tell me what old Ted's been up to out in California."

Eli delivered as best he could, remembering the names of a couple of golf courses and a number that he thought was Ted's current handicap, a hotel he'd mentioned on Catalina Island, some information about the Getty's latest acquisitions and Ted's fairly strong opinions about them, which were a mix of favorable and irate.

Toward the end of the second Negroni, Eli shifted course. "I do have one more question. There's a restorer in town, Johanna …"

"Ah, yes, Ms. Kosar."

"She's done some work for you, I take it."

Fontenot held out his hand in the stop gesture. "No offense to this fair city, which after all is my home, but there is no one local I'd trust with any part of my collection. I'm sure Ms. Kosar does fine work, and I know that Felicia's outfit has directed items her way. And Felicia knows her business well, so I'm not implying otherwise. But my collection is, well, it's very important to me, and there are only a few people in the world I would let near one of my paintings."

"But you do know her—Johanna, Ms. Kosar."

"Not really, but we have met. She's one of my son's friends. I don't know where he finds them, which is not to say that she's one of the worst. Seems like a lovely young woman, in fact. Far too good for the likes of my son, if you ask me, though the fact that she has anything to do with him does not speak well of her judgment." He laughed now, as though he had been told a joke a minute ago that he'd just got, even slapping his thigh with the realization of whatever it was he found funny.

Eli stared at the amber dime of liquid in the bottom of his glass, his own realization not at all humorous: Johanna had probably lied to him about how she knew the Fontenots. Eli was certain that Fontenot was giving him a mix of truth and lies—or, maybe more likely, small truths that created and hid a greater lie—but when he said Johanna had not worked on one of his paintings, it had the ring of plain truth. Sometimes when people overexplain, they're lying, but Fontenot had just been bragging.

The rich man leaned back, and for a moment Eli wondered whether the tall chair would hold his shifted weight. "Out of curiosity, may I ask how you arrived at the idea that I have ever hired Ms. Kosar? Is that something she told you?"

Eli locked up in a way that was probably obvious, though he recovered enough to down the last sip of his drink as a stalling tactic. He was pretty sure he was mostly mumbling when he said he thought Felicia had said something about that, but it was entirely possible he'd got it mixed up. "Must have been someone else." He searched for a name. "Prejean, maybe."

Fontenot laughed. "Entirely possible. You do know, don't you, that Ted and Prejean had a major scuffle a few years back?"

Eli took the opportunity to change the subject and laughed. "Now, I did hear something about that. How did they leave it, if you don't mind my asking?"

Fontenot repeated a version of the story that was more favorable to the Lost Art Registry and less favorable to Prejean's museum than the version Eli had gleaned from Felicia. "Not that I'm saying old Ted's above that kind of thing.

Hell, I wouldn't put it beyond him to steal a painting just so he could be the one to find and return it."

Fontenot hadn't let him beg off a second Negroni, but he pushed the third less strenuously, and Eli was able to stumble back out into the bright day. He walked a block away from St. Charles before he realized his mistake and turned around.

He was still walking—indeed he wasn't even back in the French Quarter—when Ted called to tell him that he had it on good authority that an art restorer by the name of Johanna Kosar might be in possession of the missing painting. He said it in a way that didn't acknowledge that Eli had mentioned meeting with Johanna in the progress reports he'd sent to Ted and that avoided referring to the conversation he'd just had with Gerard Fontenot.

"I have no evidence that that's the case," Eli tried. "Nor where the painting might be even if Ms. Kosar and the paintings did cross paths at some point." Her last name felt strange in his mouth. He'd only ever called her Johanna, and it felt almost as though she were that single name, a name whose consonants even sounded like vowels, a name that echoed like wind in his mouth, nothing like the curt and definitive *Kosar*—a hard word that sounded like it could inflict pain.

"You were hired because of your very particular skill set." Ted's voice was loud through the phone now. "Use those skills."

Eli went back to his hotel to sleep off the drinks Gerard

Fontenot had insisted on paying for and that Eli had let him pay for, figuring that was between him and Ted, a kind of jockeying between rich men that Eli wasn't interested in parsing. He woke from a dream set in Puerto Rico—or, more accurately, a minimalist set depicting Puerto Rico—realizing what Ted had directed him to do. Still too tired to contemplate a response, he delayed his consideration and succumbed again to sleep. This time he was in the real Puerto Rico, swimming in the waves off Rincon. What woke him from this dream was not a realization but a sound: Someone was knocking on his room door.

Through the chain, he saw blond hair, turning, and then Johanna's face. Even though she had already seen him without clothes, from nearly every angle, he rushed to pull on pants and a T-shirt before letting her in. He invited her to sit on the bed while he closed himself in the bathroom to splash water on his face and brush his teeth thoroughly.

The daylight out the window had diminished, and the clock verified that it was now evening. He invited her to dinner, but she shook her head, saying, "Maybe later" and pulling his shirt right back off.

Again they made love several times, and he realized they were even more well matched than he'd thought. But of course sex is always better after the first time with a person, better with a little knowledge and experience.

When both of their stomachs growled simultaneously, she consented to dinner.

As he watched her dress he saw this time the fragility

of her control, realized, too, that what she hid in her daily life was not only her passion but also her fear: fear of losing what she had so carefully crafted as her life. As herself. She may have stolen the painting, but she had killed no one. She might even want to kill someone, but he felt sure she didn't have the right combination of traits to go through with it.

Eli still had no idea what he would tell Ted, but he would not break into Johanna's place, and he would never take anything from her that she didn't want to give him. Even if he was wrong about some of the facts, even if Johanna had killed the man who'd died in the Hotel Richelieu, he would never hurt her. If she'd lied about Fontenot, then she'd had a reason for doing so. And if she'd killed a man in the very hotel where they had just made love, then it must have been a man who needed to die. Eli was sure of this as he felt his moral compass align with Johanna and Johanna alone.

Clay

PERHAPS it was simply because his book was finally finished, but Clay began to notice things that were whole. The moon was gibbous and waxing, soon to be full. His sight was drawn to bulging shapes: ripe oranges, a water-swollen newspaper straining its rubber band, the thick books squeezed into the full shelves of the Fontenot library. Despite the ongoing presence of ruin in the city, the sense that the people whose paths he crossed were in the middle of a work in progress, Clay's world was dominated by a feeling of wholeness and completion.

It had been difficult to get the phone number and harder still to convince the man on the other end of the line that he was not a nut job or a reporter. "It would be a first," the man told him on their third phone call, and Clay could tell from looking into the IP addresses on the websites mentioning him that someone in England was checking into him. "Generally people are seeking products made from materials sourced elsewhere," the man said, his vocabulary no doubt ginger by design and through practice. "There are legalities to consider as well as practicalities and logistics."

Clay had learned a few tactics from his father. One was to make the person you're negotiating with think that you are the one hesitating, that you are the one with concerns and about to back out. "Obviously," he said, "I would need an iron-clad contract to make sure that my instructions are followed to the letter."

By their fourth conversation, they were talking numbers, and Clay knew by then that it was just a matter of naming one high enough, which he would very soon be in a position to do. Even his father had brought up the subject of his trust, though he failed to understand that Clay having access to his inheritance changed the nature of their relationship completely. His father, it seemed, believed that Clay was bound to him by something other than financial need, perhaps the fabled filial affection or duty or else some sad desire for parental approval. For days Clay had been grinning in the mirror when he imagined the moment when his father happened upon the realization that this was not the case.

It was this fourth conversation that his father interrupted, and Clay cut it short to follow him outside. Unlike most large homes in New Orleans, or perhaps even most small ones, theirs did not have a front porch. As a child, Clay had wondered how much that defined them, made them less friendly, their lives more occluded, their motives more sinister. But of course his father had chosen the house, not the other way around.

They sat in the back, looking over the semiformal gardens that the landscape-maintenance company had quickly put right after the storm. His father took pride in the variety of roses, many of them rare, but not enough actually to touch dirt himself. Clay had never liked the roses, which seemed too obvious and smelled too sweet when blooming. Either too full or straggly and forlorn. In the afternoon light now they looked like hands, aged or deformed, twisting through the earth at the air.

His father surveyed the roses and the lawn beyond them with a sweep of his hand. "A party in the spring, perhaps. Pimm's cups and croquet, that sort of thing. Maybe we can even invite some prospects for you. There's got to be some young woman willing to overlook your obvious defects, given the imminent size of your bank account."

This was the second time that his father had acknowledged that Clay was about to come into his money—a date that he'd been able to delay five years but could delay no longer. Thinking about how wrong his father's vision of what that meant for the future was sustained Clay's happy smirk as his father—cliché that he always was—lit a cigar. And Clay needed that moral sustenance because he'd guessed correctly that his father was about to bring up Johanna again.

"I know you like the blond, and there's no reason a man can't keep comfort on the side, but we need to find you a good New Orleans girl. A well-bred girl from a good Louisiana family."

Clay nodded, wishing his father would offer him a cigar so that he could turn it down.

"Speaking of Johanna, by the way, I feel quite certain she's in possession of that small painting I might have mentioned to you earlier, perhaps something she inadvertently carried out of Belgium back when."

The hatred Clay felt for his father was cold. Of course he would again try to use Johanna against him, having identified her as a weakness much more exploitable than any physical abnormality Clay had been born with and more effective than any verbal jabs at a mother Clay had never felt much affection for. "I'm quite sure she does not," Clay said, his voice as stony as he could make it, "but even if she does, so what?"

"Some men ..." his father said, pausing to puff ostentatiously several times on the fat cigar, as though he had an audience other than Clay. "For some men, their possessions are a point of pride. Naturally they wish to maintain them. No one wants something taken from him due to a moment of weakness or a moment of indulgence. You see, the missing object will then remind him forever of that moment. Its safe return returns the world to order. A place for everything and everything in its place, as your mother was fond of saying."

"She was talking about my toys, about cleaning my room."

"Yet even so, I have no doubt that she understood the wider implications of the sentiment. Things that are true in a specific moment very often transfer into excellent general principles, I'm sure you would agree."

It was something his father had always said: *I'm sure you would agree* rather than *Do you agree?* Clay knew that he was close to the name Johanna wanted, and he also knew that he could not simply ask for it. He asked a less direct question: "So what's in it for you?"

"Sometimes when a man is helpful to another man, there is a reward of sorts. Maybe a man wants a piece of property returned, and another man can make that happen. And maybe the former has something the latter would like to acquire, but money alone isn't enough to pay for it. Maybe such a favor will smooth the way, create the conditions for a comfortable financial transaction. Plus there's just the general satisfaction of order restored, I'm sure you would agree. I'm sure *this city* would agree." His father again gestured with a sweep of his hand, first with the empty hand and then with the cigar.

Clay turned the eyes he knew to be cold onto his father, stared at him. "Is that why you killed Ladislav?"

His father actually laughed, coughing around his cigar and taking a moment to regain his breath. "Come now, we both know that was your handiwork, you little turd, you lying little piece of shit."

His father's tone was friendly, almost amused, though Clay knew that was an affectation masking genuine disgust. Clay pursed his lips, gladdened to know he could produce such a strong response in a man who rarely resorted to profanity as a rhetorical strategy.

"I gave you a chance to come clean, and you did not take it. Yet I have kept you out of trouble nevertheless. Lucky for you, I knew you were lying to me even as you sat there and swore on your poor homely mother's grave. In exchange, you are going to put things right. You are going to take something to Belgium, and you are going to bring something home."

Clay pressed himself to remain calm at the realization that his father, after all the gamesmanship, might simply hand over the final means for Clay's revenge.

"Don't fret," his father continued as Clay held his expression still so as not to reveal his glee. "I'm not entrusting you with the money for the latter. That's what wires are for."

Clay was careful not to agree too readily. He wanted his father to believe he was bullying him into the plan. "This is the last time," he said, turning his voice slightly adolescent for effect.

"I am well aware of when your birthday is," his father said. "Believe it or not, I was there the day you were born. Sometimes I let myself fantasize about the old days, when during a difficult birth the father was given the choice of whether to save the mother's life or the child's."

"I think you got that from television," Clay said, still feigning petulance to cover his victory.

His father puffed harder on the cigar, surely for effect. "For what it's worth, I would have chosen yours."

Clay decided he might as well beat him to the punch line. "But I'm guessing that's not the choice you would have made then if you knew then what you know now."

"I don't think that's true, Clayton. I would have been happy to have rid myself of your mother sooner than I in fact did." He smiled affably, as though he was discussing sports with a friend.

"How 'bout them Saints?" Clay spit out.

"Who dat?" His father winked at him, his smile now looking more malicious. "You'll leave in about a week. I'll even arrange you an upgrade, and God knows you could use an upgrade, even if you don't need the extra leg room on both sides."

Clay nodded to acknowledge the insult. "But I'm guessing from the prelude to this conversation that you don't even have the thing I'm supposed to take."

"I will soon; I guarantee you that."

Clay's gladness was short-lived, and he left his father outside when he realized the prerequisite on which his father's plan depended. He climbed the stairs as fast as his uneven gait would allow. He pressed the key that speed-dialed Johanna, but she did not pick up.

Johanna

S H E put on a dress and stained her lips a dark pink with the only tube of makeup she still owned. This felt at once like putting on a uniform and going undercover. Of course Gerard Fontenot knew exactly who she was, in biographical outline if not detail, but there was also this: She was beautiful in a way that men notice and react to.

She'd refused his invitation to the Fontenot home but agreed to meet him at the Crescent Club, which, owing to the fact that most of its members lived uptown, was located not terribly far from Audubon Place. She felt like she was going into enemy territory. Whether this was silly or not, she couldn't be sure. Clay's father had helped her, or at least had helped Clay help her. Holed up in a small Brussels hotel, knowing that the passport she kept under her pillow while she slept was not enough to start the new life she wanted, she had been saved not only deportation but trips to consulates and embassies. Papers had appeared, tickets had been purchased, paths had been smoothed.

Clay believed he had bought these things for her by giving up five years of financial freedom—that his father cared enough about keeping him under his thumb that he would go to such lengths. But the cynical have their blind spots, too, which often have the same source as everyone's: an unsupportably large sense of self-importance. Johanna had never believed the father's claim to altruism or the son's version. If Gerard Fontenot had helped her, it was because it had been in his interest to do so. She had not interrogated his motives at first because she needed what he offered. She could also admit now, from her stronger vantage, that she had been in a traumatized state—not making much sense of anything but just putting one foot in front of the other and trying to move forward. As she thought about it months later, she surmised that the father was trying to protect the son from the likes of Ladislav and so himself from scandal. Now it struck her that there was probably much more to it than that. Perhaps he had been protecting himself from blackmail. Perhaps that was why Ladislav was dead. Perhaps she was worth killing, too. Perhaps that was why Eli was here. Perhaps. Perhaps. Perhaps.

Gerard Fontenot might well be able to give her the name she wanted, but to ask for it would be to imperil herself. This she understood as she applied another coat of the lip stain.

Twenty minutes later she was sitting in a nook of the Crescent Club. She sat on the edge of a huge leather armchair that would swallow her if she scooted back even a couple of inches. There was no door in the doorwaylike opening into the main room of the club, yet the angle of the little room made it private. She could hear the sounds of glassware but not the voices of the few people she had passed on her way in. She could hear the pianist's hands producing a particularly innocuous "Moonlight Sonata," but she could not see the black baby grand being played.

Clay's father's suit looked chosen to match the gray in his hair. His face was smooth with fine pores, his hands manicured yet not feminine. She requested a mineral water, but he ordered them both a gin and tonic, naming a brand of gin she had never heard of. His smile covered his teeth as he nodded to the bow-tied server and waited for him to leave after he delivered the drinks.

He turned sharply toward her, his tone sinking deep. "You have something that does not belong to you."

Holding the very full drink level with two hands, Johanna stared straight at his eyes and shook her head very slowly.

"Are you saying that you don't have it, or are you saying that it belongs to you?" He stirred his drink and then removed the thin straw to drink directly from the glass.

"I'm saying that I don't know what you are talking about." Johanna shifted so she could set the drink down. She knew she should taste it, at least pretend to have a few sips, but she couldn't bring herself to. The room was kept at a temperature comfortable for men in suits but too cold for the bare-shouldered women they brought with them. Holding the drink was making her shiver.

"A man you know—or, better, let's say *knew*. A man you knew died about a block away from you. He should have been in possession of three … three items. Instead he was in possession of two. Add to this information the fact that this man whom you know, whom you knew, is someone you very likely wanted dead."

Again Johanna shook her head. "Your son thought I should want him dead, but he is not the man I want dead."

Fontenot studied her. "I think I see; you're the sort of economist to focus more on demand than supply."

It did not surprise her that he was quick to understand. "The demand creates the supply. You only have slaves pick cotton if people want to buy cheap cotton—to use a Southern analogy."

"On that subject, let me assure you that my family managed to be on both sides of the war between the states, which of course is the only way to make sure you're on the winning side. By which I mean the profitable side. But let's confine ourselves to contemporary history, shall we? One might surmise that you'd like to see me dead as well, albeit on somewhat different grounds."

"To be honest, I hadn't considered the possibility." Johanna scooted back in the seat just a little, stopping herself before she fell into the wide and deep concavity created by decades of the larger and more powerful. She held her back straight, her shoulders back, her chin ever so slightly lifted, her bare knees together. "My focus has been quite singular, so I would have to give that some thought before I could give you an honest answer."

He laughed, and it sounded to Johanna like genuine amusement. She met it with her usual stare; a reaction only gives someone something to use against you.

He eyed her drink, its condensation soaking the cork coaster even in the refrigerated room. He put his own drink down, clasped his hands together, and leaned forward, elbows resting on his now-spread knees. "Yet surely you credit me for setting things right."

Johanna maintained the eye contact he had established. "I'm thinking that if I were you, I would avoid terms such as *right* and *wrong*."

"Fair enough, but back to why we're here: I don't give a damn what happened at the Hotel Richelieu or what you've done or haven't done or why. I have even less interest in seeing any harm or trouble come to you. You're a friend of my son, and it seems to me you've lived a nice, quiet life here for a good decade. Really, all I want is to see your life remain as nice and quiet as it has been."

"You think I killed Ladislav."

"As I said, you more than anyone else I can think of would have wanted him dead. Or perhaps needed to defend yourself against him—surely that's what I would believe. Clearly we would be talking about self-defense. No one would blame you for that, and to involve the authorities would be an unnecessary use of your time. You would be compelled to discuss topics you might prefer to avoid. As I said, what I really want is to see your life remain as nice and quiet as it has been."

"I don't think that is all you really want, if you will forgive me for being direct." In her words, she heard his intonations, his way of making some words shorter but drawing out certain vowels. It was something she knew she did: mirror people. Perhaps it came from having to learn new languages, make people like you in those languages. She knew this was why men often fell for her—they could believe she was like them—though she knew it was also because they could sense that she did not really want them. She decided to speak very softly. "You think I killed him and took the painting."

He pressed the tips of his fingers together, leaned back, and nodded. "I do."

Now she smiled, and the pleasure in his error was a real one. This allowed her to be more straightforward. "If there were three paintings missing, then Ladislav had at most two of them with him in New Orleans. And not only did I not kill him, I didn't even know he was here until after he was dead."

Fontenot cocked his head. While ordinarily a gesture of surprise, it struck Johanna that he'd already known what she would say. "I'm telling you the truth," she said.

"How do you know he didn't have the third painting?"

Johanna tasted the small bit of victory in the moment, tried to feel it as something tangible on the tip of her tongue. "Because he lost it more than ten years ago."

Gerard nodded, granting her the point. "Well, whatever the case may be, it needs to be returned to its rightful owner, an act which will restore contentment to all involved."

"Who is its rightful owner?"

"The man who bought it."

What she wanted more than anything was the name of that man, but she knew the worst thing she could do now was to name the thing she most wanted. "That's one definition," she said.

"It's the legal definition."

She could feel her goose bumps and smoothed the fine hairs on her forearms down, one at a time, forcing a pause on the conversation. "So why have you not taken the legal approach?"

"As I have already said, calling in the authorities would complicate things unnecessarily. Why should you get in trouble over a small misunderstanding? All that really needs to happen here is that the painting be returned."

"To its rightful owner?"

"Precisely." Now his smile bared his teeth. He leaned all the way back in his chair, holding his drink on his stomach as though the glass was not wet.

Again she mimicked his way of speaking: "May I ask what your interest is in this matter?"

"That doesn't concern you."

She knew she shouldn't, but she couldn't stop herself any longer. "Tell me who this 'rightful owner' is, and perhaps I can see that you get the painting."

"That doesn't concern you, either."

"On the contrary."

"You won't be getting that information from me, and—trust me on this—you don't really want it. Let's just make this go away, and you keep leading your quiet little life."

That he thought her life was little was no surprise, but something else about his words did not calculate properly—and precisely because he thought her life had no consequence. She tried it out loud: "If you didn't call the authorities, it is because you didn't want them called, which means you have something to protect or to hide."

"Maybe I want to protect my son. Or at least protect the Fontenot name."

Johanna swallowed as slowly as she could so that it would not be visible, realizing too late that this probably exaggerated the motion by giving him time to register it.

He went on, "But you're right. I don't think you bashed that goddamn rodent's head in. You're tall, that's for sure, but you don't look that strong."

"Maybe I would surprise you."

"Not your style, anyway. You'd be all about premeditation. You would have poisoned him or at least brought a knife. More than likely you would have covered your tracks much better. The police wouldn't even know it was a murder. Anyway, I bet you evacuated before the storm. I'd guess you'd be more than willing to take your chances against the wind and water, but you'd be afraid of the men who stayed behind."

Now his words froze her, and she could not even swallow.

"I hit on it, didn't I? You weren't even in town when our Czech friend hit his final wall, and yet you'd let me think you were a murderer. So now I ask myself why. At any rate, I've assumed for some while now that it was Clayton who lost his cool. No doubt in my mind that you were the reason for it. Probably thought he was protecting you. Maybe you can return the favor and see that that painting lands in my hands so that I can get it where it needs to go and he can keep leading his sordid little life. Truth is, I'm quite curious to have a look at that particular piece of artwork before I do. Anything that generates so much interest has to be worth a gander."

She considered avenues of protest and knew it was too late to take any of them. "As I implied, I will see that the painting gets to you if you will give me the name of the man you plan to return it to."

He winked at her—a clear act of aggression. "Let's play it this way instead: You get me that painting, and I won't tell him your name."

Marion

THE vinyl felt cold through the thin smock, but otherwise she was comfortable, finding the pain more fascinating than unpleasant this time—not erotic like the pain Clay delivered yet revelatory in its own way, each tiny bite into her skin a clue to who she was.

This time, too, she had a mental image of the result, could feel her wings or fins or wing-fins spreading across her back. She relaxed and listened to the loud Mozart string quartet, the satisfying hum of Eddie's gun, the low beads of his voice when he talked, which wasn't often or for long.

How strange it must be to work on skin rather than canvas, to make art on an object that moved. The canvas just sat there, stony in its silence, never talking back, never resisting but never cooperating, either—its own form of resistance, really, in its refusal to participate.

"Did you hear about those kids in the warehouse?" Eddie asked after a while. "I've been worrying it was that couple with all those dogs that are always parking themselves out-side. I feel bad because I wished they'd go away, but that's not how I meant it. Six people died, and four dogs. They were just trying to stay warm."

Marion's shoulder blade tensed under Eddie's hand, and he asked her what was wrong, his voice gentle. "My broth-er," she whispered under the music and the noise, and he stopped, laying a cool hand flat on her back.

Dressed, shirt covering her now-itching back, Eddie told her what he'd heard and she told him about her brother's return, their last conversation.

"Don't worry until you know," Eddie told her. "The odds are against him being there."

Perhaps Henry had been right about family connection because the possibility that he was dead sat metallic in her stomach. She'd always assumed they could repair their rela-tionship later, much later. Her vision of it was vague, and in it their hair was gray, their faces fallen or pinched, but still it was something she held in her mind as a piece of her future.

Eddie reiterated, "The odds are against it, and even if he was there, some who were made it out."

Marion nodded, but her throat constricted with her ef-fort not to cry.

"You got to work later, right?"

Marion nodded.

"Let's walk you down there and get you a drink. Maybe folks will be there who know something."

Marion nodded again and let him lead her down Decatur toward Molly's, grateful to be told what to do.

The dark-haired bartender from the lounge across the street was peering into Johanna's workshop's windows, white towel hanging out of the back pocket of his jeans. He turned to them as they approached. "I saw some guy come out of here earlier—just didn't look right. Johanna didn't come across for lunch today, either."

"Maybe she just had a visitor, you know," Eddie said.

"Something about the guy didn't look right, the way he looked around when he left. And who comes down here in a suit anymore? Anyway, I knocked hard and I rang the bell and she didn't answer. Place is locked up and looks okay, so I guess all is fine. Kind of saw it out of the corner of my eye, anyway, while I was serving a table."

"You hear about the warehouse fire?" Eddie asked him.

"Yeah, bad thing, really bad thing." But, no, he hadn't heard anything about the identity of the kids involved other than that they were homeless, or something similar, who'd come to New Orleans, and that they'd had dogs with them. "Some people got out," he said. "If any good can come out of such a bad thing, maybe it'll inspire some of these kids to go home and make peace. Or at least do something if they're going to stay here, you know?"

Marion tried to remember the faces of the couple often squatting on Decatur but couldn't. The girl had blond dreadlocks and was pretty filthy-looking, but Marion's memory would fill in no more detail. A couple of the dogs she remembered, though: a black-and-white border collie mix and a tan terrier-type dog with wiry fur.

"You didn't do any work on them, did you?" she asked Eddie.

He shook his head. "Nah. That couple with the dogs came in once and asked about prices, but they never came back. She had some nice ink on her already. One of them I recognized because no one except this guy in Copenhagen draws like that. Never travels over here, so she went to him. The guy's tats were pretty run of the mill. You know, you could create a chronology of trends by working up from his ankles or wrists. Tribal first and then all that followed. Tribal, my ass." Eddie's laugh was small and disdainful, but the disdain didn't seem to run deep. "But her—she'd shown some originality. Plus the money to back it up."

Eddie walked Marion to Molly's. "I'm going to come back and get you at the end of your shift, okay?" He waited for her to nod. "So you stay here until I get here. And you call me if you hear anything." He took her phone, flipped it open, and pressed buttons. "I'm 7 on your speed dial, for good luck. You make yourself a drink before you make one for anyone else."

Inside the girl with pin bangs was working the bar. "We're both on—finally got enough business. Which half you want?"

Marion shrugged, trying to remember her name. "Hey, Suzette?"

"Yeah?" The girl raised her plucked eyebrows higher.

"You hear anything about that warehouse fire?"

The eyebrows lowered and knitted slightly—an expression of sympathy Marion was unused to. "Sorry, but no."

The shift wasn't busy, but it was steady. Marion kept moving, glad to have time passing. Occasionally she and Suzette met in the middle, but mostly Marion worked the back and Suzette the front half of the bar and the window orders. That meant that Suzette had higher turnover, Marion had more locals and heavy drinkers, and they each earned their half of the tip jar.

"It's nice not to have the whole stretch for a change," Suzette said while they were splitting the cash. "And you're good."

"Thanks." Marion tried a smile.

"Hey, want to get a drink with me sometime soon? I have a mad crush on a bartender across the way. I'm dying to see what's there, but I don't want to come on too strong or have him think I'm the kind of girl who drinks alone in the afternoon. Come with me—maybe one day next week?"

It had been years since Marion had had a girlfriend and a long time since she'd had a friend at all unless she counted Clay or Eddie. She was starting to think she *could* count Eddie, but it would be nice to have a friend who didn't want to go out with her. "Yeah, that sounds good." Later she wished she'd said *fun* or *great* or something more enthusiastic than *good*, but she'd done the best she could for a girl whose only brother might be dead. Maybe she'd follow up by reminding

Suzette about the drink or even getting her phone number. Eddie had made a calculation when he'd made himself 7 on her speed dial, but that had been generous. There was no one at all between him and 1, which was nothing but her voice mail.

Eli

HE imagined, perhaps even planned, a painting of a city block containing an apartment building with the facade missing to reveal the rooms. In the middle of that building was a room containing him, Johanna, a bed, a table, books, flowers. The other rooms, indeed the whole rest of the city, would not be detailed. Those nearest them would be suggested in brushstrokes, while those farthest away would be only smears. An unfinished world, containing only them and the things they touched. This represented how he felt when he was alone with Johanna, the rest of the world pushed away. Or, more accurately, they were the whole of the world, or at least the only part of it that signified. In the painting, the flowers near the bed would be bright—the only yellow in the whole painting.

This vision and the feeling that came with it had allowed him to avoid thinking about Ted and Ted's request, but after Johanna had left for her meeting, that darkness cloaked him. It turned chilling when his phone rang.

Though he expected the call to be from Ted, he was not surprised to see the Puerto Rican phone number. When bad news is coming, it often arrives from multiple directions. His sister, presumably, or some other relative, calling to tell him that his mother or father had died or was in the hospital dying. He'd never thought about it consciously, but he realized when he saw the glowing numbers that it was a call he always expected, perhaps because it was the call he'd most feared in prison: the call for help when you are helpless to offer any.

The voice on the other end was not his sister's. It was soft and low and had the same stirring effect on him it always had. He pictured again the contrast of black curls against a pale collarbone, the near-fatal shape of perfect lips.

"I'm calling because I'm worried about you," she said.

His pause was long. "More than decade in prison and not one visit, not one call, not one letter. And now you call."

"You told me that was the better way, but the point now is that no one called me while you were in prison to voice their concern about your well-being. I do care about that, no matter what you believe."

"And now someone has called you." He sat back on the bed, stretched his legs out on the floral bedspread, and leaned back against the wall. "To say what?"

"To say that you're distracted, to say that you might make a bad decision because you're distracted."

"And the solution was for you to call, as though that's not distracting?"

The stir in his loins that had always been automatic at the sound of her voice quelled. He would not have believed this was possible, not for the stretch of time before he was convicted or his first several years in. He realized that he was going to hang up on her and made himself delay, made himself first say good-bye and wish her well.

"Wait," she said. "Do you still care about me?"

"I don't know." He sighed. "That painting—the one of you, the one I stole—"

"I've hardly forgotten."

Her call was poorly thought out, but he doubted it was poorly intended, not by her. Instead it was merely casual in its concern. She wouldn't board a plane, but she'd dial a few numbers. "Well, I wouldn't know whether or not you've forgotten, now, would I? What I'm trying to say is that you're like that painting now. It once meant a lot, and I invested a fuckload of time into it, so I have to still care. But it's in a frame I didn't pick out, in a museum far away, and I like the idea of it being there."

"What I'm trying to say is that if you still care about me at all, and if you care about yourself, then you should just do what you're supposed to do to stay out of prison."

"And your interest in this is what?"

"Don't you think I felt like shit the whole time you were in? When you finally got out, I decided I could stop feeling guilty and get on with my life."

"And now I might be inconveniencing your plans?"

"I know you're not an asshole, Elizam, so stop pretending to be one."

"Good-bye," he said. "I wish you well. If they call you back, tell them to go fuck themselves."

"Stay out of trouble, Eli. If they send you back, it's not on me this time."

Now he did hang up on her, but she wasn't the person he was mad at. Her call had had the effect Ted no doubt wanted, though: It had alarmed him. Ted had gone to at least some trouble to track down her name, or maybe he'd had that little trick in his pocket from the beginning, just in case his new employee didn't conform to expectations.

Eli didn't know what he was going to do, so he decided to maintain appearances, keep to his schedule. He had just enough time to shower and make the auction Felicia Pontalba had invited him to attend.

This time Eli had better taxi luck; the driver stayed awake at all traffic lights and delivered him to the front door of the auction gallery. Felicia met him just inside and walked him past a man who seemed to be some combination of greeter and bouncer.

"The lot is small today, which is good news for your time, but perhaps less interesting for you."

She was packaged well in a dark blue tailored dress and heels, minimal makeup. Her hair had dried curly this time but was pinned back. Again Eli saw beauty in occasional glimpses and angles, but mostly he saw affability, affirming his first impression of her.

"Now, you've met the Broussards already, if I recall correctly." A bit more Southern accent slanted into her voice with the standard politenesses.

"Characters, the both of them," Eli said, returning to the platitudes that Felicia enabled and that had seemed to satisfy her before.

"This city has a knack for that. Anyway, they're probably the only folks on the list I gave you who will be here today, since it was mostly a painting-related list. The Broussards are unusually catholic in their acquisitions, so they come to a lot of the smaller estate sales. They're here today for a lot that will be mostly silver, and they'll return Friday for porcelain."

She escorted Eli to a refreshment table at the far end of the foyer and served a ladle of some sort of punch into a plastic cup. "For the larger auctions, we serve champagne—actually a knockoff, prosecco or cava or whatever's on sale in quantity—but today I'm afraid all we have is punch. It does have a bit of a kick, though." She winked as she said kick.

Eli thanked her and took a sip, the carbonation of some ingredient slightly stinging his upper lip. "Tasty," he said, though it was nearly awful.

Felicia smiled. "Actually, I lied to you. Well, not technically, because he wasn't on the list, but his father was."

Eli raised his eyebrows and forced himself to sip again from his cup.

"I do believe I just saw Clayton Fontenot walk in. I told you about his father."

"Yes," Eli said, "I met his father."

"But not the son?"

Eli tried to match her wide smile, but it felt tight around his words. "But not the son."

"Catch me before you leave, then, and I'll make the introduction. Odd that he's here, really. The father uses him as an errand boy sometimes, but Mr. Fontenot wouldn't be interested in anything here today. Plus I hear the son is about to turn thirty, which according to the most reliable local gossip means he's about to come into all his money."

The Broussards toddled over to greet him, calling him "Mr. Elizam," which he did not correct, and Felicia took the opportunity to slip on to the next person.

"We're hoping you can settle an argument for us," Fatty said. "There's a new chef in town whose gumbo has the darkest roux we've ever seen, bowl after bowl of it."

Mignon picked up for him: "And we just couldn't imagine how he could afford to pay people to stand around and cook a roux that dark, not to mention the risk of burning it."

"And so we inquired and were informed that he darkens the roux *in the oven*." Fatty whispered the last three words, holding his hand to one side of his mouth as though he were telling a shameful secret.

"In the oven!" Mignon exclaimed, making no attempt at secrecy.

"Here is the cause of much disagreement in the community. Mignon and I were at first as horrified as anyone, but then we thought about it and decided it's actually a very clever idea. A wonder that others haven't thought of it long ago."

"But not everyone agrees?" tried Eli.

"Going against tradition, you know, in a place where tradition *matters*. And so we're wondering how you, as an *outsider*, feel about it."

Eli had no idea whether they were talking about how to make gumbo or talking about something bigger that he didn't understand, but the word *outsider* confused him. He decided to stick to the literal but allude to something grander, just in case. "I'm of the opinion," he said, imitating their intonations as best he could, even though he knew from prison that trying to fit in is a mistake and that it's better to win respect for your differences, "that in most things in life, the outcome is the best means for evaluating the process."

"I like that!" Fatty said. "And I can think of no better way to get a roux that dark without burning it."

"Except, dear, the problem is that the resulting gumbo just doesn't taste quite right. Roux is not meant to be *that* dark. I guess what I'm saying is that sometime there are no shortcuts worth taking."

"Well, I say the darker the better, so long as it's not actually burned."

"It was great to see you again," Eli said, backing away slowly and then more abruptly.

He found a seat inside the auction room, toward the back and left side, where he could watch those attending— people who wore their wealth in different styles and levels of ostentation. He figured the richest man to be the under-dressed man in worn corduroys and sloppy lace-up oxfords, but that was an uneducated guess. Besides the Broussards, he recognized two faces, both of which belonged to antique-shop keepers he'd met on his second day in the city and neither of which acknowledged him.

The auction itself was fairly dull. Many of the items were bid on by only one person, as though the attendees had worked out in advance who wanted what. A few items were bid up, but Eli sensed none of the tension or passion of art auctions he'd seen in movies. There were no jetsetters, no international spies, no obscenely wealthy men from enemy nations, and Felicia Pontalba was the best-looking woman in the place by a good bit.

He felt more at home than he would have expected, yet also vaguely disappointed. He had been able to ditch most of his punch in the men's room, but the few sips had soured his stomach. He hadn't been eating enough, he knew, and he knew it was because of Johanna.

His watch showed that she'd likely be home by now, but he knew that he should stay and meet Clayton Fontenot.

In the end, he'd delayed for nothing. Clayton Fontenot had slipped out before the auction even started, Felicia told him when she came to say good-bye. "I'm not sure how much longer you'll be in town, but I am expecting you to take me out for a drink." She held both his hands, and he realized she was full-on flirting with him.

"Something with a kick," he tried, but he couldn't get himself to wink.

Out front, while waiting in the short taxi line even though his inclination was to sprint toward Johanna as fast as he could, Eli fielded a call from Ted. He moved down to the farthest bench flanking the semicircular drive in front of the elegant old auction house and sat under an oak tree, cool from the stone bench pressing through his trousers.

"It's done," Ted said, "so you won't have to take care of it."

The discomfort in Eli's stomach magnified.

"I could tell by the sound of your voice that you weren't going to take care of it. Before I recruited you, they told me your weakness was women. A philanderer is what I asked them, but they told me no, that the problem was serial at best, that you were the worst kind of all—the falling-in-love kind."

"What do you mean? You got someone else to do the job?"

"What I mean is that I spared you from making a poor decision because I like you. The painting will now be returned to its rightful owner."

Johanna's name caught audibly in Eli's throat.

"No harm will come to Ms. Kosar if you behave professionally."

Eli saw that Ted had planned his final sentence carefully, that he figured he had Eli with it. "Why'd you even send me to New Orleans if you could have taken care of it here all along?" he asked.

"Honestly, I had no idea where the painting was, and it's also the case that we didn't realize there was already a supportive player on the ground there. He was away due to the storm, it turns out. Had we known we would have someone on location, we would never have sent you there at all." He said *on location* as though it were code and not merely a synonym or euphemism. "But the point here is that our work on this case is done."

The cold seeping into the backs of his legs and ass was uncomfortable now, yet Eli stayed seated, letting the chill spread up and through his torso until he felt genuinely cold all over. He would not have guessed that the city held so much winter so early.

"Take the rest of the week off there, if you'd like. Keep the hotel on the company card, our treat. Or better yet, we'll get you a room at the Ritz or the Monteleone. You've earned it, and I know for a fact you haven't had much fun of late, and by *late* I do mean the last decade or then some." Ted paused. "So enjoy yourself, and we'll expect you back in the office next Monday."

Ted's tone didn't match his words—he sounded more annoyed than anything else—and Eli found it strange that he had adopted the plural first person. Ted had always been more of an *I* than a *we* sort of man.

"You said that no harm will come to Ms. Kosar," Eli said slowly. "Can I assume that means legal as well as physical?"

"No harm of any kind will come to Ms. Kosar so long as things proceed smoothly. The client will have his painting returned to him, but he's paid only for that and not for the story of where that painting has been. We are not in the law enforcement business. We're in the recovery business."

Whether Eli believed Ted or not really didn't matter because Ted could not speak for Gerard Fontenot or the man whose painting was being restored to his questionable ownership. And these seemed to Eli like men who might very well bring harm to someone.

Johanna

JOHANNA had agreed to meet the client because she was uptown anyway, but she would have canceled if she'd had his phone number on her. On the other hand, it bought her a little time—if only a delay that could make what she had to do feel like a decision and not something coerced. She hated the idea of losing the painting, but she hated almost equally the idea that she was being forced to do anything by someone who had power just because he was a rich man. The thought that Elizam could save her occurred to her, but she knew she would have to give up the painting. If she could get the name she needed, it would be worth it. Maybe Elizam would give that to her after all. Or Clay. In the end, it didn't really matter who.

The second meeting was peculiar. Its location was a small coffee house that sat next door to a small residential-neighborhood-style gas station that had been hit hard by the storm—its lot buckled, one pump down and one removed. The husband had wanted to discuss the work Johanna was doing to restore his drawings and also to apologize for his wife's withdrawal of her work from Johanna's care, which was new information he presented as though she already possessed it. "She's high maintenance," he explained, "and she needs to blame someone other than herself or fate or the weather. She does better with a human target, and even better if that human target is female."

"It isn't a problem for me," Johanna said, "though I do expect to be paid for the work I did."

"Frankly, between you and me," he said, leaning in over the coffee drinks he had ordered and carried to their table, "between you and me, it's more a matter of being downright difficult than merely high maintenance."

Johanna was familiar with this move: a man seeking sympathy for being married to someone he had chosen to marry. It occurred to her that he might think she'd worn the blue dress—which was modest in its neckline but short enough to show her knees when she sat and made of a snug-fitting knit—because of him. She wasn't above pursuing such men. Married men were usually easier to get rid of quickly. But not always, and then they were the biggest problem of all because they felt entitled to whatever it was they thought they were exploding their lives to obtain.

"You should tell her," she said, "to use better materials for her work. She is very talented, and she knows what she should be using, so it seems intentionally self-defeating."

The man jerked back as though this idea had really never occurred to him. "Maybe it gives her an excuse," he said, "something to blame if her work fails. I doubt it's conscious, though."

Johanna shrugged. What the woman thought was not her concern. Only her actions mattered, and her action here was to take away some of her work. She wished she could drop the husband as a client, also.

"At any rate," he went on, "I feel dreadful after you went to our house while we were out of the country and everything."

"No good deed goes unpunished," Johanna said, repeating as softly as she could another of the lines she had heard people at the Mojo Lounge use to describe similar situations.

"Of course I'll pay you for all the work you've done." He pulled out a wallet. "I need to finesse this a bit at home, so I hope cash is all right."

Johanna shrugged again. Cash was fine, so long as he realized he was paying for nothing but the work she had performed. If he wanted to think of it as their secret, he could, but it was not a secret to her. What it did feel like was a waste of time; the man could have dropped the money off at her studio.

"Let me escort you back," he said, standing quickly as soon as she pushed back her chair. "I can drive you. Or if you drove, I can ride with you and get a cab back up."

"No, thank you," she said, intentionally withholding an explanation or excuse why not. She owed him nothing.

"Can I call you?" he asked, his hands stuffed into the

front pockets of his jeans, his expression like a catalog version of sincerity.

She gathered her cup and saucer to put in the self-busing tub by the door. "I'll give you a call when your drawings are ready. Cash will be fine again—or whatever is easiest for you."

She knew something was wrong as soon as she opened the door to her workshop. Nothing had changed that was visible to the naked eye, but still she knew. She had learned to trust her instincts, to believe in her subconscious interpretation of events. Perhaps she could see, without knowing that she could, disruptions in the patterns of dust. Perhaps there was some other way of her knowing, but someone had walked through her studio while she was out. She was certain.

Even though she was sure that whoever had entered had also left again, it did no harm to take extra precautions. She set her bag down on one of the worktables, slipped off her shoes, and extracted the small switchblade, which she tucked into the elastic between the two cups of her bra, and the small can of pepper spray, which she palmed before going upstairs, her index-finger pad on the spray button. The thought occurred to her that she *should* call Elizam, or that at the least she *could* call him, but this thought was painful, a contraction in her stomach. He had known about her meeting—that she would be away—and what was he, after all, but a thief?

A question for later, but once again an idea was reinforced: She was alone in the world, and that was good.

Upstairs her impression confirmed her earlier intuition. Someone had been inside her apartment, and he—surely it must be a he—was no longer there. Nothing was exactly out of place, but one sofa cushion sat higher than the other, as though it had been lifted and replaced. The bowl on her kitchen counter that held her mail and any odd object that needed a location before she decided to throw it away was a millimeter or so to the left of where it had sat before. She wasn't an artist, but she knew perspective and composition better than many of the artists she had worked with. The bowl was definitely if ever so slightly *wrong*.

She went directly to the filing drawer of her desk and was relieved to see her few essential papers, including her lease and tax forms as well as the Social Security card Gerard Fontenot had arranged. He had arranged for the newer passport, too, though she had allowed it to expire bearing only the departure stamp from Belgium, the stamp in Amsterdam, where she and Clay had changed planes, and the entry stamp made in the Atlanta airport, where she'd changed planes a decade ago and caught the very last flight she had taken: the one that ended at Louis Armstrong airport. Since then, she'd never gone farther than a short drive. Even for the storm, she'd made it only as far as Arkansas, biding her time in Little Rock until she could point her van back toward New Orleans.

She looked next in the closet. The carefully wrapped painting—the only other thing she cared about aside from the documents that allowed her to continue her life—was gone. She tried to console herself with the fact that she had already resigned herself to relinquishing it, but it was worse that they hadn't even let her have that bit of dignity. The meeting with Gerard had been a ruse, more or less, a way to get her out of her place. Instead of letting her give up the painting, they had taken it from her with no opportunity to see it one last time. She didn't even have a photo of it, though she didn't need one. She would remember its every detail for the rest of her life.

Next she interrogated the word *they*. Surely Gerard Fontenot comprised it, and the man she wanted dead most in the world. For them she felt hatred, black and heavy and hot. But the other likely member of the *they*, the one who would have the dirty hands of actual work—for him she felt something else. *Betrayal* was the only word she could attach to it, but it was insufficient.

She sat on the sofa, rocking her torso gently, and cried.

Clay

CLAY drove one of his father's cars to the Lower Quarter, where his knock on Johanna's locked door went unanswered. To kill time while waiting for her to return, he skulked around the block and peered through the crack in the gate behind the old Ursuline Convent. The convent had stood since 1725 and had never been left empty until Katrina, its nuns sticking out the wars and yellow-fever epidemics that had come to their new city. But in August they—women in their sixties, seventies, eighties—had left by boat when the floodwaters rose. The roof had sustained serious damage, Clay had read, but the sisters were returning a few at a time.

November occupied their gardens, which had been cleaned up after the storm but were now austere rows of hedges. The statues of praying nuns and one monk were arranged in a V. Each looked toward the sky, and Clay imagined them looking into the eye of a hurricane rather than beholding the face of their God.

He tried knocking again, loud enough to be heard up-stairs, and then calling, though Johanna almost never picked up when he phoned. He crossed Decatur to the bar across the street and ordered a beer.

"Saw you knocking across the street." The bartender looked and sounded like a Cajun, but he was on the tall side if that was true.

Clay heard the protective tone and wanted to spit on the ground, wanted to tell him to stand in line.

"You're not the first guy hanging around her door today."

"She does run a business," Clay said. "Any repeat cus-tomers?"

The bartender leaned on his forearms. "There's one guy who comes around quite a bit, and it's about damn time, I'd say. But that's not who I saw coming out of there earlier—guy in a suit who looked like he shouldn't be there. I was worried, to tell you the truth, but everything looked fine. Anyway, you can ask her yourself."

Clay turned and saw Johanna's silhouette in the window. He left his full beer and five dollars. The bartender's parting words followed him: "I'll be keeping an eye out." He crossed the street without looking in either direction, though he vaguely listened for cars.

When Johanna turned slowly to face him, he experi-enced the physical desire he always did when he saw her, together with the shame he always felt when she returned his gaze. The stain of tears on her face deepened his shame.

"Are you hurt?"

She shook her head. "But they took something."

"I can get your painting back," he told her.

She leaned back on one of the tall worktables. Her fingers were stained white, and there was a smudge of white on her face. "That probably would not be good for me," she said. "They would just come back for it. I would always be worried that they would come back."

The street outside remained traffic-free and quiet, creating a strange sense of alteration through absence more subtle than any change caused by addition. Clay could hear Johanna's stereo playing softly: violin over an orchestra. He couldn't name the composer. Good music, like birds, was another thing she knew much more about than he did despite his education, which was both more extended and much, much more expensive than hers.

"What if they wouldn't?" he said. "Come back, I mean. What if you knew that no one was looking for the painting at all anymore, and you could just have it?"

"If you can get the painting back, you can get me the name that I want." Her look stabbed him. "You can give me his name."

Clay nodded, though he knew he would never tell her the name of her living enemy—knowledge that could only ever be a threat to her. The means for her revenge were also the means to her self-destruction. This he understood better than she could. Just because you have been a victim of power doesn't mean you understand how it works or know how to imitate its methods. Because she was an innocent, she had no idea that she was an innocent. "Maybe I will," he said.

"There is one other thing I want to know, which is who your father hired to break into my home."

Clay shook his head because he didn't know.

"I want to know if it is a man named Elizam." She looked at the ceiling for a second and then produced a last name.

"I can try to find out, but my guess is he used a cop." Clay laughed. "It's what he would do. Plus only a cop wears a suit in such a way that it's the thing about him that people notice."

"He wore a suit?" Johanna's voice lifted slightly with the question, but she set her mouth quickly tight. "Either way, I never want to see you again, and I want you to tell your father to leave me alone."

Though she followed it with the request about his father, Clay knew in the moment that the first part of her sentence was the important part. She'd been watching him, and he saw the decision arrive on her face before she said it. He also knew that its recent arrival made it no less solid or enduring. *"Never."* He mouthed the word soundlessly and found it remarkably soft in his mouth. "Are you sure about that word?"

"You want to be punished. Your punishment is banishment."

Johanna turned away from him and twisted the volume dial on the stereo, hitting him with the concerto like a blunt force, unable to hear the last thing he would ever say to her.

Marion

I N the end, it was not a customer who told her that Henry was alive and well enough but Henry himself. "Calling to take you up on dinner," he said, and the long night of thinking that he might be dead shortened into a single moment of relief.

When Marion asked him about the fire, her voice still precarious from the fright, he repeated what everyone was saying: "Terrible thing, terrible thing. But, no, not my crew at all, though I think I crashed in that same warehouse one night."

She cordoned off her anger as irrational and allowed herself the pleasure of relief. Again she had a brother, perhaps a less-than-copacetic sibling, but it was at least a tether to someone, proof that she existed in relation to something else, that she had a history, a genealogy, a family of origin. "Sure," she said.

She mentally combined the scant contents of her refrigerator and thin cabinet that held the rest of her food. She'd read a book once, a memoir of a formerly starving but now successful artist who'd once survived several days on flour and an onion by making a flour-and-water crust and baking it with a topping of caramelized onions. Delicious, he'd written of the makeshift tart, but she suspected he was lying about his hard times because he also seemed to be drinking a lot of wine on those same several days. Wine was never free, nor was the gas and electricity to run an oven, and poverty was never romantic and tasty.

Once in college she'd heard from an acquaintance about a cheap market run by an elderly woman in a sketchy neighborhood. After finding it, she'd eaten a horrible meal of oily canned mackerel and rice for three days. The memory of this meal—welcome as it had been at the time—raised her older, more rational anger at Henry, and she wished there was a shop nearby that sold canned mackerel so he could see how he liked it. But if he was straight edge now, he was probably vegan—a comical notion given that she'd never known him not to give in to an impulse or craving, culinary, pharmaceutical, or otherwise. She tried to remember how she'd felt about him when she'd thought he might be dead, which softened her a little.

In the end she sautéed garlic in olive oil and boiled spaghetti and thawed frozen peas and stirred it altogether. Henry ate appreciatively as they sat across from each other at her small Formica table. Dark bangs slanted across his forehead and partway over his eyes, and for a second she saw in him the boy he had been back when they were something like brother and sister, back before he'd discovered his large talent for taking drugs. Even as children, though, they had generally gone their separate ways, not connecting even enough to squabble.

"So that could have been you," she said midway through dinner.

Henry smiled, his mouth closed around a mouthful of food. "I'm glad it wasn't."

Marion knew she was supposed to say that she was also glad, or something like that, but she just chewed her food and swallowed, taking small sips of water between bites.

It was while he was washing the few dishes that she realized she'd decided something. "You should stay here for a while," she said.

He stopped, dried his hands, and faced her. "You don't have much room, and I haven't been a very good brother."

"Just for a while, until it warms up," she said, looking down and away. "All I have is the couch—I'm sure as hell not giving you the mattress—but you can crash here if you want. It's not like I'm saying you were a good brother, just that you can put this roof over your head for a while. Maybe until it gets warm again. Let's just see how it goes."

He embraced her, and she loosened into it only a little as he whispered the two words thank and you, not as a single phrase but as two distinct words, *thank* and *you*, over and over.

Eli

HE opened his room door without asking who it was because he was so sure it would be Johanna, who had not answered the ten times he had called. "Johanna," he said as he opened the door, and Detective Mouton laughed and pushed by him.

"Don't worry," the detective said, sitting on the unmade bed and motioning to the only chair for Eli to sit across from him. "She's fine. I can't promise she'll stay that way, but she's just fine right now."

The earnest, slightly beleaguered demeanor the man had displayed over gin fizzes had been taken over by something cockier and more reckless. Eli couldn't guess which facade, if either, was the real Mouton.

"I take it you were the man for that job," Eli tested.

"I guess we're a lot alike, the both of us on the dole as repo men."

Still in his boxers and a sleeveless undershirt—his prison pajamas—Eli glanced around for his jeans and remembered they were on the side of the bed, out of his current line of sight. "For some it's a higher calling than for others," he said.

The detective laughed, still cocky. "Nope, men like us, we just take orders and cash our paychecks. Whatever you once were, that's not what you are now. I've seen your record, anyway, and I guarantee you that you're out of your league here. You're a boutique thief, and I'm a hack, but that's not the distinction at stake here."

"You win either way," Eli said, "so why are you here?"

"Because I hear you're more about stealing back than stealing. Boutique thief, like I said. So this is a courtesy visit to save you time. Time among other things."

Another prison tactic: Let the other person speak again before you do.

"I think you understand. I'm here to let you know that whatever it is you're planning to do next is something you should plan not to do after all."

"I'm guessing you got a big *or else* for me."

"I got two of them. One is *or else you go back to prison.* The other is *or else one badly hurt blond lady.* Put them together and you get *one badly hurt blond lady with no shoulder to cry on.*"

The cop stood up, and Eli stood to take the man's relative measure. His same height, thirty pounds heavier, maybe equal strength, but you never can tell. Nothing on the right hip, but, yes, a southpaw: holster bulge on the left.

"Speaking of women," Eli said, finding his own version of reckless, "how's your wife's vow of chastity going?"

"Vow of silence," the detective said as his fist found Eli's nose.

Eli reeled back, regained his balance, sat down in the chair, and watched the spread of blood drops—not many but a few—on the chest of his undershirt. "You held back," he said in a husky whisper.

"You probably think I hit you because you insulted my manhood, but if you do, you're wrong. I'm glad my wife is finding herself or whatever the fuck she's doing. I love my wife, and what she wants, I want. If it's to not talk, well, between you and me, so much the better. The reason I punched you is just so you'll remember our conversation next time you look at yourself in the mirror and try to decide what to do next. You look yourself in the nose, and you think of all the hits you'll take when you're back in prison, and you think about what Ms. Kosar's face would look like dripping blood. Then you cash your paycheck and go home, and I'll be doing the same."

Marion

WHEN she heard the knock at the door, just after Henry had gone out to apply for jobs, she figured he had forgotten his key and returned for it. It took several seconds to register whose face she saw instead of her brother's, so out of context it was.

"How do you know where I live?" she asked, though of course Clay could find out whatever he wanted to, and the city was now even smaller than it used to be if you counted by people and not square miles.

He asked if he could come in, and she stepped aside so that he could fit through the door with the large messenger bag he was carrying.

"Every time I see you these days, you're with a different guy." He sat down on her sofa, which was still covered in the sheet and blanket that made it Henry's bed.

"Are you stalking me?" she asked, preferring pugilism to any other strategy at the moment.

He shook his head. "Just coincidence, mostly, though I

did want to catch you alone. Today I'm here to ask you a favor."

Marion sat across from him on the beanbag chair but didn't say anything.

"I can pay you for your effort, too."

She waited, deciding to hear what he was asking her before agreeing.

He patted the bag. "I know that you know Johanna, the art restorer on Decatur. Can you hold on to this for two weeks and then give it to her? Bring it to her workshop?"

Clay looked thinner than ever and hospital-pale against the green couch.

Marion shrugged, a noncommittal gesture. "Why don't you give it to her since you know where to find her?"

"I've got to go on a trip, and I don't want her to have it just yet."

"If I say okay, is this something that's going to get me in trouble?" Marion asked.

He rubbed his hands on the knees of his cords. "No, I don't think so."

"'No' or 'I don't think so'? They aren't the same thing."

"I'm pretty sure not. For one thing, no one will have any idea that you have it, which is why I chose you in the first place. No one can connect us unless you told someone about us, which would surprise me. Plus, by the time you tell Johanna, it won't matter. Thus the two-weeks part. Just so you know, it's something that belongs to her."

Marion contemplated his request as well as the idea that

Clay would not be returning from whatever trip he was going on. She couldn't have said why she thought this was the case, but there was a sense of finality clinging to him. She also had the distinct, peculiar sense that she was a loose end he was tying up. *Two birds with one stone*—another of her father's small stock of unoriginal phrases.

"Please," he said, and in his voice she heard the desperation that she'd heard in it that day she'd hidden in the closet while he talked to his father, the day he had lost the attraction of power.

Marion squinted at him, as though that would allow her to see something else in him. "You could just mail it or something."

"But I trust you," Clay said very quietly. "Which isn't something I say to very many people."

"Okay," she answered.

He moved into her, his mouth close to her ear. "Can I make love to you before I go?"

To her surprise, she wanted to, if only for completion, a way to ravel her own loose end. Also to her surprise, what they did in her bedroom was more like lovemaking than anything they had done before. Clay was gentle, almost in the extreme. His sweat dripped on her face and chest, and his hips trembled when he was close to coming. When he finally did come, it was with a great shudder. After, they lay side by side, close but not touching, for a long time. The deep breath he took before sitting up to dress sounded like a gasp.

"I'm sorry," he said.

"I've got to go to work anyway."

He shook his head. "No, sorry in a bigger way."

"It's okay," she told him. "It's really okay."

At the door, he kissed her on the mouth. She pointed to the bag. "I like her, by the way. I'll make sure she gets it."

"But not for two weeks."

"But not for two weeks," she repeated, smiling.

Johanna

FOR the first time since she had found her vocation, she could not work. Instead she walked, fast and for hours at a time, when it was not raining and when it rained hard. She couldn't place her problem in a single location: the absence of the painting, the intrusion into her space itself, or the confusion represented by the short word Eli. Perhaps she was just sick from having the possibility of revenge presented and then yanked away after so many years of wanting. If she had the painting and the name—or perhaps even just one or the other—then a plan might still be made. But she had neither, and anyone who might help her would not. Whether their motives were to protect her or thwart her mattered little, if at all; it was what they did that mattered. The person most likely to be able to help her was also the least likely to want to, and if there was any element of protection in the motives of Gerard Fontenot, it was self-protection.

And so there was also this for Johanna: a loss of control and thus fear.

When a check arrived from the artist couple for her final work on the husband's pieces, she experienced a vague disappointment. If he had stopped by with an envelope of cash, then she might have seduced him. An act of control and a small act of revenge against Clay, against Eli, against her situation. Would she have done that? Probably, but her destructive impulse was not strong enough to survive the additional step of calling the man and arranging an encounter. It would have needed to be easy. Peter across the street crossed her mind, but he had done nothing wrong. She felt compunction there that she would not have felt toward the unsavory married artist. There was also this: She was done with men she might actually like. They led nowhere happy, either.

So she channeled her anger into her feet and walked and walked and walked. After two days of walking, she felt considerably better, and her pace slowed a bit. She included more stops: a cup of coffee, a bottle of lemonade, a postcard that caught her eye. She lingered to watch some renovations in the 600 block of Chartres Street, at the carriage house where six-foot-tall Storyville brothel owner Rose Arnold had lived in the 1920s. History called her "Aunt Rose," but Johanna doubted anyone in her line of work deserved a term of benign familiarity. If her girls called her "aunt," it was probably out of fear or loathing, maybe jealousy—the desire to change places. Her stops lengthened: an hour in an exhibit on the Louisiana Purchase at the Cabildo, pre-Mass music at the Cathedral, lunch near the window of the newly reopened but mostly empty Muriel's.

It felt in wisps as though the city remained vacated so she could tour its history. At other times it felt like an off-hours movie set, though Johanna knew full well that the world was not arranged for her. She had never allowed herself more than a minute of magical thinking. People are good or bad; the world does not care.

Walking behind the Cathedral, Johanna noticed a sign announcing the reopening of a bookstore famous, she knew, for the author who had once lived there. Damage to the outside of the building was still evident, and the walls inside were stained. Johanna walked through the tight cases and read the book titles that lined the walls.

"All new?" she asked the man behind the counter.

He shook his head. "We lost parapets and fixtures—and a lot of money by the end—but the books survived."

Johanna's vocation took over. "How on earth?"

"First, we were lucky. Then my wife took over. She's her own force of nature." His smile was gentle. "We found a contractor who was able to get in right away. He cleaned the air-conditioning ducts with bleach and got the air back on. Otherwise it would have been a tragedy of words and pages."

Johanna asked him to recommend a book on French Quarter history, and he guided her by the elbow to a shelf. "You pick," she said. "Three or so."

Soon she was walking back down Decatur with her books, ready to take herself and her fictional history back inside, into the private space where she belonged. First, though, she stopped for a bottle of bleach, figuring that, if nothing else, the smell of it would help purify the place of her work, of her life. Then she would be ready to get back to that work, the work that was her life. A new client's project would mark her return.

Eli

THOUGH Eli had assumed the young man had intentionally avoided him at the auction, it was Gerard Fontenot's son who had called him. Eli had picked up right away, without glancing at the incoming number, again assuming it was Johanna, who had not answered his calls all day. "Johanna," he'd breathed into the phone, and the male voice on the other end had replied, "She's safe." It disconcerted Eli that this was almost how his last conversation with Detective Mouton had started.

"Don't come here," he'd said. "Let's meet somewhere open."

Clayton Fontenot had not seemed to mind his paranoia. "I hate the Hotel Richelieu anyway. Definitely won't be going there again until they do something about the bar. And don't even get me started on that thing they call the pool." It seemed to Eli that Clay had gone out of his way to let him know he'd been to the hotel before, but he also knew from experience that there are as many false confessions as real ones. People will cop to all sorts of terrible deeds, but they hate to admit those sins they've actually committed.

Now they sat on a bench facing St. Louis Cathedral, between groups of pigeons and their human equivalents. A caricaturist working on the ground nearby occasionally hawked his goods to a passerby, but the skinny kids in hoodies walking by didn't look like they had money to spare for a sketch. The other sounds were indistinct, and even those sources nearby sounded as though they were crossing a distance.

"I don't really have time to determine whether you are a good guy or a bad guy," Fontenot's son said.

Eli was debating whether to argue that he was a good guy or to tell this guy to go to hell when Clay held up his hand, pressing back his response.

"I did my research, don't get me wrong. If I didn't *think* you were a good guy, at least where Johanna is concerned, I wouldn't be here. But I don't have time to test my conclusions. So I'm going to hope you are a good guy, but I'm not going to tell you anything you'll find useful if you're not. As I say, I don't have a lot of time. What you need to know is that Johanna will not be safe if she has the painting—"

"So people keep telling me." Eli moved to speak more, and again Clay Fontenot pressed the air in front of them with his open hand.

"I know you know what I'm talking about. What I don't know is whether you were the one who took it from her place. I'm guessing not."

Pigeons approached and pecked at the ground near his feet, yet still the small noises they made sounded farther away. As loathed as they were, as dirty as they were considered, they were beautiful animals in their dozens of gray. No longer trying to speak, Eli just shook his head in response to the implied question.

"Either you did or didn't, and either way, you may or may not be planning to get it back for her. First, you should know that you can't. You don't have those kinds of skills—trust me, I'm familiar with the security—and pretty soon you won't even know where it is. Second, and maybe this is more important, Johanna can't have the painting while other people want it."

Eli had interviewed the wrong Fontenot, obviously, and wondered if that had been his own oversight or if he had been steered that way by Ted. "It isn't even worth that much," he said. "Not worth enough to account for all the drama."

"You really don't understand how people operate, do you?" Clay hooked an elbow over the back of the bench and opened his chest more fully toward Eli. "People are scum. They care about money, of course they do, but also pride and power and revenge. Even Johanna, you know, cares more about revenge than she'll ever care about the likes of you or me."

The sounds of the square rushed closer, as though they'd been held behind some barricade and then released en masse.

"It's more complicated in her case," Eli said.

Clay shook his head. "It's more sympathetic, but it's really not more complicated. What do you know about her?"

"I don't want to know anything she doesn't want to tell me. I have too much respect for her for anything else."

"No, not respect," Clay said, narrowing one eye as though sizing him for a suit. "You are in love."

Eli nodded. "Yes. Yes, I am."

"Would you die before you hurt her?"

"Yes. Yes, I would."

"Would you go back to prison before you hurt her?"

The question didn't surprise him, and he nodded. "Yes, I would."

Now Clay closed himself off, leaning forward onto his knees, palms clasped, face cast down and shown to Eli only at an acute angle. His question was barely audible: "Does she love you? Can you make her happy?"

Eli thought carefully before saying, "I don't know, but yes, I think so."

Still Clay didn't look up, but he spoke louder now. "Then you need to stay calm and wait. While anyone cares about that painting, Johanna is in danger—from herself as well as from others. You get that, right? You're not stupid?"

Again Eli nodded even though Clay wasn't looking at him.

"When that's no longer true, no one will care about her."

"There's a cop, too, looking into the dead man."

"Mouton?" Clay laughed. "Mouton won't do anything

he's not paid to do. He's got a stack of cases to last his life-time. No way is he going to take time to solve one no one wants solved. People are gunning each other down not so far from here, yesterday and today and tomorrow, and he won't solve those murders, either."

"Well, he seemed more than a little interested, and very recently at that." Eli pointed at his nose. "Anyway, what about your father? I assume he's writing the paychecks you're talking about."

"My father will continue to be the asshole he has always been, but by next week his interests will no longer include the later work of Eugeen van Mieghem. As you said, the painting isn't worth that much money. Speaking of Mouton, by the way, when you see Johanna, tell her he's the one who did the footwork. Assuming is wasn't you, and I suspect you didn't pack a suit for this trip if you own one at all. You probably own exactly one, right? Anyway, you'll be putting her mind to rest on something and doing yourself a favor in the process by telling her it was Mouton."

Eli closed his eyes and let Johanna's face resolve on the backs of his lids or his mind's eye or wherever the physical location of visual imagination lies. Eli liked to think of it as a place. He opened his eyes abruptly on the pale young man. "If people operate by pride and greed and power, what do you get out of all this—whatever this is?"

"You left revenge out of your list. What I get is my own version of revenge. But sometimes some of us are capable of a little more, something bigger than ourselves, at least if it coincides with self-interest. I guess the word for me is justice. Revenge is part of it but not all of it. There's getting even but also making things even."

Eli nodded. "Okay."

"Just so you know," Clay added, "the only reason you're getting anything out of this at all or playing any part at all is because I ran out of time. My hand was forced early."

"Okay," Eli said again. "I can trust in duress a lot more than I could ever trust in generosity. Or justice."

"You may be a good man—that's probably what I would decide if I had time to test my conclusions—but I am not a good man. You've got nothing to worry about there. It's the one thing you can trust me on."

Clay

HAVING sent in the page proofs of his final book, made plans for the money that would be left after his orders were followed, and decided that his only farewell to his father would be by mail, Clay was finished with the city. As he watched it turn murky below him, he regretted that he had only ever taken it for granted. He had traveled to many places that might have given him perspective, had lived overseas, yet he'd only ever thought of New Orleans as his family's home. He'd always blamed the city for that, which was a mistake now too late to rectify. He drank his first-class wine and allowed himself the pleasure of a regret merging with nostalgia, savoring how maudlin it all was.

The shimmering hues of Johanna's hair in an autumn light dappled and waved by the flora of Ochsner Island produced a sharper regret, a pain no less real because it was vague, but he swallowed it away with the nectar of the gods. As soon as the seatbelt sign was extinguished, he would ask for another glass.

In the overhead compartment rested an architect's bag holding the frame of an empty canvas nearly the exact size of a modestly well-known Belgian artist's painting of a young woman waiting to depart from a dock in Antwerp—a painting that would not be recrossing the Atlantic to its home country because it sat in a poorly furnished shotgun duplex in the Bywater. That black bag and his father's name would gain him entry to the residence of a very wealthy man living between Brussels and Antwerp—a man whose familial power and affluence dated back far beyond the Fontenots of New Orleans, very nearly to the Middle Ages.

It was a family whose name was well enough known that Clay could depend that the man's mysterious stabbing ("Nothing stolen!") would make at least a few European newspapers and that he would be able to purchase one from the safety of a country that was not Belgium—the country where his British contact would meet to take care of his final business, his final human remains. It would be this man who would mail two copies of the newspaper story to New Orleans. One would go into a card together with a small leather bookmark inscribed with Clay's full name. The envelope would bear his father's name. The card would bear Clay's handwriting but not his signature: "Sorry you won't be able to buy that thing you wanted after all." The informality of it delighted Clay. The other clipping would go to Johanna, part of his final gift to her and evidence of the other portion of that gift.

The stabbing itself was the only variable he could not

predict in all its details, but he trusted his research and his choice of method. Most of all, he trusted his resolve. And his experience: Even if the first death by his hand had not been planned, he knew at least that he could take human life. The man's painting, the one his father so badly wanted, would remain in the stately home, perhaps in the very room Johanna hated above all others, to be embroiled in an estate war that might well outlast his father's arteries. Clay guessed, too, that any investigation into the painting's provenance might point to a more rightful owner. An accidental good deed done on the side, perhaps making up for some small harm he'd caused in his life's work without realizing it—some unknown collateral damage with his name on it.

After draining his glass, Clay worked two fingers between the buttons of his shirt and made contact with the soft, flawless skin of his stomach—his most beautiful material.

Marion

HER shift was busy, her mood strangely buoyant. Whenever she caught herself trying to dissect the buoyancy, she stopped, telling herself to enjoy floating on the surface of her life for a change.

On her way home, she walked her bike the first couple of blocks, pausing to look into Johanna's workshop, which was empty. She saw the light on in the upstairs window and figured that Johanna lived up there. She imagined her making tea, or reading, or washing her face. All guesses—she knew nothing about Johanna's life even though she had envied it, or envied what it might be. She wondered what Johanna was to Clay and Clay to her, but it didn't really matter. She liked both of them, in the end, yet she would also be glad to be done with them and with everything else the storm had brought into her life. Eddie was the exception; she had chosen him.

She pedaled the rest of the distance home, enough tips in her purse to treat Henry to a meal out. Maybe she'd call and invite Eddie, too, though she wasn't sure she wanted to mix friend and family just yet. She and Henry were building a new relationship, not resuming an old one, and so they still circled carefully, practiced a civility that would remain artificial as long as it had to be practiced.

Her place was dark when she got home, and she felt the prick of small disappointment. Usually she kept her bicycle inside, but since Henry had moved in she'd taken to locking it to the front stair railing to give them a little more interior space. She was risking theft, but her bike wasn't worth much, and she'd sprung for a good lock.

She decided she'd work for an hour to see if Henry showed up and then go eat either way. Her growing tattoo had inspired a shift in her work, and she was sketching for a painting more stylized than anything she'd done before. Still Biloxi but cleaner in its lines and more exaggerated. One day soon, she thought, maybe after she finished this one, she was going to turn her attention to New Orleans. The trick was to find a new way to depict such well-trodden territory, to see the city in different colors. Or maybe she could make it new because it was new—no longer that place it had been before.

When she heard people in front of her house, she was about half an hour into a sketch of a particular block of beachfront Biloxi before it was leveled. Telling herself a secondhand bicycle wasn't worth getting shot over, she peeked out her front window through the split in her curtains. What she saw wasn't a thief but a woman and small girl bringing a cat carrier and a large box into the house across the street.

Marion stepped out. When the woman gazed at her, she felt self-conscious. "Need any help?" seemed like the best response.

"We got it," the woman said and turned back to the house, which looked undamaged by the storm but long in need of fresh paint. It had been blue once, perhaps a turquoise now diluted by the bare wood emerging through the paint. "You didn't live here before," she said over her shoulder.

Marion shook her head in agreement. "The place I use to live is no more."

The woman faced her again, hip popped out to one side. "You and a lot of people. Next thing you'll be telling me is that white kids are moving into the Desire Projects."

Marion laughed a little because the woman's face was softer than her words. "I don't think that's happening any-time soon."

The little girl took the cat from the woman and disap-peared inside, but the woman stayed out front. "I thought my house would be worth even less now than it was before, but you make me think I got a chance of selling it."

"I'm about the last person you should take advice from, real estate or otherwise." Marion lingered, half expecting the woman to have some sage words for her, but she just made a small grunting sound and said, "I'll keep that in mind." She turned around again at her front steps and added, "And I guess I'll be seeing you around."

As soon as Marion walked through the kitchen, she realized that something was wrong with the third room, which she'd started calling, just to herself, the studio instead of the bedroom. What she wasn't sure of was whether the composition had changed in the few minutes she was outside or whether she just hadn't noticed when she'd got home from work because she had been mired in her thoughts.

Regardless of when it had been taken, the knowledge that the architect's bag was gone lodged in her esophagus. She'd looked into the bag within minutes of Clay's departure—perhaps curiosity is the simplest human impulse, even if its consequences are so often messy—and so she knew that it contained a small and expertly done painting. It was the kind of painting people pay real money for, though from what she could make out of the signature, she had never heard of the artist. While it was possible that Clay had got her in over her head, she settled on the more likely conclusion. She had been failed by Henry, and as a result she would fail Clay and Johanna. To trust another was to be made untrustworthy yourself. She was a victim of both her own stupidity and the paltriness of her origins.

She was rocking herself on the floor, arms around her bent legs, when she heard Henry come in. Though she'd turned off all the lights, he walked straight through the house and stood near her.

"I've got to tell you something," he said. "I've done something I'm not sure I can fix."

Marion cradled her knees harder. "No kidding. Why did you come back?"

"To try to fix it, or at the very least to give you the money."

"You sold it?"

"I was going to buy, but I worked my tools and I want to stay clean. They taught us that it doesn't have to be automatic, that you can stop the process by thinking about it. It's not something I could have done a year ago, and I'm not sure it's something I can even do tomorrow, so I want you to take the money and put it where I can't get it. It's important that you don't trust me."

Marion laughed and said that maybe they were biologically related after all. Though the envelope Henry handed her was fat with money, and money was what she most needed from the world to make a new life, she found herself calling Eddie with the idea of trying to close things right. She focused on the simple steps of doing this and allowed her positive impulse to remain as unexamined as her baser ones always had been.

Johanna

EVERY emotional hue but the strong one she could not name washed off her like sand when Elizam walked through her door. The light outside was bright but diffuse, and his face loomed dark before her, his features vivid and deep despite the backlighting. With her eyes she could recall the feel of his hair, which looked wiry but to the touch was thick and soft. She took in his eyes, his lips, his badly swollen nose.

She whispered the one ugly syllable: "Thief."

"It wasn't me," he said. "I didn't take your painting."

What happened next surprised her: She believed him. "Why not?" she asked. "Why didn't you?"

"Because I would never do anything to hurt you."

"But what if you thought it was in my best interest to have the painting gone?" she asked.

"I wouldn't make decisions for you. If I had believed you would be better off giving up the painting, I would have tried to talk you into it. I wouldn't have just made it happen." He bracketed her shoulders, moved his head to find direct eye contact.

"What if I was suicidal and asked you for a knife? Would you give that to me?"

"But you aren't."

She waited for him to say more, nodded in agreement when he did not. "But I need that painting. You are a thief. You can get it for me."

Elizam was shaking his head before she finished. "I can't."

"You *will* not. You want to avoid prison and save me from myself and live happily ever after."

He reached for her hair, but she pulled back.

"Repeat that to yourself, Johanna, and ask yourself if that's a bad thing to want. But even so, I would do anything for you anyway. I would go to prison for you, right this moment. The thing is that I don't think I *can* steal it. A matter of ability. To have a chance, I'd have to know exactly where it was. I would have to hire people, probably from out of town given that the connections seem to run deep and unpredictable around here."

He went on talking, but she stopped following the details. After catching the brunt of his message, she was doing what he'd asked: repeating to herself the happy ending she had accused him of wanting. He was right: It was not such a bad thing to want.

They were interrupted by Marion and a man she'd seen on the block quite a bit lately. After Marion caught her breath,

get SARA ERWEN RIDING LESSONS?

PITKIN COUNTY library

inspire lifelong learning

Checked Out Items 12/7/2015 14:19
XXXXXXXXX0502

Item Title	Due Date
1130003402819	12/28/2015
1. * The lower quarter / Elise Blackwell.	
1130003384264	12/20/2015
2. The truth according to us : a novel / Annie Barrows.	
1130003422312	12/20/2015
3. Away in a manger / Rhys Bowen.	

* Indicates items checked out today

.

.

Manage your account online at
http://pitkin.marmot.org/MyAccount/Home

she told her story, which was as surprising to Johanna as anything that had happened since the storm: Clayton Fontenot
had given her something to hold on to and then give to Johanna, but her junkie brother had fenced it before remembering that he was in recovery. He had repented too late.

"I'm really sorry, but Clay said it was important that I
hold on to the painting for two weeks, that I wasn't to give
it to you right away. All that my fucked-up brother knows
is that he sold it to some fence who said he had clients in
the Marigny."

Eli straightened, seemed brighter or lighter than before.
"The Marigny—are you sure? I thought it was in an alarmed
safe uptown."

His voice stirred something in Johanna, which she only
slowly recognized as hope.

Marion looked sideways and cocked her head before
straightening it. "I'm not sure that it's right, but I'm sure
that's what he said."

"What day is it?" Eli asked no one in particular.

"What do you mean?" Marion asked. "You mean what
day did he sell it?"

"What day is it today?" Eli asked and then answered his
own question. "It's Thursday." He turned back to Johanna, a
smile now small but growing on his beautiful lips. "I think I
can help after all. I think I can actually help."

It took her a long time to tabulate what had happened,
and after she had managed that, she still did not know what

it meant. A day earlier, even an hour earlier, she would have welcomed this moment as a herald of revenge. Now she believed that Eli's misunderstanding had been instead a deeper understanding: What she really wanted was not a name on a piece of paper or a canvas that would be a means to an end but rather the return of the painting itself.

Eli

WHILE it might have horrified him only a week ago to think that he'd return to his old profession, Eli felt free and light as he rounded the pink house and pried open the window next to the back porch—the easiest entry he had ever encountered, which somehow made sense for a house containing such a reckless collection.

The odds were against it, of course, but not by so very much. The Marigny was not a large neighborhood, and surely the Broussard house accounted for at least three-quarters of its art. Its collection, too, was a hodgepodge and likely sloppily sourced.

Johanna had not wanted to leave her place unguarded, and Eli was unwilling to leave her alone in it overnight. She resisted his staying over, at first. "I'm not equipped for guests," she said, and finally told him that no one but she had ever slept in her apartment, with the exception of the small dog she had taken in temporarily. Eli had told her he didn't mind sleeping on the sofa, but she said that wasn't the problem.

"Gerard Fontenot will realize that the painting is gone, and then he will look for it," Eli told her. "The chances of him looking for it here are very high."

"Clay said two weeks, and his fault has never been stupidity," Johanna said, but Eli's argument was still persuasive. She showed him the drawer with her knives, her can of pepper spray. They asked Peter to call the police if he saw the man with the suit. That this man probably was the police made this a faulty backup plan, Eli knew, and so he hoped that a backup plan was all it was. He weighed the risks, though, and knew that he could never get the painting back if it wound up in one of Gerard Fontenot's safes somewhere in the world, unless perhaps he made it his life's work at the Lost Art Register.

Johanna's bed was small and their situation unsettled, but he found it surprisingly easy to fall asleep. He woke very early, though how early he wasn't sure because his watch and phone were across the room and Johanna didn't seem to have a clock.

Lying as still as possible so he wouldn't wake her, he watched her sleep and thought through his plan, such as it was. Her nostrils flared slightly with each inhale, but she was silent and otherwise motionless in her sleep.

Eli was glad he knew the Broussards, or at least had conversed with them twice. If they surprised him, he might even be able to talk his way out of it, particularly if they were guilty of buying stolen goods. Cats, he remembered, and was glad that there had been no sign of dogs. He had not seen any evidence of an alarm system, but neither had he conclusively determined the absence of one. His former self would have been disappointed; he had become an amateur.

He made love to Johanna again after she woke up, holding her waist and looking down at her, again failing to understand his great good luck that she would have anything to do with him at all. That his status with her might be temporary hurt, but he would accept whatever was given to him and on any terms.

Afterward, while she made coffee, she asked him about the painting. "If Clay had the painting, then that means his father stole it from here."

Eli nodded and said that he thought so. He waited for her next question, but it did not come. He answered it for her: "Detective Mouton."

She paused and looked at him. "I hate it that he was in my flat, that there are molecules of him in the air."

"We'll run your filter more," Eli said. "I'll vacuum and scrub. I'll wipe everything down over and over."

They drank their coffee in silence for a while, and then Johanna told him about the zoo in Audubon Park, which was scheduled to reopen soon. She described the tigers in greatest detail, and next the birds in a rookery in the park outside the zoo. She told him of a dream she'd had in which the birds had disappeared one night, and the next day when everyone noticed, no one knew why they were gone. In other words, this was the best morning of his life.

Fifteen minutes before the porcelain auction was scheduled to begin, Eli was walking down Decatur wondering why Clay had let him believe Gerard Fontenot still had the painting. Apparently he'd trusted Eli's goodness but not his patience. He hooked a left up Frenchmen Street and then a short right before climbing through the window he pried open.

He figured he had at least an hour and probably two before there was any chance of Fatty or Mignon Broussard returning from the auction gallery, but it only took him about ten minutes to eyeball every painting in the house and another fifteen to ascertain that the house had no safe. If there was stolen art there, it was on plain display, which made sense to him, having met the Broussards.

He sat down at the computer stuffed into a nook off the large, busy kitchen, but he didn't even need to turn it on. Sitting right next to it, under an ugly paperweight containing a replica of a Degas ballerina distorted by the convex curve, was an Art Auction Gallery business card and a four-figure check bearing not the name of the auction house but the personal account information of Felicia Pontalba.

Marion

THAT your fellow?" her newly returned neighbor asked as Marion gave her the new garbage pickup schedule.

Marion looked up to see Eddie climbing out of a large, dark brown Pontiac half a block down the street. "Maybe."

"He ain't half bad," the woman told her. Once again Marion had forgotten to introduce herself in the proper window of time, and now it felt too late to just ask the woman her name. Of course the woman hadn't asked for hers, either.

"Not even half bad," Marion said.

As Eddie and Marion drove across the smear of Slidell toward what she had heard childhood neighbors call *the real Gulf Coast*, Marion told him she hadn't known he had a car but that if she had, she would have guessed it looked just like this.

"I guess my low-rider days still show. I figure I'll get rid of it soon, but I wanted to make sure things worked out here first, that I wouldn't need to be driving out again."

"I'm glad they worked out," she said, and he squeezed her hand on the vinyl seat.

She was unprepared to see the coast, plot after plot either empty or a pile of rubble that used to be a house she envied. Miles and miles of destruction. She tried to find some pleasure in the fact that for once the wealthy had fared worse than the poorer people who couldn't afford to live on the water, but the effort failed. It was all carnage.

"Once in college I brought a guy home," she told Eddie, "and he said this was the most boring place he'd ever been to."

"Then he was an idiot," Eddie said. "For one thing, no place is boring, least of all this one."

"Now this place is just gone."

They parked in the new casino's half-full lot and walked along the beach, which had been cleaned to immaculate for maybe half a mile.

"What about where you're from, what's interesting about it? What about your family?" Marion asked as they took sand-slowed steps.

"As for my family—not boring. That I can say. I got a dealt a raw hand there, and part of that meant living in a lot of different places. But at a certain age, you're responsible for yourself, and maybe you get to pick your own family. That's why I came to New Orleans. Seemed to me like a place that's starting over is a good place to start yourself over. What I mean isn't just that it's easier or puts you in a lot of company but that it makes you part of something bigger than yourself, so it's not just about you. Intentional community, or something."

"I read somewhere that New Orleans used to be called the accidental city."

"Some people make the most of bad happenstance."

The line was obvious and nearly straight: fine, pale sand on one side and rubbish tangled in kelp on the other, as far as they could see. Here and there a gull sat atop a heap, a pelican on a precariously perched toilet seat or window unit. It was like the opposite of a still life, with the animals representing not decay but life and the inanimate representing not the static but the transitory, the destructive passage of time. She felt like she had found it: a way to start painting about New Orleans that was new. It surprised her that she looked forward to the work itself rather than to anywhere it might lead in life, which was probably nowhere.

And maybe the art growing across her back would inspire what she put to canvas. She imagined herself alone in a room, painting something darker and more stylized than she had done before. She saw a long, multicolored alligator swimming in brown water, dark, jagged birds making the sky over the river near her house marvelous with their terrible numbers. She would need a large canvas for that.

She startled when she noticed Eddie staring at her.

"This is a date, right?" he asked, his voice muted by the soft wind coming off the water.

"Not exactly dinner and a movie," Marion said, but she let him move in to kiss her.

The Pontiac overheated when they were almost back to Slidell. As Marion sat in the car with Eddie hidden behind the opened hood, she felt happy—actually happy for the first time that she could remember.

Clay

CLAY assumed that his first encounter—the first of the two deaths—would be difficult and the second easy, but they were reversed. The man he met in Luxembourg was both fastidious and nervous despite his thuggish appearance. He was particular about the wire transfer, the details of what was more or less a last will and testament, the preparations for the death itself.

"It must be a suicide and not a homicide—not even an assisted suicide," the man instructed in perfect but heavily accented English. "This is not The Netherlands."

Clay smirked, not quite sure if the added bit was an attempt at levity or not.

"But it is crucial that you proceed correctly so as not to damage the material." He nodded, perhaps confirming that they both knew *material* was one hell of a euphemism. "We make beautiful products, and this situation, while out of the ordinary, will be no exception. I'm sure that's the way you want it."

As he nodded his agreement, Clay imagined Johanna's long fingers, her short, clean nails.

There were papers to get to his publisher and addresses to verify: Johanna's, of course, and his father's, and Marion's. He had not forgotten about dear Marion. Because he knew Johanna would not touch his money, would feel besmirched by it and angry to have it presented to her, Marion was going to be a very wealthy young woman. It fitted their relationship, which, after all, had begun as a monetary exchange.

Maybe she would do some good with the money—Clay sensed in her an unrecognized affection for New Orleans and, he assumed, for wounded things of various kinds—or maybe she'd blow it on tattoos and Jell-O shots and absurd jewelry. He really didn't care. The point of giving her the money was letting her do with it whatever she wanted.

It all took several days more than expected, so he was glad he had told Marion to hang on to the painting for a full two weeks. Even though Johanna was no longer in danger, it felt right that the whole affair be settled in its details and then completed posthumously.

He assumed it would be her face he saw as his vision darkened and permanent sleep seeped slowly in, but he knew that the last face he imagined might well belong to the second defendant whose death he had made literal.

Everything in Belgium had gone as planned, as he had imagined it on the plane, right down to the ready rental car with its accurate navigation system. The bachelor had even answered his own door, a door his ancestors had walked freely in and out of for several hundred years. He wasn't imposing, nor was he a once-strong man declined to old and frail. Perhaps because he had watched too many movies in his life, these were the two alternatives Clay expected. Instead he was very nearly ordinary, though a first impression of kindliness cleared quickly to an obvious smallness evident in the overly tidy haircut. A puniness of character or mind or self—Clay didn't worry about the terminology for the thing that a person is, the thing he intended to take from this man and render nonexistent.

"Monsieur Fontenot the Younger, I assume?" Even his voice was smaller than it should have been, the words pinched off, leaving too much space between them.

His eyes, though, while small were deep. They were dark and mean, and Clay wanted to cut them out of his face.

Clay nodded in response to the man's question and just that easily entered the mansion with the architect's bag containing an unpainted canvas and a recently acquired hunting knife.

Eli

H E stood, and Felicia Pontalba sat cross-armed at her desk.

"Was it for a finder's fee?" he asked.

To her credit, she made no show of feigned ignorance, uttered no denial. "Once, at a lunch when I thought something might bloom between us, I told you the secret to my profession."

"Having something others want." Eli sat on the chair she had pointed to.

She lifted her breasts with her hands, squeezed them together to deepen her cleavage. "I suppose I was hoping you'd want this."

"I can't deny the aesthetic value," Eli said, cautious.

"Not the area you collect in, though."

"Not anymore, though my younger self is ready to punch me in face just about now."

"Thing is," Felicia said, "that what you *do* want, other people also want."

Eli scanned the room as inconspicuously as possible, noting two possible locations for a hidden safe large enough to hold the painting even as he realized it wasn't especially likely that she'd have it here.

"But I have it on good authority," she continued, "that at least one of them thinks it's no longer missing. Which is to say there's no reason everyone can't be happy." Cleavage subsided back into her gray wool dress, Felicia again looked all business. "And I want to be happy."

"You seem pretty happy."

She squinted at him. "Maybe I want to be happier."

"And what would make you really happy?" Eli asked. "More money?"

"Curiosity can torment, at least a person like me. When I was little, I would find every last one of my hidden Christmas presents, open them, fondle the merchandise, and then rewrap and retape everything so well that no one ever knew."

"Or else they just let you think you got away with it."

"Maybe, but the point is that I'm unhappy with you because you left my curiosity unsatisfied."

Eli resisted the urge to draw back, and he held his tongue while maintaining the eye contact that was making him want to run.

"Never fear," she said. "It's not that big a deal, and I can get laid by good-looking men for free. No need to resort to blackmail for that."

Eli remembered one thing he'd learned from his family: the importance of preserving female pride. Anyone's pride, really, but it was particularly tricky when it involved a woman's sexual allure, at least according to his father. "Men are used to being turned down. Accuracy through numbers," his father had advised.

"No fear there," Eli said, "or at least only the best kind of fear."

Felicia had already moved on. "I suppose you could call what I'm proposing a more modern transaction. You may recall I mentioned a Mr. Prejean? He and your boss had a bit of a squabble a few years back?"

Eli nodded.

"Well, a painting was loaned to Mr. Prejean for an exhibition but has never been returned. I think he's hoping all was forgotten with the storm and all."

"I don't have the skills or the crew to get into a museum," Eli said. "The technology has changed, and I don't have the contacts here." He continued when she said nothing, "Seriously, I cannot do it, and I really don't want to go back to prison. It's pretty awful, you know, maybe even worse than you imagine."

"I can imagine that it is pretty awful, but you're in luck, because what I'm looking to reacquire is not in a museum. It's in a storage unit. Prejean is not so much as a thief as a hoarder. Sad, really, but his diagnosis is not really our concern here."

"It's still a crime. You could report it."

"The police in New Orleans are busy."

"One of them manages to make time for me." Eli touched

his nose involuntarily but quickly returned his hand to his knee.

"You may find that he's recently lost interest. Anyway, this isn't a matter for the authorities but a small situation—an in-family kind of thing."

"But my job here is done. Ted'll be wanting me back in Los Angeles."

Felicia smiled wide, and he saw that the trick to her trademark was stretching out a mouth that was more square than it was any other shape. "Let's just say you'll be doing Ted a favor, too."

"If you're so tight with Ted, why aren't you telling him about what you recently bought from the Broussards?"

"As far as I'm concerned, a painting no one thinks is missing isn't missing. One key to being part of something bigger than you is just to remember the simple fact that you are. If and when that particular item reenters the category of 'missing,' I won't know where it is anymore, and no one will know I ever did. Meanwhile, I'll have taken care of another matter, and people will be all the more impressed because they won't know how on earth I've done it. 'And so quietly,' they'll say."

For the second time in a week, Eli found himself a recidivist and a thief, and once again he found that the city wasn't nearly locked up enough to keep its valuables safe. Though *storage locker* was a misnomer for the elaborate, climate-controlled facility where affluent New Orleanians kept the art and wine and fur they didn't have room for at home, it wasn't hard to sweet-talk the woman at the front desk, who was clearly beleaguered after several months of hysterical and often berating phone calls from those same affluent New Orleanians wanting to know the condition of those canvases and bottles and coats housed in a suburb that had seen extended and repeated power outages. Kindness and a simple lock pick were the only tools Eli really needed for this job, which made him think it was a good thing his determination to make a life as a nonthief was strong.

The next day he was back in Felicia's office, trading one canvas for another.

The photograph he'd seen of the Van Mieghem had not done the colors of the painting justice. Even in the awkward fluorescent light, the red of the young woman's dress glowed like embers, and the colors of her skin managed to convey that she was cold as she looked out over the Atlantic.

Felicia interrupted the art appreciation. "If the other collection you're starting doesn't work out, maybe you'll stop by sometime and cure my curiosity."

Eli felt good about lying because he liked Felicia. "That'll be the very first thing I do."

Half an hour later, he relished the peculiar sensation of walking down the street with a missing European painting in the middle of the day. But no one on Decatur—which was as crowded as he'd seen it—gave him or what he was carrying a second look. He had a secret no one in this place cared about. The closer he got to where he was going, the faster he walked.

Johanna

Eli stayed with her for nearly a week, until they both felt sure that no one would be coming back to look for the painting. Sometimes she startled to a sound in the night, reached toward her phone or her pepper spray, but increasingly she trusted that Clay had taken care of things—had somehow got her the painting in such a way that no one knew she had it or that permission had been granted. Maybe he'd traded another five years of financial liberation. She'd called to ask him, but he never answered. Finally Eli called the policeman, just to feel him out, he said, just to be sure.

Johanna found that she didn't mind having Eli around. She liked how he was compact in his movements, how everything he had with him fitted into one small and neat bag, how he always removed any traces of himself from a room before he left it. This meant they shared some essential quality, even if she was unable to explain or even name it.

When his employer called from Los Angeles, Johanna listened to one side of the conversation. "Yes, I know I was supposed to be back," he said, and the conversation stretched long. At last Eli said, "Yes, I can do anything for two years."

After he'd hung up, he told her he could visit her from Los Angeles but not from prison. He did not ask her to go there with him, but his eyes posed the question.

She stroked his hair. "I've merged my history with this city's," she said and then told him about the types of people she imagined, the dapper Frenchman who liked to attend the French Opera House and the people who'd preceded her in the Lower Quarter. "It's like having roots, even if it's not quite the same thing."

Telling him this felt far more intimate and revealing to her than if she'd given him the details of her actual history, told him the kinds of things that people usually want to know about someone else, told him the secrets that are true but accidental, that were not of her choosing at all.

He said he understood. "I felt good here almost as soon as I landed. Like being at home, except better. I'd move here if I could." He looked at her in a way she decided was hopeful. "But for now I'm stuck with the job I have—a parole of sorts, an extended confinement."

"I'm not going anywhere. Two years is not so long." She started to lean into him, but her words were clear enough.

"I'm probably going to have to do some things I won't want to tell you about."

"Thief," she said, almost a laugh, but then she nodded more somberly. "I won't ask you about them. We have other things we can talk about."

"And right now we have two more days before I go," he said, moving into her, his lips finding hers.

As he waved from the back of a taxi crawling up Decatur Street toward the interstate, toward Louis Armstrong Airport, she felt happy.

It was easy to sink back into the life she had made, working while listening to music, eating her lunch across the street, working some more, making her supper, and reading herself to sleep, most often with some history about the settlement of New Orleans or a novel written by a writer who'd lived in the city, usually in the Vieux Carré.

One day in the run-up to the city's first Mardi Gras after the storm, she walked to the bookstore.

"Got a new history title you might like," the bookseller told her. "Nice illustrations, too."

She shook her head. "Actually, I was thinking of trying something new, maybe something about how the city is now, or maybe I will browse through your art section." She looked down at her fingers, which were resting on a stack of paperback novels.

"Science fiction, local author," the man said. "Kind of a dystopian future of Louisiana after it's mostly underwater."

"I guess some future is better than no future, right?" she said, and the bookseller laughed as she turned her head to read the spines of the books lining the wall.

Later that day a package arrived with European stamps, and she felt afraid until she realized the stamps were British, from a place where she knew no one at all. She opened her other mail first and then turned to it, using a box cutter to pierce the heavy tape.

The package contained a small bound journal: pale in color, finely grained, softer than any leather she had touched before. She opened it, and tucked inside its thick ivory pages—all of them blank—was the obituary of a wealthy Belgian industrialist whose murder was still under investigation. Fatter and older than she remembered, now clean-shaven. But even the poor quality of the newspaper's reproduction of his official photograph did not disguise his small, cruel eyes. Stuck to the obituary was a yellow Post-it note that read, "He knew it was from you. He knew it was for you."

Johanna sat with the photo a while before tucking it back into the journal, which she placed in the file drawer that held her documents of identity and survival.

After a slow cup of coffee, she retrieved her toolbox from downstairs and located a new nail and the smaller of her two hammers. She removed from the closet her favorite object in the world and freed it from the layers of butcher paper protecting it.

She considered each of the walls in her flat before hanging the painting across from the sofa, where she could look at it whenever she wanted.

Acknowledgments

I am beholden to the great city of New Orleans and apologize for taking small liberties with its geography and post-Katrina chronology. Thanks to New Orleans photographer and writer Louis Maistros for permission to use the cover image. (More of Louie's work can be viewed at www.louismaistros.com.)

This novel was written with the partial support of a University of South Carolina Provost's Grant for Creative and Performing Arts, for which I am grateful. I also want to thank the College of Arts & Sciences and everyone who participates in The Open Book.

I am indebted to family (including various Blackwells and Bajos) as well as friends and colleagues (including those who are both friends and colleagues).

I would not have books in the world without help along the way from many writers. Some of them know who they are; others have helped me through their work alone.

Thanks to my editor, Fred Ramey, for being a better reader and person than a writer could invent; to my agent, Terra Chalberg, for her editorial insights and professionalism; and to everyone at Unbridled Books for their unwavering commitment to books.

My life would be much less rich without the amazing Esme Bajo, and I'm lucky to even know her. I am grateful to David Bajo for more than a quarter century of good literary company—and for helping me restore the thing most worth saving.